FOOL ME TWICE

FAMILY TIDES
BOOK 1

SYDNI LYNN

Book Cover by Sydni Lynn
Edited by Shelly Jay Shore

PLAYLIST

Last Chance (Alternate Version) by CHPTRS
Quitter by Cameron Whitcomb
My First Heartbreak by Myles Smith
Believer by SYML
July by Far Caspian
Passenger by Noah Kahan
Bullet From a Gun by The Script
Safe by BANNERS
Suncats by Hazlett
Feel Something by Joshua Bassett
This = Love by The Script
Know Love by RKCB
Would It Be Ok by AFSHEEN feat. Angel Taylor
HARD LOVE by NEEDTOBREATHE feat. Andra Day
Hear Me Say by Jonas Blue feat. LÉON
Let Go by BANNERS
Sunshine by Lily Meola
DtMF by Bad Bunny

To my Grandma, whom I never got to share my stories with.
I miss you so much.

CONTENT WARNING

Fool Me Twice includes depiction of abuse, microaggressions, death, suicide, and nonconsensual outing of sexual preferences. For a full list of content warnings, visit www.sydnilynn.com.

Please read this story with care.

PROLOGUE

NINE YEARS AGO

REMEMBER TO BREATHE.

Mommy doesn't say it, but I hear the words in her voice. It's what she always tells me, when I get so excited that I start holding my breath.

But I can't help it. I'm too excited to breathe. *He's here! He's really here!*

Mommy smiles at me over her shoulder, but her brows pull together as her eyes sweep across my face. Instead of opening the door, she turns to look at me. I practically fall over my own feet trying not to crash into her. I bite back a squeak of protest.

Why would she stop? He's on the other side of the door! What if we don't answer quickly enough and he leaves?

I want to jump past Mommy and open the door myself. As if reading my mind, Mommy shifts on her feet, then stands very, *very* still, until, finally, my eyes focus on her. She raises her hand palm-up in front of her stomach as she takes in a deep breath, and mouths *one, two, three, four* before flipping her hand over and lowering it like she's pushing some great force into the ground as she breathes out. I press my heels into the carpet, trying to stay still as I follow along. I can almost hear her telling me what to do:

Breathe into your nose. Breathe out through your mouth. Nice and slow.

Again, Mommy mouths. I do it again, and then again, until my shoulders drop down below my ears and my feet remain firmly planted. Finally, the flurry of butterflies in my tummy goes quiet. I look hopefully up at Mommy. "Now?"

Mommy's lips twitch, like she's trying not to smile, and I know I've done it right. She opens the door, and there he is: Uncle B. My favorite person in the world, not counting Mommy.

"It's really good to see you, B," Mommy breathes.

"You too."

Uncle B wraps an arm around Mommy's shoulders as he leans against her, their heads bent together like they're sharing a secret.

Siblings do that sort of thing. Sharing, I mean. At least, they're supposed to. That's what Gia and Lux's mom, Ms. A, says. Mommy says the same thing goes for me even though I don't have a sister or brother to share with.

Not that I haven't asked for one. I'd be the best big sister *ever*. Just like Mommy.

Looking past Mommy, Uncle B takes in the decorations the birthday fairy left last night. Mommy says she only comes when you're sleeping, and you can always tell she's been there by all the confetti she leaves behind. "What's with the balloons?"

Mommy's smile disappears. "Brody." She tugs on the sleeve of his t-shirt, but he bats her hand away. "*Brody*."

"We can talk later, Fin." Brody cranes his neck like he's trying to see past her, and I know he's looking for me. "I can see someone special waiting for me."

"Brody—"

Uncle B ignores her, ducking down and sweeping me off my feet, tossing me into the air. "Crew! How's my favorite girl? Tell me, what's with the balloons?"

I giggle as the air rushes around me, my curly hair flying into my face. Uncle B catches me, and I press my hands into his cheeks, beaming. "It's my birthday, silly!" His bright blue eyes, so much like Mommy's, widen slightly. "That's why you're here!"

"Well, I mean, yeah!" He glances quickly at Mommy before looking back at me and returning my giant smile. "*Of course* it is! Would I miss my favorite niece's birthday?"

"Uncle B, I'm your *only* niece."

Setting me back down on my feet, Uncle B puts his hands on his hips. "So? You can't still be my favorite?"

"I can tell you that at this moment, *you're* definitely not *my* favorite," Mommy mutters, walking past us and back into the kitchen, where we had been admiring the cupcakes the birthday fairy delivered before Uncle B knocked on the door.

"Fin—"

"Not now, Brody."

I tug on his sleeve. "Are you in trouble?"

"Yeah, Crew-girl, I think I may just be," Uncle B says quietly.

"Maybe you should say sorry." Ms. A always makes Gia tell me sorry when she hurts my feelings. Gia doesn't like to so much, but that's okay. Lux always gets her back. That's what he promises, and Lux and I *never* break a promise, *ever*.

"Your uncle doesn't know that word," Mommy tells me, slinging a dish towel over her shoulder as she leans against the doorframe.

I look at her and back to Uncle B, frowning. "You don't know the word *sorry*?"

Uncle B scowls at Mommy. "I do, too."

"Well, maybe you'd like to use it in a sentence sometime."

She's using her snappy voice. I frown at them. "Are you two fighting?"

They look at each other, and then Mommy crouches down in front of me. "Not at all, sweetheart. We're just...bickering. Fake-fighting. It's something siblings do. Like Lux and Gia, right?" I nod. She tugs gently on one of my curls. "Why don't you show your Uncle B what the birthday fairy brought before Lux comes over?"

"Is Gia coming, too?"

Mommy smiles a little. "No, she's hanging out with friends today." *Good*, I think. I don't want Gia to come. She won't play Barbies with me anymore, and she's always calling me and Lux babies, even though she's only two years older than us. Lux says she just wants to be cool like her new friends, but I don't see why. She never *looks* like she's having fun with them. "Now go on. Show your Uncle B around."

I beam up at him, bouncing up and down on the balls of my feet. "Yes! Uncle B, you have to come see." Grabbing a hold of his hand, I dig my feet into the floor as I pull for him to follow.

"Fin—"

"Go spend some time with your niece, Brody."

"Uncle B, you have to see the number balloon!" I squeal, pointing to the large silver "7" swaying in the living room, standing out in the middle of the rest of the bouquet of colorful balloons. A banner tacked to the wall just behind it reads, *Happy Birthday!* "See? It's a seven, because I'm seven today!" I stop in the middle of the living room, tilting my head sideways to peek up at him. "How old are *you*, Uncle B?"

Without looking away from the decorations, he answers, "Twenty-five."

I scrunch my nose. "Twenty-five?! That's old!"

"What?" Uncle B drops to his knees, clutching at his chest. "Old? Why I ought to show you—come here!"

Grabbing a hold of me, Uncle B's fingers skate across my ribs in a tickle attack. I shriek, trying to wiggle out of his hold. When he doesn't stop, I let out a little roar and grab for him. *Always fight back*. That's what Lux taught me. Even though sometimes I think he lets me win.

"Sailor," Mommy calls out. Uncle B and I freeze, but when I look up, she's standing in the hallway, watching us with the big smile she gets when she's trying not to laugh. "Try not to hurt him, okay?"

"Hey," Uncle B protests, but I double my efforts in taking a swing at him. Uncle B is ready for me, tackling me back down to the floor until I'm wheezing with giggles from his tickling fingers.

"Do you give up?" Uncle B asks, his eyes sparkling just like Mommy's. I wish I had their eyes. Then maybe I would look more like them. But Mommy says I have the prettiest green eyes to go with my brown curly hair. She says it makes me *unique*. But I don't want to be unique, I just want to be like Mommy.

"Never!" I growl. An idea comes to me, and I fake-whine, "Uncle B, I can't breathe!" His grip on my arm loosens right away and I use the new wiggle room to crash my entire body into his—arms and legs going everywhere.

"Oof!" He crashes back to the ground with a wheeze. "Okay, killer, I give, I give! I'm surrendering before your next move gets the jewels."

"Jewels?" What jewels? Like a crown? Princesses wear crowns. I scramble upright at the thought. "Uncle B, did you get me *jewelry*?"

"Jewelry?" Uncle B sits up, his eyebrows pinching for a second before they quickly shoot up his forehead as he laughs. "No, I, um, I didn't get anything like that for you."

"Then what *did* you get me?"

Uncle B pats his pockets. "I definitely got you something. Let me just—okay, it's not much, but..." He pulls out his wallet, and I stare at him, eyes wide, as he starts tugging out money. *Wow*. "I, um, know I've missed some birthdays and Christmases even, so um, here." He hands me the cash and I try my best to count it.

"Wow, thanks, Uncle B—"

"Oh, wait, are those singles?" Uncle B looks at the money in my hands. *Singles?* He holds up a finger, takes the stack from me, and shuffles all of the "1" dollar bills back into his wallet before giving the rest back, muttering, "I'm gonna need those for the strip club later."

I blink. "What's a strip club?"

Uncle B freezes, his eyes darting over my head to find Mommy. She must've left the room because Uncle B lets out a breath. "Never mind that." He waves it off. "Why don't you tell me about this Lux kid. Is he your boyfriend?"

"Eww! *Gross*, Uncle B!" I shudder. "Lux is my *friend*."

My *best* friend. My only friend, if you ask Gia, but I don't think that matters. Lux is the only friend I need.

PART 1

FOOL ME ONCE

ONE

NOW

THE EVER-PRESENT ACHE in my jaw should be distracting, but I barely notice it anymore. I still feel as numb as I did the day I texted Brody after Mom's heart monitor flatlined.

Sailor: Mom passed away this morning. Thought you should know.

He never did answer. Not that I expected him to.

If it had been up to me, I would have left it alone. File our relationship away as a fleeting memory, and try to move on with my life. Instead, I found myself boarding a plane earlier today with my social worker Priya at my side, on our way to my new residence—or as Priya keeps insisting, my new *home*—in Siren's Cove.

The only place left for me. The one place I don't want to go.

Mom, apparently, had other plans.

"Sailor?"

I blink slowly, skimming the empty plane. *When did everyone get off? Hell, when did we even land?*

"Sailor?" Priya repeats. I wince and turn to meet her worried brown eyes. Giving her a smile I hope looks reassuring and not fake, I draw my bookbag from under the seat in front of me and get to my feet. I pull my small duffel from the overhead bin, the little pineapple keychain swinging back and forth as I throw the strap over my shoulder.

Priya watches me from the aisle, her own bag already in her hand. "Got everything?"

My hand tightens on the strap of the bag. Do I have everything? No, not even a little bit. At least, not what really matters. But with Mom gone, I just had to hope like hell that the things I grabbed would make me feel close to her. These two bags can't even possibly start to fill this hole in my heart, but it's all I have left. My entire life—and Mom's—reduced to a couple of bags. I swallow back the threat of tears and nod. "Yeah. That's everything."

Priya hesitates, her gentle features pinching slightly as she studies my face, before starting off the plane. I follow silently as we bypass baggage claim and go right to the rental car counter. I reach for the mermaid tail on my necklace, zipping it back and forth in a steady rhythm as music continues to play in my ears while Priya talks to the desk agent. I keep the volume low enough to never miss a word from Priya, but unwilling to tug the headphones off in my need to drown the silence in my head.

"We're all set," Priya announces, brandishing a set of keys. "Come on."

A light breeze greets us as we step outside, not nearly cool enough to mask the wall of high humidity after the air conditioned airport. The sky is rapidly darkening, thunder rumbling above us.

How fitting.

We make it to our assigned car before the first drop of rain. Priya's hand flits around the tight knot atop of her head, her usual headwrap secured and thick black hair in a high ponytail, as we settle in our seats. "I guess it can't always be sunny in the sunshine state! I think hurricane season has started too."

Fisting the charm on my necklace until my nails bite into the palm of my hand, I struggle to ask the question that's been plaguing me since Priya booked the flight.

As if she can read my mind, Priya pauses with one hand hovering over the gearshift. "Sailor? What is it?"

My mouth opens and closes a few times, nearly unwilling to ask but desperate to know. "Are you sure he's expecting me?"

"Brody should be waiting on us at the center. I talked to him myself earlier this week." *Should.* Such an operative word when it comes to Brody.

"With Daniela?" Child services assigned me a new caseworker since Priya isn't licensed in Florida, and even if she were, it's too far for her to come for check-ins as frequently as the state requires.

"She prefers Dani, but yes."

Tightness pulls at my chest, and I try to keep my breathing under control. "I can still contact you, right?"

Priya smiles and I feel its warmth seep into my bones. "You won't be getting rid of me so easily. I'll be keeping in touch. But if you ever need anything, don't hesitate to reach out. Okay?"

I nod and rest my head against the seat, my eyes fluttering shut as I release a deep breath. At least something will stay familiar.

Priya backs the car out of its space, and we set off.

There's no turning back now.

Not that I'd have anything to turn back *to.* Safe Harbor Group Home for Youth had grown on me, but it would never have been *home*. Still, I'd found peace in helping with the younger kids—even some of the ones my own age too, if they weren't too hardheaded to accept my company. I'd miss some of them, but even though a few of the kids had offered to give me their numbers, I hadn't taken them up on it.

Keeping in touch does nothing for this weathered heart. I've learned my lesson.

The roar of the highway eventually gives way to silence. We leave the rain behind us, driving into the almost blinding sun. I close my eyes against the light and accidentally doze off.

A sudden shift from the sun to shadow wakes me sometime

later, the car already slowing down. I blink, shifting to look out the window. We're no longer on the highway. Large palm trees sit on either side of the road, like one large covered driveway. A sign shaped like a mermaid tail, nearly as tall as the closest palm, sprouts up from the red wooden mulch. The writing on it is bright and clean, like it's been recently repainted.

WELCOME TO SIREN'S COVE!

I want to yell for Priya to stop the car and let me out, but we continue forward, following the directions from her GPS until it's abruptly interrupted by an incoming call. With practiced ease, Priya slips on an earpiece, pressing a button to answer the call.

"This is Priya." Her calm demeanor shifts to something hard, her eyes slightly narrowing as she listens to the person on the other end. "I see."

I finger my necklace, eyes darting around. The bay of palm trees open up into a quaint beach town, full of vibrant hues of pink, yellow, green, blue and orange. The open storefronts and homes are painted in cool tones, some with boldly saturated colors that impressively work, others a simple white, standing out starkly against the buildings embracing them.

It looks like a secluded little paradise. Siren's Cove is a popular location for surfers and divers, from what I read online. It's bursting with life, full of smiling faces and people strolling leisurely up and down the streets—many skateboarding or biking, a flurry of activity everywhere I look. There's a perfect view of the ocean as we drive down the main strip.

The quieter streets on the outskirts of town are wrapped by an alcove of towering palm trees. Dropping my necklace, I lower the window and place my hand just outside, letting the salt-scented wind caress my skin, the sun's warmth kissing me in greeting. I release my first steady breath in what feels like hours.

"Okay, we'll meet you there." Priya ends her call, taking off her earpiece and tossing it into the center console. The little huff of breath she lets out as she does it is the only giveaway of annoyance. I brace myself, the brief moment of ease vanishing. "So, there's a slight change of plans." Priya briefly meets my eyes, offering me her social worker smile, the one that says *everything will totally be fine*. Automatically, I start grinding my teeth again. "We're going to head over to the shop."

"The surf shop." The place that proves Brody can commit to *something*. Just not, apparently, me. "What happened to meeting at the community center?"

"Yes, well, it would appear that he never showed." Priya's steadfast refusal to shy away from the truth is one of the reasons why I'm incredibly grateful she was assigned as my caseworker. She's never afraid to have tough conversations, leading with compassion and a gentleness that never makes me feel like I'm being coddled. It's one thing to be able to read a room, it's another to be able to read the person in front of you. In Priya's line of work, I think it's incredibly important to know how to do both. She does it well. It's why I trust her.

"Okay then." I nod, trying to sound as confident as Priya does that everything is going to be okay. I probably don't pull it off. "Let's go."

The road turns from pavement to gravel to crushed seashells, the beach rolling closer and closer. A bright yellow hut sits right on the sand, palm fronds decorating the sloped roof and hanging over the edges. Surfboards of all sizes and colors sit upright on stands or tucked into racks. Small round buoys hang from the pillars holding up the overhanging roof. There's a surfboard propped next to the door, its polished surface replaced with what must be chalkboard paint. Someone has written the week's sales and specials in handwriting that's way too neat to be Brody's.

I grab for the door handle at the same time that I finally catch the shop's name, and suddenly, I forget how to breathe.

Nailed into the drywall, where the roof meets to form a triangle, is a neatly-carved wooden sign. Staring back at me are two words:

TOP FIN.

TWO

FIN.

Fin?

Did Brody name the shop after Mom?

The question is right there, on the tip of my tongue, but I swallow it down. I don't understand. *Why would he—?*

Maybe it has nothing to do with Mom at all. Top Fin could have any and everything to do with the fact that this is a surf shop and we're on a beach. But...

I press my hand into my thigh, dragging it back and forth as uncertainty eats at me. I don't know if I'm trying to keep myself grounded or keep myself from punching Brody in the face the moment I see him. My skin feels too hot and too tight, my throat burning as I fight back tears. He wasn't there for a moment of Mom being sick. None of it. And he, what? Thinks he can slap her name on a building as homage, and that'll make everything okay? My heart thunders against my ribs.

"Sailor?" Priya's voice is hesitant, but gentle.

I stuff my churning emotions down and drop a wall over my face. I will *not* give this man another piece of me. If he wanted me to feel something, he should have stuck around. Once I'm sure my face is unreadable, I roll my shoulders back and lift my head.

"Let's get this over with." I jerk open the car door and step out, only to be immediately accosted by a tiny whirlwind of dark curls and outstretched hands.

"Sailor, you made it!" The woman who sweeps out from the shop's awning has a lilting, enthusiastic voice, kind without being overbearing. She almost seems too small for it, short and shapely with a round, smiling face. She flips her hair with ease I could never achieve with my own wild curls, her long black hair tumbling down her back.

"I'm Dani," she says, smiling broadly as she shakes my hand, her grip firm but friendly. Other than the tiny smile lines at the corners of her eyes, her face is totally smooth—she could be twenty-five or forty-five. I have no idea. I know Priya is in her twenties, and she feels more like a big sister rather than some adult with no idea how to relate to me. Or worse, someone who's going to try to act like the parent I don't have. "It's so nice to meet you."

I nod as I return her handshake, not sure how else to respond. To say it's nice meeting her too would be a lie. Nothing about being here, except *maybe* the familiar smell of the sea, is nice.

And even that can't make up for everything else being wrong.

Laughter spills out of the open shop, and we all turn toward the sound of voices. *At least someone's happy to be here.*

"That would be the boys," Dani explains. When I blink at her, bewildered, she adds, "They work for your uncle. Good kids, though Lord knows they're loud about it. Come on."

I drag my feet over the gravel as she gestures for us to follow her inside, falling a few paces behind them when Priya quickens her step to catch up with Dani, speaking to her too softly for me to hear. I can't help glaring at the shop name again, staring it down until the awning cuts off my view.

The store is orderly and neat, considering it seems to have a bunch of guys running it. The store's walls have large floor to ceiling sliding glass doors, all of them currently open to let the sea salt air carry on the breeze. We weave through racks of clothes, and with every brush of fabric, every step forward, my body stiffens further. I swear it gets hotter, too, the pounding in my temples matching the pace of my heart. The floorboards creak underneath our weight and I pause, looking back the way we came.

It's not too late.

I could leave right now. Take off while they're not looking.

But where would I go?

"Guys!"

The familiar voice freezes me before I can take a single step.

"It doesn't sound like much work is getting done." It's light, teasing, all fake anger and real affection. It shouldn't make me feel like I want to throw up, but it does. "What am I paying you for anyway?"

For a second, I'm standing in the hallway of my childhood home, staring after a man who promised to never leave. Nothing more than a rushed apology from his lips as he gave me his back.

The last words he ever said to me, the words that still haunt me to this day.

"I'm sorry, kid."

I think I'm going to be sick.

"Hey." Priya's soft voice draws me out of my head, her hand on my arm bringing me back into my body. "Hey, it's okay. Look at me, Sailor." Dani stands just behind her, her brows drawn with worry. "Take a deep breath." I do. It's muscle memory.

Mom's voice rings through my head. *Remember to breathe.*

"I'm fine." I'm not. Far from it. But what does telling the truth change? Priya and the South Carolina Department of Social Services believe it's in my best interest to be placed with someone I know—however loosely—than to stay at Safe Harbor until I turn eighteen. "*Group homes are meant to be temporary,*" Priya had explained when she initially brought up the idea of relocating me to Siren's Cove. "*You deserve something permanent.*"

Yeah, right.

"If you need to take a moment, Sailor, we can step back outside," Dani offers.

I shake my head. “I’m good.” Then, remembering my manners, I tack on, “Thank you.” Wiping underneath my eyes to make sure there’s no trace of tears, I nod towards the sound of voices just beyond them. “Let’s go get this over with.” Priya searches my face for a few seconds longer before starting forward. Dani shifts back until she’s at my side, and while I’m not sure if she’s lending me strength or support, I’m grateful either way as we step out into the middle of the shop, my nails biting into the palms of my hands as whatever the guys had been joking about dies on their lips. *If nothing else, at least I got lucky with my caseworkers.*

There was an ever-revolving door of caseworkers at Safe Harbor, some more burned out than others. The younger ones came in with fresh faces and kind smiles that disappeared a few months into the job. You were lucky if you got one who knew how to maintain their optimism. You were even luckier if you got one who remembered your name.

I once asked Priya how she handled it all, worried that at any moment she’d leave me too. “*Talking to someone helps*,” she told me, though I’m not sure if that’s really the way she copes or if she just grabbed the opportunity to ease me into the idea of going to therapy.

“Hey, why’d it get so quiet? You guys know I was just jok—” Brody halts at the sight of me, frozen halfway through stepping out of what must be the back room, his familiar floppy blonde locks poking out from underneath his ball cap. He stares at me, his wide eyes still just as cerulean as Mom’s.

Every interaction with him over the course of my childhood plays on a sped up reel, so fast, so fleeting—much like our relationship. The phantom smell of cigarettes burns my nose and it scrunches on its own accord, my lips curling in disgust.

I never thought I’d be seeing his face again after he walked away six years ago. I swallow thickly.

Adjusting the hat on his head, Brody rubs the back of his neck as he looks between me and both caseworkers. "Wow, you've... really grown."

And you look exactly *the same.* "A lot changes in six years." I don't bother keeping the sarcasm out of my voice.

"Crew—"

My head jerks back, as if I'd been slapped. "*Don't.* Don't call me that."

There's a beat of silence. Finally, he says, "What do you want me to call you?"

"Just—Just Sailor. Call me Sailor."

"Sailor," he says, as if trying out the name. Like he can't possibly imagine not calling me by a nickname he hasn't bothered using in years. But *Crew* no longer exists. She hasn't for a long time.

"Mr. Lehmann." It's weird to hear Priya refer to Brody by our shared surname. As far as I'm concerned, he stopped being a part of our family the night he walked out on us. We might still share a last name, but that's about all that keeps us tied together. Otherwise, he's no family of mine. "Nice of you to finally join us."

"Oh, um, shit, time must've gotten away from me." *Liar.*

"Yes, I'm sure." Priya sounds far from it, and Brody shifts where he stands, his eyes cutting away from us.

He's always been easy to read. And he's always been a liar.

An alarm beeps briefly from the back room, followed by a slam of a door. A new voice calls out, "What is Brody's truck still doing here? *Please* tell me he made it over to the center—"

I stumble forward without thinking, because this time, the sight of a familiar face *doesn't* make me want to cry—at least, not in a bad way. The green eyes I'm used to only seeing through a screen widen at the sight of me as another man steps out of the back room. His salt and pepper hair is a maintained buzzcut since his Army days, the only change being the neatly trimmed beard he's grown.

My eyes water, and my voice cracks on my whispered, "*Kelly.*" Before I can think better of it, I close the space between us, knocking into Brody as I pass him to throw my arms around Kelly's waist, burying my head into his chest as the weight of the last month comes crashing down.

Kelly—freaking—Foster. Mom's best friend. A man I've often thought should have been my actual uncle, instead of being the stand-in for a man who never bothered to fulfill the role himself. And now, my only life raft in the choppy seas where I find myself drowning. *God am I grateful to see him.*

Kelly doesn't hesitate to hug me back, his tattooed-covered hands rubbing soothing circles on my back. Where Brody is lean, Kelly is all broad muscles, and I feel strangely safe in his embrace. "I got you," he says quietly, just loud enough for me to hear him.

It's a relief to not hear another platitude. I've heard *it's going to be okay* so many times in the past six months that I think I may just scream if I hear it again.

Pulling back slightly to get a look at me he shakes his head. "You gotta stop growing, kid, you're making me feel old."

I chuckle, a slight rasp to my voice giving way to my choked up feelings. "As if." *He's what now? Forty-five?* He was closer to Mom's age than Brody's. Kelly laughs, knocking his fist lightly against my jaw playfully before fixing his attention over my head. His eyes narrow as he meets what must be Brody's, but he says nothing.

"Why don't we step into the back and have a little chat," Dani says. Her tone is pleasant, but it's clear she isn't asking. As a matter of fact, it sounds like *someone* is in trouble. I duck my head, smiling to myself. They couldn't look more different but Dani almost reminds me of Mom.

"I think that'd be a good idea," Kelly's square jaw is even squarer when it's clenched like it is now. His face softens as he shifts his attention back to me. "I'll be right back."

Priya lays a hand on my arm as she goes to step past me, searching my face. "Will you be okay to wait out here? I could stay with you, if you want."

"I'll be okay."

"I would hope so," Dani says. "You're in good hands with the boys, I promise. I gave birth to two of them, and the other two are my honorary sons." She cuts her eyes to the guys all around the shop, though I count only three of the four she mentioned. They all shift where they stand, straightening up slightly as if uncomfortable under the scrutiny of this one tiny woman. "Let me know if they give you any trouble."

She shoots them all one more firm look, gives me a much gentler one, and on that note, the adults clear the room, leaving me with a bunch of boys I have no desire to talk to.

Maybe I'll just wait outside.

Before I can scoot back toward the entrance, one of the guys steps forward, a broom in one hand and the other pushing dreadlocks out of his face, an easy smile lighting up his soft brown eyes. He's several inches taller than me, with brown skin and a baby face to adore. "Sailor, right? We've heard a lot about you. I'm Milo."

I swallow thickly. What am I supposed to say? Nice to meet you too? Hope you enjoyed the front row seat to my family drama? Lovely weather we're having?

I'm not here to make friends with a bunch of surfers or play nice with Brody. All I need is to get through this year and graduate high school, and then I'm gone.

Undeterred by my lack of response, understanding swimming in the depths of his eyes, Milo gestures to the two other guys in the shop. "The tall one is Banks—"

"Hey!" The shorter one protests, but the smile on his lips gives away his amusement.

"And that's Griffin," Milo continues, grinning. I try not to stare at him. Is there some sort of prerequisite in which all employees must be surfer-model worthy to work here?

Where did Brody find these guys anyway?

I study them again. Banks and Griffin are way too similar in looks to not be related, with their deeply tanned skin, full lips, square jaws and nearly white-blonde curls. There's something familiar about them, and I puzzle over it for half a second before I realize why. They both have Dani's eyes. Dani's reassurance of being in good hands floats through my mind, *"I gave birth to two of them." They're definitely her sons.*

She birthed *them?* But she's so *tiny*.

As if reading my mind, Griffin grins at me. "We take after our dad."

For all their similarities, the two of them are far from identical. Banks has his hair up in a man bun that really works for him, showing off his guarded hazel eyes. Griffin's expression, in contrast, is bright and carefree, and he's nearly bouncing on his feet, his curls left to sweep across his broad shoulders with every movement.

"Don't mind him, crankiness comes with age," Griffin jokes, ducking from behind the counter as he dodges his brother's punch to the arm. His hair falls to the side with the movement, revealing a long white indented scar running down the right side of his face. "I'm the only Marshall brother you need to know. My friends call me Griff, by the way. I'd ask if you have a nickname, but, uh, it seems like that's not your thing."

Just how old is Banks? He doesn't look that much older than any of the rest of us. And...what was that about nicknames?

My head nearly spins with the pace in which I try to keep up with Griffin's conversation. "No, it's not my thing. And, I'm...not really here to make friends anyway." I can barely look at him as I say it. *It's like kicking a puppy.*

"Well, that would be unfortunate," someone says from behind me. "If it were true."

I freeze at the new voice.

I turn around, my stomach tying itself in a knot as I stare up into familiar gray-blue eyes—eyes I used to be able to read as well as my own. Eyes I haven't seen in over three years.

I blink slowly, as if time has come to a crawl, and a ringing starts in my ears.

"*Lux?*"

THREE

NINE YEAR AGOS

SOMEONE KNOCKS on my bedroom door, and I pull my eyes away from my book, ready to complain about being interrupted *again*—but instead, I find myself lighting up. "Uncle B!"

"Crew!" Uncle B spreads his arms wide, and I leap out of bed, tackling him with a hug. His arms wrap around me, and I rest my head against his chest, listening to the steady beat of his heart. "What are you doing here?"

"Well, I mean, if you don't *want* me here, I guess I can go."

"No!" I squeeze him hard, digging my feet into the carpet. "Please stay, Uncle B, please."

Uncle B chuckles. "Don't worry Crew-girl, I'm not going anywhere."

Something in my chest tightens and I peer up at him. "Promise?"

His eyes search my face before he squeezes me back just as hard and drops a kiss on top of my head. "Yeah, Crew, of course I promise."

I smile and snuggle further into him before scrunching my nose. "Uncle B!" I pull away. "What is that smell?" Something in the back of my throat tickles and I cover my mouth to cough.

Uncle B's cheeks redden as he rubs at the back of his neck. "Oh, um, it's probably the smoke."

"Smoke?" *Oh!* "Smoking's bad for you!"

"Yeah, so your mom likes to remind me."

"What about your mom?"

Uncle B blinks at me. "What?"

"Your mom. Doesn't she think smoking is bad too?"

"Um, yeah, probably." Uncle B walks past me, stopping beside my bed. "What are you reading?" I bounce after him, barely breathing as I explain the magic adventures. Uncle B takes in the stack of books in the corner of my room as I continue talking, nodding his head and sometimes asking questions—kind of like Lux does when I start chattering like this. Lux always wants to know what I'm reading.

I try to get him to read too, but he says he loves it when *I* tell him about the book instead. He says he likes it even more when I read aloud to him. He can be so silly sometimes!

Suddenly, Uncle B stops, staring at the photos on my nightstand with a look I don't understand, and I go quiet.

I like those pictures. There's one of me and Mommy on our recent road trip to West Virginia. It was so pretty—and the pepperoni rolls were really good too! My favorite photo is the one of me and Lux with our backs to the camera, holding hands. Ms. A took the picture on our first day of kindergarten at the bus stop. Lux was crying, and Ms. A said I walked right up to him, grabbed his hand and told him everything would be okay. She likes to say that he's been stuck to me like glue ever since.

Uncle B narrows his eyes as he grabs a picture, bringing it closer to himself. Leaning against his side, I try to see what he's looking at. It's Mommy and me making funny faces on a video call. Somewhere on the other side of the world, in a green uniform, Mommy's friend made a funny face too, and took the picture. He travels a lot. "That's Mommy's friend!"

"Kelly," Uncle B says. There's something weird about how he says the name.

I look up at him. "He's your friend too, right, Uncle B?"

"Sometimes."

"Are you fighting with him?" Uncle B's eyebrows scrunch together, like a caterpillar. "You and Mommy fight a lot..."

"You catch that, huh?" Uncle B looks over at me, his lips twitching, but his eyes are gentle. "We're all okay, Crew."

"You're all friends again, you mean?" Uncle B doesn't say anything, instead he looks back down at the photo. I'm so good at knowing what Mommy's feeling just by looking at her face, but even though they look alike, I can't figure out what Uncle B feels at all. "Uncle B?"

Clearing his throat, he puts the photo down and picks up the book I dropped instead. He sits down on my bed, holding the book out to me. "So, where did you leave off?"

I can't help but smile as I take the book and sit beside him. Uncle B throws an arm behind his head and lays back. Folding my legs, I flip the book open, the pages flying fast as I try to find my place. I *always* use a bookmark, but I kind of forgot when I saw Uncle B.

Peeking over at him through my curls, I frown. *He looks sad.* His eyes dance around my room, always going back to the photos. *Does he want to take a picture too?* Maybe that's what we can do this weekend! I'll ask Mommy.

My knees stop bouncing and I fix my eyes on the words in front of me. As I start reading aloud, Uncle B releases a deep breath like I do when I finally catch mine. I stop reading to lay my head against his side, my feet pressed against the wall, and fall back into the magical adventures of a treehouse.

I WAKE up to the sound of voices in the hallway.

"It's not like we were hiding anything from you," Mommy is saying.

Rubbing my eyes, I spy my book beside my bed and Uncle B

gone. I push myself up until I'm sitting, a blanket falling to my lap.

"I thought there was nothing going on between you two." That's Uncle B. He sounds upset.

"There isn't." Mommy says. "Even if there was, it's none of your business."

"I just think it could be confusing for Sail."

"Like an Uncle that comes and goes when he feels like it?"

"What the hell does that mean?"

"You only show up when it's convenient for you." There's silence, and I shift on the bed, holding my breath as I try to hear them. I thought Uncle B said everything was okay. Why are he and Mommy fighting again? Did I do something? "Tell me, do you even remember it's Father's Day Weekend or did we happen to luck out with your presence since, coincidentally, there's a huge NASCAR tournament in town?"

There's another moment of silence, then, "Why would Sail care about Father's Day?"

Mommy huffs, and my chest tightens. My hands grab a hold of the blanket, fisting tightly in the fabric as I release a shaky breath. "Sometimes you're so oblivious I could scream." She pauses, then says,"Sailor's been asking questions."

"About what?"

"Brody...you're one of the two closest male figures in her life. And God knows that little girl loves the hell out of you—even when you don't deserve it. I want you to know your niece, really know her."

"I *do* know her," Uncle B protests. "Just because I'm not here every day—"

Mommy cuts him off. "You're hardly here at all!"

"Oh, and Kelly is?" Uncle B challenges. "I didn't realize he could take leave from the Army whenever he feels like it."

"He may not physically be here, but he still shows up for Sailor in all the ways it counts."

Silence fills the house and a trail of goosebumps flares across my arms.

"You mean he shows up for Sailor *and* you." Uncle B's voice sounds weird, like when he said Kelly's name earlier today while staring at the picture. "And, what, I don't?"

"Brody, I need you to open your eyes! You're not a kid anymore, but Sailor is and I need for her to know that she can rely on you."

Mommy says something too quietly for me to hear. But it must be something bad, because Uncle B is a lot louder all of a sudden, and I jump when he says, "Don't talk like that!"

"Brody, keep your voice down!" Mommy hisses.

"No." Uncle B's voice sounds farther away. "I'm not talking about this."

"*B.*" Mommy's voice seems to follow him. "We can't just ignore this. Please talk to me."

"No. I'm done talking." The front door slams shut, the walls seeming to shake. *One, two, three, four*, I can almost see Mommy mouthing the words as I try to take in a breath. Tears fall down my face but I don't move to get rid of them, staring at the light spilling in through my door as I breathe out.

Again, I can practically hear Mommy say.

I try my best, but this time my shoulders never drop down below my ears. I feel like I'm falling, and I'm scared.

FOUR

LUX FREAKING ARMSTRONG. Here. In Siren's Cove.

What the actual hell?

I thought the biggest problem coming here would be facing Brody, but now I'm not so sure. After Mom died, I'd thought there was no way my world could shift any further off its axis, but at the sight of Lux...

I rub a hand across my chest as Milo drives us up the coast, alongside the beach.

Mom would've killed me for getting in the car with a stranger. But what's one more wrong decision?

I needed an out, and with the adults still talking in the back, Milo came to the rescue. Well, Milo *and* Griffin. He refused to be left out, nearly tripping on the heels of my feet as I stumbled past Lux in a rush.

Milo swiped Brody's keys with a familiarity I tried hard not to fixate on and we climbed into the beaten-up blue truck I haven't seen in years. The one Kelly had been talking about when he walked into the shop.

"What is Brody's truck still doing here?"

Better question: What am *I* doing here?

I should have known it was too good to be true, no matter

what he told Priya and Dani. Living up to a promise has never been Brody's strong suit.

By the strain in Kelly's voice, he knew it, too.

The truck is littered with empty cigarette packs, the smell of smoke still in the air. Milo and Griffin made quick work of swiping a few random shirts onto the back floor in a pile, laughing at a pair of women's underwear they found, and stuffing some crumbled papers into the side doors. With a few half-drunk water bottles and gum wrappers strewn about, I scrunched my nose as I swiped them aside and got in, trying not to suggest that I just walk instead. His place can't be too far.

The guys transferred my bags into the bed of the pickup and we took off—leaving Lux in the rearview, his body tense as he watched us go.

He's changed. No longer the boy I knew, but nearly a man, all broad shoulders and long legs. His floppy black curls are gone, his hair cut close to his scalp.

And he's tall. God, is he tall. There was once a time I could look him directly in the eye.

Those days, like so many others, are behind us now. There's not a chance in getting it back—getting *us* back.

I just...don't understand. How can he be *here*?

No one speaks as we drive away from Top Fin, but the silence feels surprisingly comfortable. As the distance grows between me and the shop, my fingers unfurl from around my necklace and I bring my arm up onto the window sill, laying my head on my arm and inhaling the fresh air. The wind ruffles my curls, pulling strands of it from the messy bun atop of my head, tickling the skin on my face as it whips around in a frenzied dance. Mom had always said my curls were just like me—wild and free.

I'm not sure I know what that feels like anymore. I'm not sure I know who *I am* anymore.

"Look alive," Milo says, and I pick my head up off my arm. "We're just about there."

I brace myself for whatever Brody's living situation might

look like. It can't be too terrible if Dani signed off on it *and* Kelly lives with him. But all the same, I can't imagine it's going to be good. Not if it's anything like his truck.

So when Milo pulls into a circular driveway off to our left, closest to the beach and right on the edge of town, all I can do is stare.

Tucked away in the arching bend of the cove that gave the town its name—like some little secret—is a one-story blue bungalow. A stained wooden porch wraps around the entire house, no railing in sight. A stone pathway woven into the carefully tended lawn leads around the left side of the house. I can't help but tip my head back, taking in the strings of fairy light rigged in beautiful dips above us.

"Brody and Kelly live *here*?" I've never considered them within the same breath let alone living under one roof.

"They've been roommates for the past ten years," Milo explains as we all slip from the truck. Griffin sets off ahead of us and I round to the back to gather my things. "Oh, hold up! Let me grab that for you."

I open my mouth to protest, but instead what comes out is, "Um, yeah, okay." I take a step back to give him room. I don't care to fight him on it. I need to conserve all my energy to square off with the ones who actually deserve my anger.

With my duffel in one hand and my backpack thrown over his shoulder, he gestures me up the steps. Griffin pulls the screen door open and pushes the next door open into the house, stepping to the side with a dramatic bow and sweep of his hand as he holds it for me. "Ladies first."

I raise my eyebrows. "They just leave the door unlocked?"

Milo chuckles, "It's Siren's Cove." As if that's all there is to it, and maybe to him and the rest of the town, it is. "If, for some reason, the door actually *is* ever locked, there's a key hidden in a fake rock underneath the agave plant here." He nods his head at the blooming green plant right beside the porch steps leading up to the door.

"How original," I mutter. Milo flashes me a grin as he gives a light shrug.

"If you can't ever find the key, the sliding glass door around back is usually unlocked," Griffin adds.

I step inside, shivering as the air conditioning greets my clammy skin. Milo gestures to a hallway immediately off to our left. "Your room's this way. Come on."

I start to follow, only to come to an immediate halt at the pictures and accolades hanging on the wall to my right that leads further into the house. The display of this home's life wraps around to the hallway the guys beckon me down, seemingly reaching to its end. Sunlight spills in through the large windows that make up the front of the house, highlighting what I wish was a trick of the eyes as my feet drag down the hall.

Frame after frame, it's Brody and Kelly with the guys from the shop: at the beach, in the water on surfboards, sitting around a fire pit laughing, sitting here at the house, bent over surfboards in the shop. There's awards from volleyball tournaments, and from surfing and skateboarding competitions. Things Brody is proud of, boasting about it all for the world to see, although there's more pictures of Kelly and another man—nearly familiar, though I can't place him—with the boys than there are with Brody himself.

I take in their lives, their stories, timestamped from various portions, all of it becoming out of focus as my eyes fill with unshed tears.

I suck in a sharp breath as my gaze catches on a series of pictures of Brody with a little girl, her blonde ringlets cascading down her back, bright blue eyes mostly fixated on him. Frame after frame where she's sitting on his shoulders, where he's holding her on his hip, where he's celebrating her milestones, where he's sitting on the beach building a sandcastle with her.

Who *is* she?

I turn swiftly from the wall, my chest tight. "You said my room is this way?"

They exchange glances, and then Griffin clears his throat. "Um—yeah. Come on." I follow him, the silence no longer comfortable. We turn the corner at the end of the hall to three closed doors. "It's the door to your left," Griffin says.

I follow his pointing finger and blink. The other two doors are plain, but mine has several flowers in multiple shades of yellow painted in the center, my name written in a swoop of neat white cursive.

"I wouldn't touch that," Milo jumps in. I flinch, my hand dropping back down to my side. I hadn't realized I even raised it. "Looks like it's still wet. Lux must've just finished, it wasn't there this morning."

Lux.

My throat aches at the black-eyed Susans. He used to pick those for me all the time when we were kids. Yellow was his favorite color. He once told me that I felt like yellow to him. At the time I hadn't known what that meant.

Gia had called him stupid, saying that if anything, I was more of a brown than yellow. It didn't make much sense to me. Not when Ms. A scolded Gia, and not when I went home to tell Mom and she explained that Gia meant my skin color and not the feeling Lux had around me.

All I knew was that Lux was nice to me, and that when he used the yellow crayon in class, he smiled like he did when he looked at me.

Pretending my hand isn't shaking, I reach for the doorknob. But before I can open it, a stream of voices fills the house.

"It would seem that everyone made their way here." Milo muses.

Great.

"Sailor?" Priya calls out.

I try to clear my throat once, twice, yet I can't find my words. Griffin takes the lead and I can't help but feel grateful when he hollers, "We're down the hall!"

Priya appears a moment later, eyes skimming over us before

flicking up to the door. "You found your room, wonderful! We can look at it together."

Tension bleeds from my shoulders at her gentle suggestion, and my hand feels a lot steadier as I twist the knob.

Whatever I'm expecting...it's not this.

A large gray wicker basket chair that could easily fit several people comfortably, immediately greets us against the closest wall, paired with a little coffee table. It's filled to the brim with little decorative pillows and I can't help but smile at the one sitting front and center that reads, *Aloha, Beaches*.

Directly past the seating area, tucked in the corner is an open door leading into a closet. Two large windows, evenly placed along the wall to the closet's immediate left, reveal the pathway along the side of the house, a circular wooden mirror hanging on the wall in between the windows and a matching dresser sitting below the reflective frame. A polaroid camera and record player sit atop with records lined up beside it, a bookend on either side of the selection in the shape of an ocean wave.

A wicker-framed bed sits between two large windows to my left, looking out to the driveway and a full-length bench at its end. A large white tapestry hangs on the wall above the bed with the words *Pray for Surf* in soft pink lettering. Little potted plants hang from the ceiling in front of the windows, rocking gently in the air from the spinning ceiling fan.

"I..." I don't know what to say. I step completely into the room and turn to Milo and Griffin. Their eyes are already on me, watching with rapt attention. "Is this really all for me?"

Milo's smile lights up the room, Griffin's no less blinding as he places my belongings on the bench at the end of the bed. He turns to face me with a spring in his step, even as he rubs his hands up and down the front of his pants. "Do you like it?"

"I..."

The wall behind them catches my attention, adorned with a collage of still images I presume are all Siren's Cove and the beach. A pink pastel surfboard sits in the middle of it all, white lettering with positive affirmations painted across it and thumbtacks pressed in. I grab hold of my necklace as I find my next breath.

"It's incredible, right?" Priya chimes in. When I still can't find my words, Priya shows mercy on me. "Thanks for giving her a ride over, guys, but Dani and I have some things to go over with Sailor and Brody."

"And Kelly?" My voice comes out small, and I hate it.

I'm afraid she'll say no, but Priya's expression just softens. "If that's what you want." It is. Priya nods her head in understanding, and with a gesture to the door, leaves.

I start after her, pausing in the doorway to whisper over my shoulder. "Thank you."

Keeping my eyes trained on the floor I rush after Priya, unwilling to face the collection of photos again so soon. The hallway is a montage of a life I've never been a part of—that I didn't even know existed.

It's a clear message: I might live here, but that doesn't mean I belong.

FIVE

HOURS LATER, someone is knocking on my bedroom door.

I blink, the ceiling coming back into focus. Floorboards creek throughout the house as it comes alive with activity, voices filling the space. Deep, rich, laughter rings out, followed by an indiscernible shout. Distantly, I can smell charcoal smoke—a grill.

Memory flickers back slowly through my groggy, tear-drenched head. I remember Brody enthusiastically telling me and Dani about the cookout he and Kelly planned as tonight's festivities. To welcome me home.

I'd already been completely overwhelmed by the conversation we had just wrapped up with Dani, full of logistics and paperwork and schedules, but it was having to say goodbye to Priya that had put me on the emotional edge. Brody implying I'm "home" was the final straw.

"This isn't my home," I snapped as I left the room, locking myself in the bedroom. The closest thing to a safe space I have.

I haven't surfaced since.

"Hey, Sailor?" Another knock follows Griffin's words, but I don't move an inch. At least, I think it's Griffin's voice. "Sailor?"

"Are you sure she's even up?" The first voice must have been Griffin, because I think that's Milo.

"Why are you both standing around?" My breath hitches, because that voice, I *definitely* recognize. My stomach churns. "Where's Sailor?"

"The door's locked," Griffin explains.

Turning onto my side, I find the shadows of their feet underneath the door. A moment later, a much firmer knock pounds against the door. "Sailor!" I jerk at my name rolling off Lux's lips. *I never thought I'd hear him call my name again.* "Open the door."

I scowl. *Not a chance.* "Leave me alone, Lux." I nearly stumble over his name, a hitch in my throat as I push through it.

"Seriously? God, you are so—" He curses under his breath, barely loud enough for me to hear him through the door. A moment later, I hear footsteps pounding away down the hallway.

"Hey! Where are you going?" Griffin calls out. The sound of their voices moving away tugs at something deep within me, but I do my best to ignore it. I am not here to make friends—*especially* not with Lux. It's better he just writes me off along with the rest of them.

After all, he did so well the first time.

The window to my right creaks, and then slides open. I sit up quickly, my heart racing. *He wouldn't.*

Apparently, he would. With a thump, Lux pulls himself through the window, landing gracefully on his feet. For a moment, I can't do anything but stare. He's all golden skin and broad shoulders, with muscles bunching and rolling as he straightens up from the window. His skin is littered with scars, and my eyes widen as I catch sight of a couple of tattoos, too. My lips part as his very presence fills the space.

No. Absolutely not. I shake my head.

"What are you *doing*?"

Lux turns to face me with a shrug of his shoulders. "You wouldn't open the door."

"And you didn't take the hint because...?"

"Hey, a little help here," Griffin whines from outside. The

other window slides up with ease, revealing a head of dreadlocks, brown skin, and Milo's self-satisfied grin.

"Sure, come on in," I offer dryly, fisting the sleeves of my jacket as the guys break into my room. A moment later, Griffin spills onto the floor at Lux's feet. He immediately starts whining about the landing, like he'd fallen two stories instead of two feet, and I have to bite back a smile despite myself.

"There, see? Isn't it more fun when your pity party includes company?" Lux dryly remarks leaning back against the wall. Milo shoots Lux a pointed look and I turn to add my own glare. His eyes twinkle with a level of challenge he used to reserve for his sister.

Jerk.

Lux crosses his arms loosely over his chest, ankle hooked across the other, but there's an underlying tension in his jaw and his one hand continuously flexes open and close—his *tattooed* hands. When did he get tattoos? *How* did he get them?

I turn back to Milo. "Would you be willing to take him back out through the window? It's okay if you let him fall on his way out."

Milo smiles, ignoring my question. "Come eat with us. The food is just about ready."

"To get rid of him, I have to join him?" I ask incredulously.

"If you can't beat 'em, join 'em!" Griffin jokes, taking a seat on the couch and throwing his sandaled feet up on the table. He reclines back, hands behind his head, for all of a second before Lux clears the room in several strides and knocks his feet off. "Hey!"

Lux ignores him, turning back to me, and I'm briefly swept up in the storm of his eyes. "It's just a cookout. We're not asking to sit around and braid each other's hair." Maybe not now, but there was once a time he did exactly that, sitting next to Mom as her fingers worked through my hair, beyond captivated by the bundles of curls. I'd often find him twirling a piece around his finger, tugging gently only to watch it spring back into place. Our teachers used to scold him for it, until they realized I didn't have an issue and it seemed to keep Lux focused in class.

Lifting my head, I stare down my nose at him. "Is that supposed to make me feel better?"

"You know, I thought she'd be a lot happier to see you," Griffin muses with a frown.

I scoff. "What possibly gave you that idea?"

"Well, um..." Griffin straightens up. I follow his gaze to Lux, who looks away from me fast, grinding his teeth so obviously I feel it in my own jaw.

"We should go eat," Milo jumps in.

"I'm not hungry."

It's Lux's turn to scoff. "Sure you aren't."

"What's it to you?" I snap.

"Me?" He raises an eyebrow in challenge. "Nothing." Without another word, he turns on his heels. I grab a hold of my necklace as I watch him go, hating myself for running my eyes over his arm, the veins pronounced, as he pulls the door open.

"You know, it's amazing how many friends you have with that *winning* personality!" I yell after him.

An awkward silence settles over the room.

Griffin breaks it. "You know, I think that went pretty well."

I can't help it—I let out a laugh. Griffin beams at me.

"Come on," Milo says, giving me a gentle nudge. "Eat with us?"

The soft encouragement in his voice reminds me strangely of Priya, but still, I hesitate. My eyes trail across the room, still in disbelief at its warmth and finding yet more little gems scattered about. The bedside lamp, a white ceramic pineapple, may just be my favorite thing. I don't know how to make the thought and care that went into this room, the easy welcome of these strange, silly boys, make sense against everything I expected to find here.

"We helped fix up the room." Milo explains. "Griffin and Lux actually came up with a lot of the ideas, like repurposing this old skateboard—see? You can hang a bag on it or whatever." He gestures to the bottom piece of what's sure enough a skateboard, wheels and all, drilled into the wall alongside the collage of pictures and by the door.

I turn to Griffin, who ducks his head, suddenly shy. I almost don't recognize him. I smile. "That's pretty cool," I admit.

Griffin's head pops back up, that lopsided grin reappearing on his face. "Really?" I nod, and his eyes brighten even more. "Thanks."

They built me an entire bedroom. The least I could do is have dinner with them. I sigh. "I guess I could go for some food."

Bouncing back to his chipper self, Griffin pushes to his feet. "Excellent! It'll be nice to have a face I can tolerate sitting across from me for once."

I can't help my huff of laughter, even as Milo protests.

"Griffin, if I didn't know any better, I'd think you just called me pretty."

With a salute and salacious grin, Griffin winks at me. "Just calling it like I see it."

I shake my head, following them out of the room. Milo leads the way, and I let myself zone out to the background noise of Griffin's carefree jokes as we head up the hall, doing my best to ignore the framed photos.

Still, it's not until we step into the main hall that I can really breathe.

Directly across from the front door, past the last of the framed memories, the house opens up into a large space, a breeze rolling through the full wall of sliding glass doors currently open into the night. The open floor concept reveals a sunken living room with two steps down, the kitchen off to my left. It's currently occupied by Kelly and Banks, working at the counters. I ignore the weight of their eyes following me through the living room as I step through the back door.

The fairy lights from the front continue throughout the spacious backyard, all fenced in by shrubbery that towers above all our heads. A large table with chairs around it sits on the deck, and just below it, off the side of the cobbled walkway and to my right, is a patio area set with a grill. I nearly dig my heels in at the sight of Brody standing before it with a beer in one hand and a spatula in the other. His head tilts back, laughing at something the guy beside him says.

Quickly tearing my eyes away, I follow the trail of cobblestones that leads into the dark. Palm trees shoot up in the furthest corners of the backyard, one side housing a shed with surfboards lined up against it, and the other a circle of adirondack chairs around a firepit.

"The path leads straight to the beach," Milo explains, following my gaze.

I open my mouth to ask about the surfboards, but immediately slam it shut as Brody's voice cuts through the quiet waves. "There she is! Hey, Crew—shit, sorry, *Sailor*, hey! Come here!"

I'd rather not. Maybe I can act like I didn't hear him, slip away to the beach Milo just mentioned. But Griffin gives me a little nudge, as if sensing my inevitable desire to make a mad dash. I stumble over my feet as I muster enough strength to pick them up and head Brody's way.

Brody ignores my glare as I reach him. He makes quick work of transferring meat on the grill to an aluminum pan that sits to the side. "Sailor, I wanted to introduce you to someone." He places the spatula down and claps a hand on the shoulder of the man at his side. *The other man from the framed photos.* "This is Hank, my best friend. Do you remember him?"

Oh, I remember him. Hank Benson. Great. Someone else Brody and Mom used to fight about. My strongest memories of Hank are of Mom arguing about him in hushed voices with Kelly whenever I'd turn my call with him over to her so they could catch up. *You've got to be joking.*

Of course my little welcome wagon wouldn't be complete without the best friend Mom always believed wasn't a good influence on her little brother.

"It's good to see you, girl!" Hank tips his bottle in my direction like a toast. It's on the tip of my tongue to retort that I wish I could say the same, but I channel great restraint. "I heard you're staying here in the Cove with us for a bit."

I shrug stiffly. "Yeah, maybe. We'll see." Brody pauses in taking his next swig, eyes on me from over the bottle I'm certain isn't his first of the day. I cut my gaze to the greenery encompassing this makeshift patio. Despite the clean, salty air rolling off the waves, I feel like I can't breathe.

I need to get out of here.

This was a mistake.

I never get the chance to find the words for a quick exit. A high-pitched voice fills the backyard, cutting right through me. "Uncle B!"

Wild blonde tendrils fly as a little girl bounds down the deck steps, racing right for us. I stare in numb recognition. *It's the little girl from the photos.*

"Evie! There's my girl!" Brody beams as he moves forward to catch her. He scoops her up into the air, tossing her up as she shrieks in delight, and it's so familiar I feel sick. A sudden chill hits me, the hair on the back of my neck rising. "How's my favorite little niece?"

Their words, her giggles, all warp themselves in the roar of noise filling my ears, my heart pounding so hard I'm almost certain it'll burst from my chest. My eyes blur at the sight of Brody hugging her close, chest caving under the weight of everything I've tried to bury over the years—the grief, the searing pain, the hurt, the choking anger, all muddied by a thunderous storm of confusion, because why wasn't *I* enough for him to stay? To *try*?

Someone puts a hand on my arm, but I jerk away.

My feet are moving before I even realize it, carrying me across the yard, my hands shaking at my sides. I shoot up the deck steps and stumble back into the house. Heat flashes through me, but my teeth are chattering like I'm cold.

The last few minutes play on repeat making it that much

harder to breathe. Only once I'm out of sight, tucked in the suffocating hallway of captured smiles and too sweet memories, away from prying eyes, do I stop and hunch over, hands gripping my knees.

"Uncle B!"

"There's my girl!"

"How's my favorite little niece?"

I can't stay here. With a trembling breath, I stand up and jerk back, staring up at the wall in front of me. All of Brody's carefully-framed memories stare back, mocking me with a life Brody never thought to share.

My vision goes red, and before I can stop myself, I pull my hand back in a fist and punch the picture directly in front of me, of Brody and the little girl building a sandcastle. The glass shatters.

I thought loving Brody and Lux all my life had been the biggest mistake I ever made, but I was wrong.

It was coming here.

LESS THAN TWENTY-FOUR HOURS. I survived less than twenty-four hours with Brody before my instinct to run got the better of me.

I flex my hand open and shut, scowling at the prickling pain. I can't even be sure if there's glass in the cuts or not, more busy with grabbing my things than worrying about the blood dripping on the floor. The distance grows between me and the house, stifling numbness embracing me like an old friend. The persistent ache in my hand is the only thing that lets me know I'm awake. That none of this has been a dream.

More like a nightmare.

It's not long before I spy the yellow hut of Top Fin. Lights spill over my shoulder, but I don't bother looking back. There's been a few cars to pass by—Siren's Cove having just enough traffic to not feel too quiet, but not so much that you feel like a packed sardine along the well-kept roads.

The car crawls alongside me, and I keep my eyes forward. Some creep trying to kidnap me off the street would be the icing on the cake of this garbage day.

"Is there somewhere you've got to be?"

You've got to be kidding me.

I grit my teeth, refusing to turn my head to meet the driver's eyes. It's bad enough that I know his voice.

"A hot date maybe?" I scoff, but Lux must catch it. "Yeah, I didn't think so either."

I give in and turn my head, throwing a glare in his direction.

Lux looks back at me, eyes darting between me and the road ahead as he slowly drives alongside me in a bright red Jeep, the passenger window rolled down so he can call out to me. I think the most shocking thing about this moment is finding Banks in the passenger seat, sitting back so that Lux can call across him. *What, did he draw the short straw?*

I'm actually surprised Kelly isn't with them.

Lux tilts his head mockingly. "You think running away is going to get his attention?"

I bristle at his question, coming to a stop. The Jeep does too. "*Excuse you?*"

Lux opens his mouth to continue, but I cut him off sharply. "I've never had much of Brody's attention to begin with, and I definitely didn't expect anything to change just because we were attempting to coexist under the same roof." He, of all people, should know that.

"*Were?*" Banks pipes in. His eyes take in the bags strewn over my shoulder, before he turns his intense gaze onto me. "Where are you going, Sailor?"

I shrug my shoulders, staring down the street. I don't know where I'm headed. It doesn't matter. I start walking again without another word. The Jeep trails alongside me, and I tighten my grip on the straps of my duffel and bookbag. "Just go back to the house. This white knight act is cute and all, but I don't need your help."

I will not cry in front of them. Not a single tear.

My phone vibrates in my back pocket, catching me off guard enough that I'm already coming to a halt before the tires screech to one as well, stopping beside me.

As if knowing I needed an out, another text comes in, and then another. All of them from Priya.

Priya: Hope things are looking up! <3 Please try to utilize the support group. It can be a helpful tool if you allow it to be. But that requires you showing up in the space. Speak your truth—no one can take that from you.

Priya: You may just find that you're not alone.

Priya: Like Dani mentioned, she'll be checking in with you on a bi-weekly basis, but we'll all reconnect at the end of the summer and assess how things are going. If you believe we need to make other arrangements, we can discuss those options. But please give this a chance. The last thing I want is for you to think the only answer is to run away.

My stomach ties itself in knots, a cold sweat breaking out across the back of my neck as I reread her last words.

The last thing I want is for you to think the only answer is to run away.

She doesn't know. She can't possibly know.

But she knows *me*. Better than anyone else I have left.

The end of the summer. That's, at best, eight weeks from now. I glance back, over my shoulder, as if I can see the house from here. *Can I really make it eight weeks with Brody and Lux in the picture?* Kelly may just be the only saving grace in this chaos.

A car door slams shut, and I glance up as Lux rounds the Jeep to stand before me. His broad shoulders cut the headlights from my glare, one that rivals his own.

"I'm calling your bluff," he says finally.

I raise a brow, shoving my phone back into my pocket. "What bluff is that? You think I need saving? That *you'll* be the one to do it?"

His jaw clenches, jumping in tandem with the rapid rise and fall of my chest with each word. Swallowing past the rising lump in my throat I only just got rid of, I push on, "You don't get to step back into my life after all these years and play some sort of hero. You *left*." Before I can swallow it, a sob rips from my throat. My bags fall to the ground.

Lux moves forward, his hand reaching for me.

"*No!*" I throw out my arm, deflecting his. "You don't get to do that either."

"You think I wanted to leave you?" His words come out through gritted teeth, like it hurts him to even ask. "That I would have done anything to ever hurt you? I was fourteen years old! What I would've wanted didn't factor into the storm that blew through my life. I didn't get a choice, Sailor!"

What?

Closing the rest of the space between us before I can move, Lux clasps his hand against the back of my neck, leaning down until he can press his forehead against mine. I can sense the strength in his hand, but his touch is gentle. Letting me know I *could* pull away, if I really wanted to.

I hate that he's giving me the choice.

I hate that I don't move away.

I hate how safe I feel even more.

I hiccup, and his thumb strokes the nape of my neck. "Eventually, you and I are going to sit and have a talk." His words are a promise, a caress to match that of his thumb, and goosebumps break out across my skin. "But for now, please just come back to the house. It's late. Sleep on things for the night, and if leaving is really what you want to do come morning, we'll get you to where you need."

Unable to help myself, I ask, "You'd let me go?"

He swallows hard, his hand on the back of my neck flexing, but after a long hesitation, and looking like he hates himself for it, he nods. "If that's really what you want."

For some reason, that's what softens me. "I'm still really mad at you," I whisper.

His tongue swipes out across his full lips. I can't help following the movement. "I know."

"And I don't need any of you saving me."

His face softens from all his sharp edges and cut jaw. "I know that too," he says quietly. "But everyone needs someone willing to jump in after them."

I suck in a sharp breath, at a loss for words, and he lets me go. "Come on," he murmurs, and I try my best not to feel the immediate loss as he steps away from me, swooping down to grab my bags in one hand.

Lux moves to Banks' side of the Jeep, holding open the back door. My face flushes at the reminder of an audience, but Banks maintains a carefully blank expression.

Can I really go back with them?

The end of the summer, Priya had said. Eight weeks from now.

Eight weeks to sink or swim. Eight weeks to give Brody one last chance, even though he doesn't deserve one. Eight weeks with a pack of boys with too-ready smiles and intense eyes and a weird knack for interior design.

I can play nice till then. With Kelly and the guys at least.

Well, *most* of the guys.

"You and I are going to sit and have a talk."

What's there to talk about? He left. Case closed. There's really nothing more to say.

Except...what *had happened* to him? What had turned my shy, silly friend into this intense, tattooed stranger?

How did his mom let this happen? Hell, how did his *sister* let this happen? Even when she didn't want to hang out with us anymore, Gia still never let anyone mess with Lux except her.

Maybe we do need to talk, if nothing more than to close this chapter of our lives. Lay the weight of our friendship to rest.

I've been carrying it around with me all this time. It's heavy and exhausting. *I'm exhausted.*

"Sailor." Banks calls, pulling me out of my head. Releasing a shaky breath, I shuffle towards them. Lux helps me up the side step, keeping a hold of my hand even as I settle into the high seat, examining the cuts with a hard frown on his face. This high up, I look him directly in the eyes.

"Don't," I warn, quiet but firm.

Lux lets me go, reluctance clear on his face. "All of that anger is going to eat you alive."

Fixing my eyes on the back of Banks' headrest, I bite out, "Better to be angry than sad."

At least when I'm angry, I know I'm alive.

It's when I'm sad that I feel like I'm drowning.

SIX

EIGHT YEARS AGO

SWIPING my curls out of my eyes, I smile at myself in the mirror. Lux shifts behind me and I tilt my head as I watch his reflection next to mine. His hands open and close at his sides, his mouth doing the same, before he finally seems to find his words.

"Sail..." Lux swallows. "You look really pretty."

My cheeks feel warm as I look down at my feet. "Thank you. It's a sundress." Mommy helped me pick it out.

Well, after she said sorry.

I'd been crying when Mommy poked her head into my room, once the walls of the house had finally stopped shaking. "Why do you and Uncle B fight so much?" I'd demanded.

"Oh, sweetheart." Mommy rushed over, holding my face in her hands as she knelt in front of me. "I'm so sorry."

"I—I don't want you to fight." Mommy wiped at my tears, but they just kept coming faster. A thought hit me and I grabbed her arms, holding tightly as I asked, desperate, "Is he coming back?" *What if he never comes back?* "He—he promised!"

"Promised what, sweet girl?"

"He promised he'd stay."

Mommy pulled me into her arms without a word and held me until I stopped crying. I told her how I thought the pictures made

Uncle B sad—that I wanted to take a picture with him, too. Then maybe he'd be happy. I don't like when Uncle B is sad...or when he and Mommy fight.

"Hey." Lux's hand brushes against mine, and I blink back to now. My smile is gone. The girl looking back at me in the mirror is frowning. As much as I don't like when Uncle B or Mommy are sad, I really don't like it when I am, either.

Searching for Lux's hand, I hold on tight. He steps in front of me, eyes sweeping across my face. "It's okay, Sail."

"You don't know that."

He squeezes my hand. "Sure I do. No matter what, it's you and me. Always."

I smile a little. "Always," I repeat.

My eyes find the notebook perched on the corner of my little desk I use to do my schoolwork. I can't wait for Uncle B to come back. I'll show him the list of all the strip clubs I found. I've been looking for them like a game of I Spy every time Mom and I go out, but I didn't get to share it with him yesterday. Maybe that will make him happy.

I hope that's what he's still into, but if he's anything like me, maybe he isn't. I used to be really into dolls, but now they're tucked away in the attic, my room filled with books and a guitar I've never touched but promised Mommy I'll learn to play. Lux says he'll teach me—he plays, and he's pretty good at it. *Lux is good at everything.*

A knock on the front door sends me bouncing out of my bedroom. "He's back! He's back!" I race down the carpeted hallway to the front door, Lux right on my heels as he keeps up.

"Okay, alright," Mommy holds up a hand, stopping me in my tracks as she reaches the door before me. She looks between the two of us, her eyes twinkling. A chuckle slips past her lips as she shakes her head at me. "Deep breath?"

I inhale sharply, counting to four before letting the breath go, shaking out my hands as I do. My shoulders drop, and the excitement in me settles to a light buzz, a gentle soothing hum that keeps the smile on my face in place. *Right*. Ready.

Mommy nods at me, a small smile on her face, before turning to open the door. "Hey, B. Come on in." Uncle B's eyes fall on me for only a split second before he jerks them away. Wiping his hands across his pants, he remains at the door. Lux steps closer to my side and takes my hand as Mommy's smile disappears. "What's going on, Brody?"

She asks it the same way she always does when she already knows the answer, like when I lie about having my homework done because I really want to read the next chapter of my book.

"Um..." Uncle B looks over at me once more, before meeting Mommy's hard stare.

Mommy's lips press together. "Why don't we take this outside." *Uh-oh. Is Uncle B in trouble?* I thought Mommy said they wouldn't fight anymore.

Uncle B opens his mouth to say something but immediately shuts it with a quick, jerky nod. Mommy looks back at me, a smile on her lips, but the twinkle in her eyes is gone. "Give us a minute, Sail, okay?"

I bite my bottom lip, but I nod.

As soon as the door closes, I make my move. Pulling my hand away from Lux's, I quickly dart across the living room to the slightly open window. Staying to the side, my back against the wall, so that they can't see me, I hold my breath and listen.

"You're not staying, are you?" My chest tightens at Mommy's words. *Why would she say that? Is Uncle B still mad at Mommy?* "Who's that in the car?"

What? Uncle B brought somebody? Who? I try to peek out at his truck but all I see is a shadow. Uncle B pulls a small white box from his jean pocket, flipping it open and tapping out a stick. My nose scrunches up. He's smoking!

"It's Hank." Uncle B answers.

"I thought you stopped hanging out with him."

"No, *you* wanted me to stop hanging out with him."

Other than a lawn mower rattling off in the distance, it's silent. I look over at Lux. His jaw is tense as he glares at nothing in particular, listening just as closely as I am. I pull away from the window to lay my head on his shoulder.

Outside, Mom sighs. "Brody, he's not good for you."

"Is that what you think?" Uncle B challenges.

There's a pause, and then, "This weekend was never about being here with us, was it?" Mommy laughs, but it doesn't sound nice at all. "You're unbelievable." My eyes begin to itch as they fill with tears, and I try to keep my breathing quiet enough that they won't hear me sniffling. "You know what...why don't you do us a favor and stay away?"

"Finley," Uncle B starts to protest.

"The last thing I need is for you to come and go from Sailor's life when it's convenient for you. I want her to know you, but not like this." I rub my chest. Mommy sounds as sad as I feel.

"Finley, wait—"

"No."

"Fin—"

"Just go, B."

I can't listen anymore. Pushing off the wall, I stumble for my room and shut the door before Lux can catch up, locking it behind me.

The handle twists side to side. "Sail? Let me in. Please?"

My chest rises up and down, fast. Grabbing at the front of my dress, I ball it in my fist as my eyes fly wildly around the room. My gaze lands on the notebook, and I stomp across the room. Snatching it up, I drop it in the trash bin next to the desk.

Mommy's words replay in my head. *"Just go, B."*

Just go.

Just go.

Just go.

Just. Go.

A small cry leaves my lips and the tears I tried so hard to keep away finally fall.

"Sailor." Lux sounds so serious. "Let me in."

No. Shaking my head, even though he can't see me, I walk over to the door and lean back against it. I don't want to be sad with Lux. Slowly sliding down to the floor, I pull my knees up to my chest and hug myself, resting my head against my legs. There's a slight thump against the door, and a moment later I spy his fingers underneath the frame.

My bottom lip trembles like last night's walls but I slide my fingers over to meet his, finally finding my next breath even as I continue to cry.

SEVEN

"THERE'S MY GIRL!"

"...we'll all reconnect at the end of summer..."

"How's my favorite little niece?"

"You and I are going to sit and have a talk."

I swallow past the lump in my throat, dragging the mermaid tail back and forth across the chain sitting around my neck. Eight weeks is all I need to endure before I can leave. That's approximately fifty-six days.

Last night—coming back here—was hard.

Things can't possibly get any worse. *Right?*

As if to challenge the thought, my bedroom door opens to reveal Lux. His footsteps drown out the low hum of music coming from the record player filling my room.

Stopping short at the end of the bed, his large hand clamps around my ankle and tugs. Goosebumps awaken across my skin as I feel every fiber of the polyester bedding beneath me and I press my lips tightly together, fighting for all the world not to give in and smile at the oddly familiar roughhousing. When we were kids, smiling came easy around Lux. I used to smile all the time.

He used to smile a lot too.

"You think I wanted to leave you?"

I blink several times, the ceiling exchanged for the stormy gray dominating the eyes of my former best friend. My hand resting on my stomach flexes, itching to reach out and trace the sharp angles of his jaw.

I wonder if he still has those dimples I used to love running my fingers over as a kid. My chest tightens at the thought.

With a firm grip around my ankle, my leg hiked up against his side, Lux plants his other hand beside my head and leans in. The warmth of his body draws me into the undertow of him and I try to ignore all the places his body meets mine. *God, give me strength.* It was definitely never like *this* when we were kids. "You gonna lay around and mope all day, or you gonna get up and face the music?"

I scowl trying to tug my leg back but his hold only tightens. "Haven't you ever heard of giving a girl some space?"

His head tilts to the side, eyes skimming down my face before coming back to meet my glare. His stare is so firm, so intense, that I find myself trying to push further into the bed to escape him. The alternative would be too embarrassing.

"Yeah, well you're not just any girl," he murmurs. My fingers twitch, and, not missing a single thing, his eyes drop to my hands before looking back up at me, the blue gleaming brighter as a dare sits there in his eyes.

"What are you doing, Lux?" I ask quietly.

What am I *doing?*

His brows furrow. "What do you mean?"

"This," I gesture between us. "This was never us."

He flinches, as if I physically struck him, but he finally pulls back—and I almost regret saying it. "Sailor," he says quietly. "This was always meant to be us."

I shake my head. "Maybe it was once, but not anymore."

Lux shakes his head right back, his thumb rubbing the inside of my ankle in circles that shouldn't feel soothing. I can't take my eyes off him, but suddenly I don't feel like glaring anymore. "See, that's where you're wrong. But don't worry, Sail, I'll prove it to you."

"You two mind explaining to me what's going on here?"

The words are like a bucket of ice cold water dumped over me. I scramble upright, Lux thankfully letting go. Kelly stands in the doorway, arms crossed, taking in the two of us with a flat, disapproving expression. Lux stares back, remaining at the end of the bed like he's got nothing to hide.

I mean, we don't.

"Hey, Kelly." Lux says casually. "Is there coffee?"

Kelly stares at him without a word. I shift uncomfortably, eyes darting between them. I don't know how Lux is still meeting his eyes—I want to hide under the bed, and Kelly isn't even *looking* at me. His eyes remain on Lux as he says, "Sailor, I'd like for you to come join us on the back porch."

I frown. "When you say us, you mean...?"

"You, me, and Brody." Kelly supplies, getting right to the point. "I think the fresh air will do us some good."

"I don't know..."

Kelly nods, acknowledging what I'm saying—and what I'm not. "I know. But we should talk." His next words are obviously for Lux. "Fresh air will do you good, too—like down at the shop or over at the Marshalls'."

Lux chuckles. "Hint taken, boss."

Cheeks flaming, I scramble off the bed. "So, um, you said out back?"

A smirk tugs at Lux's lips at my obvious discomfort. I smack him in the stomach as I pass by him. Lux lets out a dramatic breath, hunching over, and I shake my head, my lips fighting against a smirk as I step out into the hallway.

It's too easy with him. Too easy to forget I'm mad. Too easy to fall back into what we once were. Too easy to remember I'm not here to make any friends.

I don't know what Kelly says, or what look he gives, but Lux's words faintly drift up the hall on a dry laugh. "Yeah, yeah. I'm going. I'm going."

I glance briefly at the frame I destroyed, and almost stumble to a halt. Someone's swept up the shards of glass, the rest of it remaining a cracked web in its frame like a million tiny cuts to match those across my heart.

Who cleaned it up?

Turning the question over in my mind as I continue on, I nearly miss Brody sitting at the table out back, sunglasses perched on the back of his head and tapping a box of cigarettes against the table in a steady rhythm. *Who wears sunglasses like that?* His right leg bounces under the table, a breath pushing past his lips in a heavy sigh. What does *he* have to be anxious about?

"Still smoking, I see." I point out, rounding the table so that I'm facing him.

The tapping against the table pauses. "I've been trying to cut back."

"It kills, you know."

Brody smiles, but it doesn't reach his eyes as he starts tapping the box again. "I know."

Before I can say anything else, Kelly appears in the doorway. He takes us both in before settling his gaze on me. "Sailor, why don't you take a seat?"

Pulling out the chair across from Brody, I do as Kelly suggests. It's only once I'm in my chair that he takes the one between Brody and I at the head of the table. At least there's *one* adult here.

There's a folder in his hand. If I'm not mistaken, it's the one Dani left with us, brimming with documents: the legalities of kinship care, the schedules of the support groups offered at the local community center for the caregiver and child, therapists covered under social services, and pamphlets packed with other resources in case we face any barriers.

Or hardships, Dani had explained, gently holding my gaze until I nodded.

I'm living with Brody. I can't see it getting any harder than that.

"Listen, Sailor, I...*we* wanted to check-in with you. I'd like to know what we can do to ensure you settle in," Kelly explains. Judging by the blank look on Brody's face, this explanation is for him just as much as it is for me. *Shocker.* "We should also go over some of the things Dani discussed, *and* set some ground rules."

So much for Brody being in charge here. The paperwork might say he's my assigned caregiver, but from where I'm sitting, it looks like Kelly's calling the shots.

Honestly, that's probably for the best.

"Sailor?" At Kelly's question, I drag my eyes back to him.

Clearing my throat, I ask, "What kinds of things?"

"For starters, the kinship support group for teens meets at—"

"At the community center, once a week." I cut off Kelly, my voice flat. "I start next Thursday." Crossing my arms over one another, I cup my elbows as I slightly hunch in on myself. "I was there when Dani discussed this." Then again, so were the two of them. Why are we sitting here talking about this?

Without missing a beat, Kelly continues, "You'll also meet with Dani—"

"Every two weeks. I *know.*" I cut him off again. "Until the end of the summer when other arrangements can be made if this doesn't work out."

The tapping against the table stops. "Why wouldn't it work out?"

My attention snaps over to meet Brody's eyes across the table. "Why would it?"

We stare at each other until Kelly clears his throat, easing his way into the unspoken standoff. "Which is why I want to know how we can best help you with settling in. Which we can't do, if you're going to run off."

Again. He doesn't have to say it but there's a knowing look in his eyes. Was he the one who cleaned up the glass?

"Wait, what?" Brody sits up straighter in his seat, dropping his cigarette pack on the table. For the first time, he looks genuinely startled, not just guilty about not doing something he was supposed to do or being somewhere he was supposed to be. Or, apparently, not knowing something he was supposed to know. "You ran off? When?"

"What does it matter?"

"It matters." Kelly answers firmly, gesturing between himself and Brody. "To the both of us, it matters." *Yeah, I'm sure.*

"But...why would you run off?" Brody looks bewildered. His sunglasses fall when he yanks his hat off his head, but he seems to hardly notice as he runs a hand through his hair, eyes wide as they search my face.

Whatever he's looking for, he's not going to find it. It's my turn to sigh. "I don't really want to settle in." I ignore Brody's question, opting to refer back to Kelly's earlier statement.

Brody shakes his head. "You don't mean that."

It comes off almost like a question. Gritting my teeth, I grip my elbows tightly, fingernails biting into my skin. "I do, actually."

Silence fills the space between the three of us, and I try to take several deep breaths before looking at Kelly, ready to check the last box. "You mentioned ground rules?"

Kelly sighs. "First...I know Lux and the others are good guys, but let's keep the bedroom door open when they're around."

I start to protest that it shouldn't matter, since nothing is happening. But then, why do my cheeks feel warm?

Brody chuckles. "Come on, Kelly, did you forget what it's like being a teenager? What's a door going to stop?"

My face gets even hotter. Kelly opens his mouth, but I cut off whatever he's about to say. "Boys are the last thing on my mind right now."

He doesn't look convinced, but after a moment, Kelly nods in acknowledgement and continues. "We'll have family dinner on Sundays. All three of us are to be in attendance, no exceptions." *Family dinner?* He's joking, right? But as he levels his stare on Brody, I know he's not. Once he's sure Brody gets the message, Kelly turns back to me. "How do you feel about working?"

I shrug my shoulders. "I don't mind it." Besides, I'm going to need money. Whether I stay here or leave at the end of the summer, I'll be eighteen in another year. The world will claim I'm an adult who can make her own choices and decisions—pave her own way. But even though that's a year from now, and I'm just shy of turning seventeen this summer, I can't start to understand how my choices will suddenly be my own and no longer someone else's.

And Mom won't be able to help me figure things out. My vision blurs at the thought. I always thought I'd have her for the big milestones of my life, and all the regular days in between. Now I just have the memory of her, and I'm afraid of losing that too.

"I think it'd be good to keep you busy for the summer," Kelly says. "You'll start picking up shifts down at the shop."

Brody nods his head, grinning. "It'll be great. A little family business action."

I start shaking my head before he can even get the last two words out. "Not even." We may be related, but we are not family. The air thickens with tension, and my leg starts bouncing furiously as I fix Brody with a hard glare. "We're not family."

His smile falls from his face. "Crew."

The legs of the chair scrape across the wooden porch as I push away from the table, slamming my hands down on the chair's arms as I hold myself in place. "I told you to stop calling me that."

"No matter what, we're family—"

"No, we're not."

"And I love you—"

Shooting up from my seat, my chest heaves up and down as I try to catch my next breath. "*Love?* You think you love me? You think you know what family is?"

Brody's mouth opens and shuts, like a gaping fish.

"Family shows up for one another. They work things out, *together*. They don't *walk away* when things get tough." My voice cracks on the last few words. "They don't ignore each other's texts and calls when someone they both love is *dying*."

My next inhale is shaky. "I've felt your love, and honestly Brody, it fucking sucks."

Without giving him a chance to respond, I stumble down the porch steps, heading right for the stone path that leads out onto the beach.

Kelly is hot on my heels. "Sailor, wait!"

Whirling around, I curse to myself as a couple of tears fall down my face. I grab at my necklace, my chest tight. "This is why I can't settle in, Kelly."

He's why I can't settle in. I don't have to say it. The tick of Kelly's jaw is all the confirmation I need that he understands. "I won't run again. I swear. But *please* don't ask more of me than I can give."

"You're hurt, and you're grieving," Kelly acknowledges. He lowers his head just a bit so that we're eye to eye, and his face softens. "*And* you're angry."

More tears fall down my face. I wipe away at them with a sniffle. "I'm *so* angry."

Kelly nods his head. "And you have every right to be, Sail." His words float between us, and it feels a little easier to breathe, just having that acknowledged. "I'm not saying this is going to be easy. But you're already here. It may be worth giving things a try."

Shaking my head, I look away. "I can't."

"You can't, or you won't?" It's a challenge, but not a cruel one. "Sailor, have you thought about why your mom assigned him custody, even after everything that happened between them?"

"I wonder all the time." Even now, I can't make sense of it. I mean, she was there the night he walked out on us. She helped put me back together. And when she probably needed him most—when *I* needed him most—he never showed. Never even answered a text message. And yet she still decided that *he* was the person to take care of me when she was gone.

How could she do this to me?

"Give it some thought." He nods towards the path behind me. "We'll be here when you're ready."

Not needing to be excused twice, I turn away, the stones giving way to sand.

Because we're on the outskirts of town, there are only woodlands off to my right, wrapping the house up in a bend that gives the illusion of our own private little beach. The nearest house is a mile off to the left.

Despite everything, it's peaceful. There's no one around but me.

Taking in a deep breath, my hands fall to my sides as I lift my face to the clear blue sky. Sea salt hangs in the air, the sun kissing my skin. Now *this*, I could get used to. A breeze rolls off the water, coming to greet me in an embrace that loosens my muscles.

Mom would have loved it here.

I can't help but smile softly, even as the tears continue to fall.

EIGHT

SOMEONE IS WATCHING ME, and I don't need to look up to know who.

A prickling sensation sweeps along my neck, but I keep my eyes on the tattered book in my hands. "I wouldn't come any closer, if I were you."

Lux hums from the doorway. "Mmm, yes, warden Kelly is not a man to be crossed."

My lips curl into a smirk, though I still don't look up. "Know a lot about that, hmm?"

"I should. My room used to be right across the hall."

That gets my attention. "What?" I shut the book as I sit up straight, my feet dropping from the coffee table to the ground. "You were living here? When? *Why?*"

Lux leans against the bedroom door frame, running a hand over the top of his head. I try my best not to be irrationally mad at him for chopping off his curls, but I can't help clenching my jaw. It's silly, really. But it's one more reminder of how much has changed—how much he's changed. "Wouldn't you like to know?"

I open my mouth, but before I can say anything else, Griffin pokes his head around Lux, his brilliant smile in place as always. "Hey, Sail! You ready to go?"

My brows furrow and I look between the two of them. "Um, ready to go…where, exactly?"

Griffin looks sideways at Lux, all accusation and faux outrage. "What have you been doing, dude?" I bite back a smile at the way Lux rolls his eyes, like he wants to be annoyed but can't quite pull it off. "Sail, baby cakes, we're headed to the beach. Do me the honor and spare me a day with a bunch of dudes?"

"As if it's *just* dudes," Lux says. "Cova's coming."

A smile pulls at his lips as he says the name, and my teeth start grinding of their own volition. *Who's Cova?* I push the thought away and look at Griffin instead. "Baby cakes?" I echo.

Griffin bops his head. "Yeah, I figured if we're going to be best friends, we'll need to give each other nicknames. I gotta try some out until I find the right one."

Best friends? I thought I was clear the other day—I'm not here to make friends. Grabbing at my necklace, I zip the mermaid tail back and forth across the chain, trying to find an excuse to say no without putting that kicked puppy look back on Griffin's face.

"Sailor?" I blink back into focus. Lux is still in the doorway, but Griffin is nowhere in sight. "C'mon, get dressed. We're heading out in five."

I shake my head. "I can't." I swallow the lump in my throat. "Lux, I'm not looking to make friends. I'm just trying to get through this."

"It's just a day at the beach."

"Today it's the beach. Tomorrow…"

"Don't worry about tomorrow. Just focus on today," Lux says quietly. "Life's too short for that."

I know. God, do I know.

Without waiting for me to respond, Lux walks off, for once giving me space without me needing to demand it. I sit on the giant wicker chair the boys filled with pillows for me, listening to his steps fade away down the hall. Taking in a slow, deep breath, I release it shakily, repeating the pattern again and again until the threat of tears subsides and the tightness in my chest loosens, Mom's voice in my head walking me through the familiar ritual.

Before I can overthink it, I riffle through the duffel on the table before me, where it's been sitting, still mostly packed, since Lux and Banks brought me back that first night. Pulling out a bikini, I make quick work of putting it on before I can change my mind.

As I dig for something to put on over my suit, my hand skims over a bundle of soft, well-worn fabric. Pulling the dark blue hoodie from the bag, I barely have time to make out the words *Country roads, take me home* before my vision blurs. I bring it to my nose and inhale deeply, unable to stop the few tears that roll hot down my face. There's still a faint smell of berry perfume clinging to the fabric, and I can almost imagine Mom still here with me. I bury my face into it for another moment before pulling it over my head.

It's the closest thing to feeling her arms around me, and I need all the comfort I can get.

Wiping my face, I toss my curls into a messy bun atop of my head and fist the sleeves of the hoodie as I brave the hallway looking for Lux and Griffin. Rapid honking from the driveway has me rolling my eyes, but I follow the sound out to the front door. The guys stand around the Jeep, surfboards strapped to the top and Banks at the wheel.

Griffin catches sight of me first and gives an enthusiastic wave. "Let's go, Sailboat! The waves wait for no one."

"Sailor." Brody's voice makes me stop in my tracks, one foot out the door.

"Hmm?" I call over my shoulder without turning around.

Brody comes into view, leaning a shoulder against the wall beside the doorframe and wincing immediately at the brightly clear blue sky. He looks like he wants to shuffle back into the shadows of the house.

My eyes cut to slits. "Rough night?"

Choosing to ignore me or maybe not hearing me at all, Brody straightens up as if he can shake off his hangover, pasting on an easy-going smile that I immediately want to wipe right off when he asks, "Could you watch Evie for a bit this evening?"

I stiffen. My gaze meets Lux's across the drive, still my anchor in the storm, after all this time. Some habits are hard to break. Keeping my tone under careful control, I ask, "And Evie is...?"

Brody grins, completely unaware of the inner turmoil stirring within me at just the mere mention of this little girl. "Evie's Hank's daughter, remember? You met her last night at the barbeque." Um, no, I didn't. And I don't want to meet her now either. He rattles on, something about split custody with the ex and last-minute rescheduling to their court approved schedule that conflict with tickets he and Hank have for a game, before finally finishing with, "So, what do you say?"

Pushing open the screen door, I don't bother looking back as I answer tightly, "Sorry. I've got plans."

Milo already has the back door of the Jeep open for me, and I could almost kiss him for it, eager to put as much distance as I can between myself and Brody. I practically throw myself in and release a shaky breath as I settle back against the seat. Looking up, I find Banks watching me in the rearview mirror.

"Nice hoodie," he greets me.

A smile ghosts over my lips as Milo and Griffin slide in on either side of me, listening quietly. "It was my mom's."

He nods to the West Virginia outline sitting just behind the song's iconic line. "You ever visit?"

My eyebrows shoot up just a little. "Um, yeah. We took road trips all the time. It was our favorite thing to do."

Milo brushes his hand across my knuckles and I blink back to here and now, realizing that I've been staring out the front window without really seeing what's there, the image of the open road and the towering heights of the Blue Ridge mountains a mere memory—just like Mom.

I'll never make new memories with her, I think, and have to swallow back tears.

"You know," Milo says quietly, "if you ever want to talk about her, we'd like to listen."

Griffin nods in agreement as Banks puts the car in gear. Lux says nothing, just sits quietly in the passenger seat, looking out the window. I frown, a little surprised that for once he's not taking the opportunity to push.

We're halfway out of the driveway when Griffin suddenly straightens with a shout of, "Wait!" Banks slams on the brakes, and the Jeep lurches to a stop. Milo throws an arm in front of me, and I dig my feet into the floor of the Jeep so I'm not completely choked by the seat belt.

"What the fuck, man?" Banks shouts as Griffin unbuckles and spills out of the car.

"I'll be right back!" Griffin hollers, disappearing into the house.

There's a moment of silence before Milo speaks up. "If you left him behind, I don't think any of us would be opposed at the moment."

The wheel creaks under Banks' white-knuckled grip. "Don't tempt me."

Lux looks back, his eyes sweeping across my frame. "You okay?"

I nod, swallowing thickly. "Yeah, I'm fine."

The door to the bungalow opens, and Griffin's already clambering back into his seat by the time it slams shut again. "Okay," he announces. "Now we can go."

He has the polaroid camera from my dresser in his hand.

"You went back for that?" I ask, too surprised to even be upset that he went into my room without asking.

"Um, yeah? We've got to document your time here in the Cove, Sail." Griffin says it as if it's the simplest thing in the world.

"I don't know if I want to remember my time here," I admit.

Griffin lightly bumps my shoulder with his and I drag my gaze from the camera to meet his eyes. "Never underestimate the power of a captured moment."

Captured moments are all I really have left of my mom. Staring at the images on my phone often till my vision blurs with tears, my hand cramping from clutching the device too tightly.

Pictures. They can hold you together as much as they can unravel you. I can still remember Brody narrowing his eyes on the framed photo as he drew it from my bedside table, the way he frowned when I'd chirped about Kelly being Mommy's friend.

I think about how I feel at the sight of the framed photos he has on that damn wall in the house. I imagine he may have felt an inkling of what I do now. Maybe it's why there was a fight that followed between him and Mom later that night.

My hand flexes in my lap, the glass shattering echoing in my ears. It had felt good, releasing just a little of the anger I've lived with for years, always simmering right below the surface ready to rear its head.

Hell, photos may very well be my undoing.

Griffin has a point. Never underestimate the power of a captured moment, indeed.

I shake my head and settle into my seat. The wind blows through the open windows, tousling the curls that escape from my bun. Milo and Griffin point out various aspects of Siren's Cove as we drive, like kindergarteners at show and tell, although Griffin's definitely winning in the excitement department. When they notice me trying not to smile at their tour guide charade, they step it up, adding extra fun facts that I think they might be making up, until I can't help giggling.

My cheeks ache from the grin on my face as they continue their double act, but a Ferris wheel in the distance snags my attention. "There's a fair?" I practically bounce in my seat, not at all embarrassed at how I squeal the words more than ask. For once, my chest feels light, almost like I'm floating. I grin, looking from face to face. After road trips, fairs are one of my absolute favorite things.

Lux turns to look at me, a knowing expression on his face. "That's the pier."

"Oh my gosh!" I can't help the way my smile widens as I look back at him. "Remember how going to the fair was the only thing Gia would ever agree with us about? And how once we were there, we'd reenact the ending scene from Grease—full song and dance?"

Lux chuckles. "You two knew every move."

You bet we did. "We only watched it like a hundred times." It was the one movie Gia and I could agree on—that we bonded over. We'd make Lux watch it with us repeatedly.

"You two were a couple of Greasers, were you?" Griffin jokes.

"Oh yeah." I bite back another grin at the memory. "One year for Halloween, Gia and I dressed up like the Pink Ladies and Lux went as a T-Bird."

The guys all laugh. "*Please* tell me there are pictures," Griffin begs.

"Yeah, we definitely got to see this," Milo adds.

Never underestimate a captured moment.

Griffin's comment rings through me, and I smile softly. "I do, actually." It's one of the few that I still have. One I fought to keep intact, when bouncing between Safe Harbor and home became too much and I began to lose things in the shuffle, or when the other kids at the group home got into my trunk of belongings.

Lux snaps around at my admission, his eyes darken with a storm of emotions I can't decipher as they flash quickly across his face. He says nothing, just holds my gaze, and I nearly lose myself in the gray clouds of his eyes. I wait for him to say something about how I'd better not show those pictures to anyone, or make fun of how ridiculous the three of us looked in our hand-painted jackets, but he just studies my face, and I can't help staring back at his.

"Wait until you see it all lit up at night." Milo's voice pierces the fog of my mind and I draw back into my seat, trying to put some distance between myself and Lux. I need to remember why

I'm actually here in Siren's Cove, and why it's not a good idea to get involved with Lux.

But even at the thought of what I've lost, I can't help wondering if maybe I have just as much to gain. *Don't I?* Being around Lux...it's just too easy with him.

Old habits are hard to break when the person you're trying to cut off is someone you love.

"Ah, there she is," Banks murmurs, beeping the horn as we pull into a spacious parking lot. A girl with the cutest purple ombre braids I've ever seen hops off the hood of a lilac punch buggy, a smile on her heart-shaped face.

We park right alongside her, and as we spill out of the Jeep, the guys embrace her one at a time. Something tugs in my chest and I hang back uncertainly, especially when Lux wraps her up in his arms, quietly murmuring something I can't hear.

"Sailor!" Milo beckons me over, and I reluctantly come closer. "I want you to meet my cousin, Cova. She's the one who gave us the pointers for your bedroom."

"You mean *graced* you with those pointers," she jokes, tossing a wink in their direction. "Although I've got to say, you all did pretty well on your own. I hope you boys don't mind that I steal Sailor for a bit."

It's not a question—her energy is magnetic. She gestures for me to follow, and my feet crunch over the gravel as we head to the back of her car. She pops the trunk, revealing an organized bin tucked off to the side, filled with sketch pads and other art supplies. A camera bag nestles behind it next to a folded-up tripod. The remaining space is taken up by two wooden crates. "I thought we could paint some crates while the guys hit the waves. They're great for bikini storage."

"I don't have many," I mumble, watching Cova wrestle one of the crates out of her trunk before pulling out a tote bag of art supplies. The sun shines across her light brown skin, catching on the rings of starfish and seashell charms clamped around her individual braids, falling down the small of her back in a cascade of purple that blends into turquoise and ends in a cotton candy pink. *Very mermaid-esque.* She's pretty like one too.

"That'll change with living here in the Cove, babe, trust me." She straightens up, smiling, and the way the corners of her brown eyes crinkle is all too similar to Milo's. I see the resemblance between the cousins immediately.

Cova hands me one wooden crate and stuffs the bag of supplies into the other, propping it on her hip as she closes her trunk. "Why are you doing this?"

She gives me another cheerful wink, but her eyes are warm and genuine. "Girl time is a necessity of life, don't you think?" She lowers her voice, so that the boys can't hear her, and adds, "Plus, I figured you might be sick of small talk, and it might help to have something to do with your hands."

With that one sentence, she's endeared herself to me forever. Except...I bite the inside of my cheek, my eyes drifting toward Lux. The guys are working in tandem, unpacking the Jeep. They all carry surfboards under their arms, the cooler's handle pulled out and ready to roll.

As if feeling my eyes on his back, Lux looks over his shoulder. I tear my gaze away.

Cova clears her throat quietly, and my eyes snap back to her, my face flushing. But she just looks amused. "I hope this goes without saying, but in case you need reassurance, there's nothing between me and Lux." She waggles her eyebrows. "Not that I wouldn't have thought about it, but it was always pretty clear I never had a chance. It's hard for any of the girls here in the Cove to compete with a childhood sweetheart."

My lips part, but nothing comes out.

Her smile softens. "I always knew you had to be something special, but Lux plays everything close to the vest. It's nice to finally meet the one person who puts a genuine smile on his face. He deserves happiness after everything he's been through, don't you think?"

Everything he's been through? I stiffen. *Whatever she's talking about, she obviously thinks I already know.* I swallow. "Right. Of course."

Cova's face grows serious, her eyes assessing me like she's trying to see if I live up to everything Lux may have mentioned about me. "Just try not to break his heart, okay?"

With those parting words, she starts for the beach. I adjust my grip on my crate and follow.

The beach is exactly what I'd expect from a place like Siren's Cove. There are volleyball nets set up at intervals along the stretch of white sand, games already underway at some of them. The lifeguard posts are an array of colors up and down the beach. Cresting waves roll into shore, not a single piece of trash in sight. There's people in the water, some surfing in the distance. Others remain on the sand, towels and tents scattered across the beach, but it's far from overcrowded. There are plenty of young faces and families, high school and college kids, even some older folks here to enjoy their summer. It's nice.

I fall back from the group, rolling Cova's words over in my head. *What did she mean about everything Lux has been through?* With Lux reappearing in my life, even with the years between us, I thought I still knew him in all the ways it counted—in all the ways in which it once mattered. But now, I'm not so certain.

What if I don't know him at all?

A lead weight drops in my stomach, because of all the things I've faced up until this point, the thought of not knowing who Lux is has to be the scariest thought of all. His words from the other night come back, suddenly so much more haunting than before.

"You think I wanted to leave you?"

So much has changed in my life. I never let myself think about what might have changed in his.

NINE

SIX YEARS AGO

MUFFLED voices filling the house pull me from sleep. I sit up, rubbing my eyes. *What's going on?* I slip out of bed and tiptoe across my room, the moonlight spilling across the floor lighting my way.

I hold my breath as I open my door just enough to hear the familiar voices.

"What the hell are you doing here?" I jump. That's Mommy's voice, but I've never heard her sound like this before. "Do you have any clue what time it is? *Ugh*, you reek. How much have you had to drink?"

"I wanted to talk to you." *Uncle B?* I perk up, trying to catch sight of him down the hall. Mommy stands with her hand raised to stop Uncle B in the entrance, the front door closed behind him.

"Oh, *now* you want to talk?"

"Finley, please," Uncle B pleads. "Just hear me out." He sounds kind of funny, like he can't help but drag his words a little.

"I don't want to hear anything you have to say!" Her voice rises with every word. Releasing a deep breath, Mommy lowers her voice. "You need to go before Sailor wakes up and sees that you're here. It'll just confuse her. Not to mention upset her all over again." What? *No!* I want him to stay.

"Fin—"

"No, Brody. I already told you, I'm done with this revolving door. You should leave. Try and sober up while you're at it, yeah?"

"I just need a little more time." Uncle B says quietly.

I frown. *More time for what?*

Mommy sighs. "You've *had* the time, B. You're the one whose chosen to waste it."

Uncle B hiccups. Is he crying? "You've never asked me to choose."

"I shouldn't have to. *God*, you're unbelievable," Mommy growls. "I'm not in the business of twisting someone's arm to do something they don't want to do. If you wanted to show up—for me, for *Sailor*—you would've."

"Oh, it's just that simple?" Uncle B shifts on his feet, coming into view, his usual smile nowhere to be found. Mommy takes a step forward and they stand toe to toe. I fist my shirt tightly at my stomach, my fingers digging into the fabric and biting into my skin.

"Don't bullshit me, Brody," Mommy warns. *Ooh, she said a bad word.* She must be *really* mad. "If you really wanted to change, you would."

Uncle B laughs, but it doesn't sound right. "Fin, come on."

"Choose."

"What?"

Mommy folds her arms across her chest. "It's your lucky shot at a second chance, and you won't get another. So choose. Us, or the alcohol. It's up to you."

Uncle B laughs again, but it doesn't sound happy. Not anything like his usual laugh. It almost sounds like he wants to cry. He doesn't say anything, and Mommy huffs.

"You can't do it, can you?" Mommy's laugh is just as unhappy as Uncle B's, but angry, instead of sad. Goosebumps break across my skin. "After everything we've been through...you can't even choose us." Her voice is a whisper now. "You can't choose *her*."

Uncle B opens his mouth, but says nothing.

"Like I said," Mommy says softly. "*Unbelievable.*" She starts around Uncle B and he reaches out for her. I freeze, eyes wide, as she yanks away from him, spinning back around to face him. "Don't touch me."

"Finley."

Mommy's face warps into something scary, her lips pulling back and eyes narrowed. "I hope losing yourself in the bottom of a bottle is worth what you've lost." Her eyes skim down his frame then back up to his face, whispering, "God, you're just like Dad."

Uncle B takes a step back like she slapped him. His eyes are wide.

Mommy doesn't even look at him as she pulls the door open. "Just go, Brody." His shoulders slump, and he turns for the door as I come tumbling out of my room.

"No! *Wait!*" I cry. He can't go, *he can't*. I want him here, with me. With us.

"Sailor." Mommy steps towards me, trying to stop me from reaching him. "What are you doing out of bed, sweet girl?"

I try to push past her. "Uncle B, please don't go."

"Sailor..." Mommy starts, but I cut her off, a hiccup ripping out of me.

"*Please*. You promised."

Mommy turns to Uncle B, who stands still in the doorway, one foot in the house and one out, his back to us. My entire body vibrates. I can barely breathe as I wait for him to say something, anything. *Please, just say something!*

"*You promised!*" I repeat, clenching Mommy's sleeve in my hand so tight I barely make out the slight tear of fabric over the roar of my heartbeat in my ears. The tears fall hot and fast the longer he doesn't say anything.

Why isn't he saying anything?

"*Brody*," Mommy says, and she sounds almost as heartbroken as I feel.

Barely looking over his shoulder, Brody slips that small white box out of his pocket and taps out a cigarette, his hands shaking. "I'm sorry, kid," he whispers.

I blink furiously to clear the tears from my eyes, but he's gone. I stumble towards the door but I don't make it more than a few feet before I crumble to the ground with all the grace of a baby deer, my body rattling with sobs. Mom's hushed words run over me, along with her hand, in an attempt to soothe me, just like she does every time I've ever fallen, scraping a knee or bruising an elbow or bumping my head.

But how do I tell her that this time, the hurt is somewhere she just can't reach?

TEN

THE SCCC: *Siren's Cove Community Center.*

I stare at the blue script across the white sign until the words blur together. It sits in the middle of a nicely kept lawn in front of a yellow bungalow elevated by stilts.

Better to look at the sign than to just sit here silently in the Jeep with Banks. Apparently, Kelly cashed in a favor, asking him to drive me over to the center, though he didn't tell me why. My guess? So that he could try and track down Brody. He's supposed to be here for tonight's kinship guardian support group while I go to the teen group.

I haven't been able to gather any sort of courage to go inside. Even though I quietly thanked Banks for the ride when he pulled into the lot, fingers wrapped around the door handle with all the intention to slip out. I've yet to move, my other hand fiddling with the necklace around my neck as I focus on breathing. *In through my nose, out through my mouth.*

With every released breath, I think to myself—for a second at least—that this is it. That I'll get out and head inside. Trail after the other teens I've watched take the stairs up to the center with its wooden wraparound porch and white-trimmed doors, opening and closing with every arrival as the minutes tick by.

"Come on." I blink several times before I comprehend Banks' words.

"What?" I look over at him to find he's already watching me.

Banks opens his own door and steps out. Slowly, I follow, unsure if this is a trick to leave me stranded in the parking lot because he's tired of my need to delay the inevitable and wants to get his car back. Instead, he stops at the back of the Jeep, popping the glass up and swinging the trunk door open.

Muscles flexing through the holes of his muscled tee, he picks up a folded fringed blanket and shakes it out. Laying it across the back floor, he hops up and takes a seat. "Are you waiting for an invitation or something?"

A huff of laughter escapes me as I shake my head. I climb up and take a seat beside him, pushing back into the trunk until its space seems to swallow me whole, my eyes trained on the building in front of us. Just in sight, but out of reach. My feet hang off the edge and I smile a little to myself as I manage to find my next breath without shaking.

After a minute, I glance over at Banks.

"Why are you doing this?"

He shrugs one shoulder. "You matter to him." *Him.* Lux. There's a steelness in his voice that leaves no room to question who he means.

"And he matters to you," I surmise. It's not hard to draw that conclusion. Their bond is obvious. Even when the four of them are together, the two of them look to each other first when it comes to sharing a joke. It's the same between Griffin and Milo.

"Well, don't you two look cozy." *Speaking of...*Milo stops his skateboard right in front of us, stepping on one end of the board to pop it upright. He picks it up, sliding it under his arm with practiced ease, and gives Banks a smirk. "You know, if word gets back to Griffin you're out parking with Sailor, you're gonna break his little heart."

"Parking?" A rumble of laughter leaves Banks. "Who even says that?"

Before either of us can blink, Milo whips out his phone, snapping a picture and then repocketing it. With a smug smile, like he's won something, he questions, "Want to comment again?"

Banks shakes his head. "So not cool."

"You're right, I forgot me!" Slipping his phone back out, Milo flips the camera view into selfie mode, holding it up at an angle to get himself in the photo. This time, I'm ready, my smile coming more easily at Banks' unamused expression. Milo meets my eyes over his phone with a wink as he looks at the photo before pocketing it once more. "That one's a keeper."

Without the teasing energy of the camera, I feel my smile fading. Milo tilts his head, a few of his dreads falling across his face and a knowing look in his eyes as he meets my gaze once more. "The hardest part is probably heading in. Especially the first time."

I look away, my hand reaching up for my necklace, tightening around the charm until my fingernails bite into my palm. "I think the first time I chose to come, I hung out in the parking lot the entire session," Milo continues. "In the back of this very Jeep, actually." He looks over at Banks. "This seems to be your calling."

"I'm setting a trend." Banks dryly remarks with a slight glance over his shoulder at me. "My mom will be so proud."

Milo chuckles, but my throat just feels tight. "I don't think I can go in," I say quietly, hating myself for admitting it.

"That's okay." Milo assures me. He leans against the side of the Jeep, and I can't help but feel grateful for a second time this night.

"You should go, though," I encourage. "Don't let me stop you."

"Nah. I'm right where I'm meant to be."

"Will you tell me about it?" I ask, and then clarify. "Group, I mean."

Milo does just that. He describes a room in the back of the house with a large sliding glass door that leads out to the porch and overlooks the beach. A private beach the center apparently owns, with a boardwalk that leads out to the sand.

They often slide the door open, letting the sound of waves spill into the space. Sometimes there's a guest facilitator, college kids that were once teens like us earning a semester credit. More often than not, though, it's run by program leader, Theo Marshall.

My mouth falls open as I look over at Banks. "Your dad?"

"Family business," he says dryly.

"And he's inside right now?" I question. I can't help but be curious about the person who contributed the other half of Banks and Griffin's DNA. Griffin clearly got his soft heart and Banks his ability to read a person's needs with a single look from their mom, but the rest of them is a mystery. Especially all that height.

"As far as I know." Banks turns to fully look at me, raising an eyebrow. "Should I be concerned by how interested you seem with this new information?"

I grin. "Do you think you should be?"

He searches my face, his full lips twisting in a slight scowl. "I don't know." And then, "He's married, just so you know."

I roll my eyes. "Oh, really? Well that completely messes with my plans of diverting Griffin's crush by becoming your step-mom." Pushing out of the back of his Jeep, I don't even hesitate in taking Milo's hand when he offers, helping me the rest of the way to my feet. "I'm just curious, that's all."

"Curious about what?"

I grin to myself. "Wouldn't you like to know?"

"Catch you later." Milo calls over his shoulder as we start for the center.

"Curious about what?" Banks calls again. I can't help but giggle to myself. "Sailor!"

I'm so entertained by ruffling Banks's feathers a little that the nerves don't hit until we're more than halfway up the steps. I suck in a deep breath. Milo gives my fingers a gentle squeeze as we take the last step and it's then that I remember he's still holding my hand. I don't let go, letting his grip ground me as my heart beats loudly in my ears as we face the front door.

Maybe this isn't a good idea.

But...how much different can it really be from my time at the group home?

Rolling my shoulders back, I release a deep breath and open the door before I can change my mind. Inside, we're greeted by a warm and inviting entryway, a middle-aged lady sitting behind the front desk across from where we stand. Sets of closed, window-framed French doors separate us from the rooms immediately to our left and right, white curtains providing some level of privacy. The low sound of voices fill the room to the right, interrupted by low ripples of laughter.

Milo waves to the lady as we move down the hall to the left of the desk, and I'm grateful to be spared any small talk. There are several doors along the hall, some closed, others open. Matching signs hang on two of the doors across from each other, an outline of a surfer on each one stating gender-neutral bathrooms.

When we reach the last door on the left, Milo opens it and ushers me in, following close behind. The room is comfortable, well-used and cared for with a large area rug in the middle. Inspirational posters decorate one wall, the other holding a bulletin board full of information and photos. For a moment, I almost forget where I am as I take it all in, the wall of photos transporting me right back to the house, as if I'm still standing in that hallway again. The ghost of it seems determined to haunt me no matter where I go.

"Who do we have here?"

The deep voice pulls me out of my head, and I look up. The room is set up with a large collection of chairs and bean bags arranged in a large circle. Most of them are full of kids my age, but there's a man whose smile is instantly familiar. With the fit build and youthful face, I would almost question whether Banks and Griffin have an older brother.

Good job, Dani, I think, despite myself. I wonder if it would be weird to high-five my social worker over her taste in husbands.

"Hey, Theo, sorry we're late," Milo apologizes, tucking his skateboard in the corner by the door.

"Don't worry about it." Theo waves him off, his next words I'm almost certain are directed to me. "This is your space. You show up when you're ready—whatever that may look like for you."

"Time is nothing if not a social construct," says a deep voice on the other side of the circle, the words gently accented with rolling *r*'s and slightly heavier vowels. I look over to the guy who spoke, and he winks at me in return. Thick brows sit atop amber eyes, a smatter of freckles across his nose pronounced against his light brown skin. "*Dime.* I didn't get your name, *sirena*."

I raise a brow in challenge. "That's because I didn't give it."

He smirks, and it pulls at the trimmed facial hair across his jaw and above his lips. Milo steps in front of me. "Okay, lay off the charm, Nico."

"Oooh, a little defensive, are we?" Nico taunts, but the words hold more curiosity than heat.

"Trying to spare you a black eye," Milo says, an edge to his voice that tells me he's not entirely joking.

"You handing them out?" Nico's tone is still light, but his eyes look a little sharper. *What is this, a pissing contest? Some sort of protective posturing?* Don't peacocks fluff their feathers to show dominance? Is that what this is? I peek sideways at Milo, frowning.

"Nope." The *p* pops with emphasis on Milo's lips. "Lux, on the other hand..." *Excuse me? Lux is doing what?* Suddenly, I recall the scars decorating his hands. Did he get them from fighting?

Nico shifts to the side in his chair, catching sight of me once more. A few curls escape the pile on top of his own head with the movement. His eyes run down my frame before folding his arms across his chest, muscles flexing, and sits back in his seat as he declares, "Worth it."

Okay. I'm starting to believe it's mandatory to be surfer-model-worthy simply to *live* in Siren's Cove. *What is in the water around here?*

Milo huffs out a laugh. "You're so full of shit." Reaching out behind him, Milo's hand brushes against mine. "Come on, let's grab a seat." I sit directly across from Nico, trying not to look too closely at the other people in the room, and he watches me silently. Milo drops down beside me, bringing the group to seven.

Seven. Seven teens. All facing similar issues. No longer in the care of someone we thought would be there all our lives. Or, at least, I did. I never imagined living in a world without my mom, and sometimes the reality of doing so is a lot harder than I can bear at times. Something heavy sinks in my chest and I grab for my necklace, my nails biting into the palm of my hand as I curl my fingers around it tightly.

It's seven too many.

"So, you must be Sailor." I tense at Theo's words but thaw a little when he goes on. "My son talks a lot about his new…'bestie,' I believe is how he put it?" I can't help grinning. *Oh, Griffin.* "However, just because my son talks to me about you doesn't mean I'd ever share anything you say here in group."

I give a quick nod of understanding. Nico, sitting to Theo's left, brings his hand up to his mouth, his thumb dragging across his bottom lip as he tilts his head a little. Almost like he's trying to solve a mystery.

"I haven't seen you around the Cove," a girl a few chairs down says, pushing her glasses up her nose.

"Um, I just arrived." I stare out the window, watching the waves lap against the shoreline.

"We're glad you're here, Sailor," Theo says, so sincerely I find myself believing him.

"*Bienvenido.*" Nico murmurs. Everyone chimes in with their own greetings, and my hand unfurls from around the necklace until I just have the charm pinched between two of my fingers.

Theo moves us through our group session with ease, some

leading the conversation with updates of how things are going with their current guardian, others opening up about their overall struggles. I nod along, taking in what's being shared and noting an array of differences in our experiences to the care and attention each of our cases are receiving. For some, their kinship placement is temporary, whereas others are permanent.

What do I want mine to be?

I think over Priya's text messages, swimming in uncertainty.

"How about you, Milo?" Theo's gentle prompting brings me back to myself. "Is there something on your mind?"

"My grandma's trying to apply for assistance, *again*." I blink in surprise. There's more animosity behind his words that I would never think he was capable of harboring. "I hate that she keeps filling out those stupid applications over and over again. It's not right."

"The system places such a hard emphasis on keeping us with family, but when the family needs help, they make it impossible to actually get any support," one of the other girls says, running a hand through her hair. She's one who isn't currently placed with family—she'd been moved into emergency foster care after a recent incident she was unwilling to explain to the rest of us.

No one pushed her to try, and that made me breathe a little easier.

"I thought your grandma just recently got approved for something," one of the boys says, genuine interest lacing his voice.

Milo sinks into his seat, like the weight of the world sits on his shoulders. Something tugs in my chest for this boy, with his carefree smile and gentle soul, carrying all this hidden pain. "She did. But anytime my mom comes around, my grandma can't help but want to take care of her. She feels guilty." Milo looks off in the distance, unwilling to meet any of our eyes. The muscles in his jaw flexes along with the opening and closing of his hands that fist in his lap. When he finds his voice, he continues. "My grandma likes to joke that I can eat her out of the house—which is true. But I try to not let her see that."

"How? By starving?" Nico questions. I shift in my seat, brows furrowed. *Is Milo not eating enough?* I think about the unexpectedly well-stocked cabinets in Brody and Kelly's kitchen, the meals for the week Kelly preps on Sunday afternoons. We definitely have enough to feed Milo if he needs it. The least we can do is invite him for dinner a few times a week. I make a mental note to talk to Kelly about it.

"It's not like that." Milo's voice is defensive. "I'm not going hungry."

Nico holds up his hands. "Wasn't saying that you were."

Theo jumps in. "I think we all just want to make sure you're okay, Milo."

Milo scowls, but after a moment, his shoulders slump again. "I eat whatever my grandma serves me. She prides herself on being able to look after me. But what she can offer...it's not always enough." He lifts his chin stubbornly. "But it's fine. *I'm* fine. I have enough of my own resources that I don't typically go without." I immediately think of Cova. Griffin and Banks, too. Probably the entire Marshall family, actually, if the way Theo is looking at him is any indication. No way they let Milo go hungry. He's got people in his corner, always.

He's got me.

I pause at the revelation. When the panic I'm expecting doesn't immediately follow, just certainty and calm, I know I mean it.

"Milo, I'd like to touch base after group," Theo says. "Let's make sure your grandmother is supported in this process and see how we may be able to help her with Cecilia. If anyone else is having similar troubles with applying and receiving assistance, please don't hesitate to pop into the center. We can help you navigate the process, maybe find other alternatives." Theo lets his words sink in for a moment, giving Milo time to consider. After a few long seconds, Milo nods. "Sometimes the most direct path isn't the quickest or easiest one, even if it seems to be. Things often take more time than we want them to. I know it's hard, but we're here to help you through it."

His words tug at something in my mind. All the arguments Mom and Brody used to have, the custody arrangements she put in her will.

"I just want more time." That's what Brody had said the night he walked out on us. For the first time, I wonder what might have happened if she hadn't made him choose.

"I just want more time."

Like he knew the inevitable was coming.

Like she told him.

Because she knew.

She. Knew.

The air of secrecy rolls in like a tide, swallowing my fear and dragging me under.

ELEVEN

BRODY NEVER SHOWED up for last night's caregiver session. Instead, I came home to find Kelly and Brody arguing, their voices loud enough that we could hear them from the driveway.

Banks gave me a wary look. "You want me to come in with you?"

I don't remember answering him as I watched Hank leave through the front door with Evie in his arms, his eyes flicking back and forth between her and the house the entire time he was buckling her into their car. I only vaguely remember slipping inside to find Kelly standing toe to toe with Brody, an array of empty beer bottles on the back porch table beyond them. A water sprinkler was running out on the grass, forgotten. I ignored all of it, heading for my room instead.

When I get up this morning, the bottles are gone, the sprinkler tucked away. The house is quiet.

Not ready to face either man, I dress quickly and am out the door before anyone can notice.

Exploring the boardwalk seems like a much better way to spend my morning than lurking around the house, especially when I remember Cova mentioning a bookstore. I look it up on my phone, and set off to escape reality in a pile of stories.

The bell above the door to Sweet Nothing chimes as I step inside, indie music playing softly. Wooden flooring creaks beneath my feet, rows of bookshelves spanning the shop, some devoted to bookish accessories and stationery items. My jaw unclenches the deeper I move into the store—until Cova's voice, almost unfamiliar in its tight, pleading tone, makes me stop in my tracks.

"Rhian, it wasn't like that. I promise."

"Are you trying to tell me it wasn't what it looked like?"

I tense at the strain in the unfamiliar male voice. Several shelves over from where I stand, a guy with a low buzz cut hovers several inches over Cova, his legs planted wide, eyes hard, and lips curled across his deeply tanned, stubbled face. *Just how old is this dude?*

Cova stands ramrod straight, clutching a stack of books. The guy—Rhian?—grabs a hold of her arm, hard, yanking her harshly against him as he leans in and says something so softly I wouldn't even know he was speaking if not for his lips moving by her ear. A chill runs down my spine at the way her entire body freezes, her expression tight and scared.

I'm about to take a step towards them, a retort on my lips, when someone shifts just behind Rhian. No, not just anyone—Nico, the guy from the kinship support group. *What is going on here? Is he friends with this dude?* He stares at the two of them, his hands loosely clenched at his sides.

Do something, I think, willing him to see what I see. *Protect her.*

As if he can hear me, his eyes meet mine from across the aisle, guarded, and I take a step back even as I fix him with an accusing glare. I only just met him. I don't really *know* him. But what I do know is that I would have never pictured him standing around with some guy who is clearly threatening a girl half his size, and doing nothing to put a stop to it. Nico looks away first, biting his bottom lip.

Fuck it. I start for them when Nico finally seems to make a decision. Squaring his shoulders, he nudges Rhian, firm enough to get his attention. "Hey. That's enough. Forget it." Forget it? How about don't do it? I bite my tongue, hoping that Nico's words—however half-assed—will get Rhian to leave. I could shake him for not stepping in sooner, but at least he's doing *something*. When the guy remains unmoved, Nico pushes, "*Vamo.* I gotta scoop up my little cousin."

I hold my breath, eyes flickering from him to Rhian. *Yes, go. Get out of here.* Slowly, Rhian nods, his eyes raking down Cova's frame and back up. "Yeah, okay." His other hand shoots up so quickly that I flinch along with Cova who loses her grip on the books. Grasping her chin in between his thumb and forefinger, his eyes darken with a promise that has me wanting to take another step back. "You and I aren't finished." Cova lets out a hiss as his fingers bite into her skin. "I'll call you later." There's an underlying threat to his announcement, like he's warning her that she better pick-up when he calls.

Cova gives a tiny nod, and Rhian lets her go, following Nico toward the door. I stare hard at the side of Nico's face, but he never looks at me. Probably a smart move—*I wouldn't look at me either.* I'd flip him off if he did. Rhian, on the other hand, glances at me as he passes. His eyes dance up and down my body, and my fingers twitch at my side to give *him* the middle finger, but I refrain. I don't want to bring any more trouble to Cova's door than she's already welcomed in.

Only once the chime of the bell over the door twinkles overhead do I cross the aisle to Cova. She's crouched on the floor, hands shaking as she collects her fallen books. I kneel next to her, gathering the rest and silently holding them out.

She pauses briefly before raising her head, unshed tears in her eyes. The fire-bright energy in the girl I met on the beach is nowhere in sight. Instead, Cova's slim frame seems borderline tiny as she hunches in on herself, her eyes flitting away every few seconds as she tries, and fails, to look at me for more than a moment at a time. Her smile, usually as bright and brilliant as Milo's, nowhere in sight. There's a tightness in my throat. It's like I'm meeting someone entirely different.

I bite my lip from asking all the questions I want to. I don't want to scare her off. I paste on a smile, pointing to her books. "You got some really great picks, but I gotta warn you," I tap the cover of the book on the top of the stack, "this one's devastating."

With a wobbly grin, Cova says quietly, "It's why I chose it."

I smile back as we rise to our feet. "If you like having your heart torn into shreds, I should probably show you some others that'll make you want to chuck the book across the room."

"Can we rank them by best fictional crushes?"

"I like the way you think."

We spend the morning browsing, sharing a nonstop conversation of favorite characters, tropes, and authors. By the time we're finally starting to think about making our way up to the register, Cova's smile is bright and steady, the slight smudges in her eyeliner the only remaining sign of her tears.

"Hey, you know, after this, we should shop for bikinis," Cova suggests. "Finally start filling up your crate."

My smile wavers, and I grip the book in my hand tightly. "How many bathing suits can one girl need?"

"In the Cove? Always one more than you currently have." When I don't reply, Cova spins on her heels and leans back against the bookcase I'm browsing. "Look, whether you're staying for a good time or a long time doesn't matter. What *does* matter is that you're here, for now, and that's all the reason you need to splurge on suits." My mouth opens, and she smiles gently. "I know a girl looking to run when I see one."

A moment of understanding passes between us.

"I'm not sure what I want," I admit quietly. "I mean..." Grabbing a hold of my necklace, I lightly tug at the charm, the mermaid tail biting into my skin. For the first time, I let myself say it out loud. "I'm not sure where I belong."

"Sometimes you've got to lose who you are to find yourself," Cova muses quietly. She pushes off the shelves, a huge grin suddenly lighting up her entire face, the shadows in her eyes disappearing as she bounces on the balls of her feet. "Forget the shopping—I just got a better idea. Come on."

Cova pays for her books and we leave the store, falling in step with each other. It's a gorgeous day, and Siren's Cove is alive with activity. Kids run up and down the sidewalk, their families calling out to them. Friends goof around and couples lean into each other, holding hands. There's cafes with an array of outdoor seating, umbrellas open to provide some covering from the sun. Vendor carts, in various sizes and colors, litter the boardwalk, one of them proclaiming itself as the official Siren's Cove Gift Shop. Dogs walk happily alongside their owners, or pant even more happily under the tables outside restaurants and ice cream parlors, catching crumbs and melting drops when they fall. Laughter and cheerful shouting fill the air above the steady hum of conversation and music spilling across the boardwalk.

"Have you ever skated?" Cova asks as we make our way towards her car.

I recall Milo's arrival to the community center. "What, like skateboarding?"

She shakes her head. "Roller skating."

The corners of my eyes crinkle with the force of my smile. "Oh my God. All the time when I was younger." There was a roller rink Gia loved that Lux and I often tagged along to, much to her annoyance. But anytime Gia wanted to go, Ms. A always insisted on picking me up along the way. Gia would take off on her skates, doing literal laps around me, laughing with her friends like they were all in on some big secret while trying to get the attention of boys. Lux remained right at my side, holding my hands as I learned to remain steady on my feet.

He never let me fall.

"Perfect." Cova pops the trunk to her buggy, depositing her

new books and retrieving a box. She holds it for a moment, worrying her bottom lip between her teeth as she shifts from one foot to the other, then presses it into my hands. "These are for you." She turns away quickly, dragging a different bag closer to herself and pulling out a cute pair of aqua skates with bright pink laces.

I look down at the box, lifting the lid to peek inside. "Um, Cova? Do you always carry an extra set of skates with you?"

"Um...no, not usually." She sits on the edge of the trunk, still not meeting my eyes as she kicks off her shoes.

I take another look at the skates in the box, laces the same color as hers, fully laced, wrapped neatly in tissue paper and not a scratch in sight. As white as they are, I would expect to see a scuff on them if Cova were renting these skates out. My eyes bounce from the box, to her, and back to the box. "Cova...these look brand new."

Her head bobs as she nods in agreement, fixated on sliding her feet into her own skates and pointedly not looking my way. "You can keep your stuff in my car while we skate. Don't worry about anyone seeing, crime is like, nonexistent around the Cove."

"*Cova*," I say, exasperated, and this time, she pauses. With a sigh, she sits up and meets my gaze.

"Don't freak out." I stiffen, and she raises a hand in almost a placating gesture. "The guys all insisted on chipping in when they found out what I was up to."

My grip on the box tightens. "And what were you up to?"

"I know you're not looking to make any friends, and I get wanting—*needing*—to keep everyone at an arm's length, but I was hoping that at least while you're here...well, that you wouldn't mind being *my* friend. For however long that looks like." She gives me a small, slightly wavering smile. "You might have noticed that I...I kind of need one."

I don't know what to say.

"I've never really had any girlfriends," Cova goes on when I remain quiet, speaking a bit faster now, like she's trying to get something out of her system. "It's always just been me and the guys. And they're great, but there are some things they don't... they just don't understand."

I think about Cova pressed against the bookshelf, Rhian looming over her. I imagine what the boys would have done if they saw it. They wouldn't have followed Cova's lead, I know that much. The bookstore would probably have ended up torn apart. I grind my teeth, the headache returning with a vengeance. I force myself to relax my jaw. "I get that. But I don't need handouts." I hold up the box. "Or bribes."

"Well, good thing I'm not doing either." She raises her chin. "Those are a gift."

"A gift?"

"Yeah, I really enjoy giving to others. Acts of service, shopping for the perfect present—it's kind of my thing. Just ask the guys."

I soften despite myself, until the memory of Rhian flashes across my mind. "Hopefully never at the expense of yourself."

She falters in tying up her laces, and I nearly regret my words at the shadows that fill her eyes. "I think it's cost me more than I care to admit," she says quietly.

Honestly.

I swallow thickly, hesitating with my next words. "Have you talked to the guys about him?"

She shakes her head before I'm even finished asking. "I don't want to involve them." Even if she doesn't...

How could they not know? How could Milo?

At the thought of them leaving her to this guy, my headache grows.

"You know they would help if you asked." I don't know if I'm reassuring her, or seeking it for myself.

She smiles a little. "In a heartbeat." Tension I didn't know I had bleeds from my shoulders as they drop in relief. At least she knows they'd have her back, if she wanted them to. "I'm just...I'm not there yet. It's complicated."

I watch her for another moment, hearing what she can't say.

In her own way, Cova must feel as trapped as I am.

More than anything else, that's what makes up my mind. I may not be in the business of acquiring any friends, but Cova is. No matter what happens next for me, I can be there for her.

At least for now.

TWELVE

THREE YEARS AGO

I SMILE at my reflection in the mirror, fixing my curls where they spring out from under my cap. The tassel swings from the corner of my eye, and I grab hold of it.

"Keep it on the right, Sail," Lux had told me, his reassurance that graduation will be okay, loosening the tightness in my chest. High school won't be so bad with Lux at my side. He promises nothing will change with us. Best friends, always.

Except lately...I don't know. I've found myself scowling anytime a girl looks Lux's way. None of them had paid him any attention before, I don't think, but this year things changed. And to some extent, so has Lux. I can't put my finger on it, but something's worrying him. He won't tell me, no matter how much I ask. I just want to help, though Lux says it's nothing for me to worry about.

A pounding shakes the bathroom door. "Sailor, hurry up in there! Some of us still need to get ready!"

Sucking in a sharp breath, my hand shakes only a little as I grip the doorknob. With another deep breath, I wipe all the emotion off my face.

Lux *hates* the mask I've perfected since being here at Safe Harbor Group Home. But how do I explain to him it's the only way to keep some of the other kids in the house at bay? I've watched them seek out those they feel are *too soft*. Sometimes it's just for taunting, but there are too many times when people go from shouting at one another to breaking out into a full-on fight.

Those are the times to really stay clear, unless you want to get caught in the crossfire—whether that's getting a fist to the face or just facing consequences for guilt by association. The first week I was here, I watched two girls go at it after one claimed the other stole her vape like she tried stealing her boyfriend. That comment seemed to push the one accused over the edge, and she paid the girl back by punching her braces out of her mouth.

"Sailor!"

I pull the door open and don't flinch as Roni's fist halts mere inches from my face, the door no longer there for her to bang on. Her eyes skim over me, her lips curling into a sneer at my cap and gown. I tense, bracing myself—for what, I'm not sure—but with Roni you can never be too careful. "It's all yours," I say quietly, stepping out of the way.

To my relief, she just nods, stepping past me into the bathroom.

Turning my head slightly to keep her within view over my shoulder, I head back to my assigned room, remembering the first lesson I learned here: *never turn your back on anyone, it leaves you too open*.

That advice came shortly after I arrived, when Roni tried to get the jump on me. She only managed to bust my lip, but it was enough for one of the older kids to take me under their wing and show me the ropes.

Never snitch. That advice came fast on the heels of the first, and it's the one universal rule everyone seems to follow in the house, no matter what the consequences may be. So when one of the house staff asked what happened and Roni eyed me from the other end of the dining room table, I shrugged and said nothing.

Things with Lux aren't the only thing to have changed.

Plopping down on my bed, I'm careful not to hit my cap on

the bunk above mine. All six beds are currently taken, but the other kids come and go without warning, sometimes in the middle of the night. One day they're there, the next they're gone.

I thought I'd be gone by now too, back home with Mom. Priya, my social worker, had assured me that this was just temporary. But when Mom collapsed last summer, her week in the hospital turned into me spending my entire eighth grade year here at Safe Harbor. Turns out she's sicker than even *she* knew, if her cries about supposedly having more time are anything to go by.

Watching her fall had been the scariest thing I've ever seen. I stood there, barely able to call her name and unable to move from my spot. I don't know what I would have done if Lux hadn't been there to call 9-1-1. But of course he knew what to do. *Lux always knows what to do.*

Speaking of...

I drop to my knees and reach under the bed to pull out the storage trunk I was assigned when I arrived. Withdrawing the key from its chain around my neck, I unlock the trunk and grab my phone. Yet another lesson I learned my first week: *keep your valuables close and locked*. Considering how many times I've seen other kids picking locks, I'm not really sure what good they do, but I guess it's the thought that counts.

Sailor: You're still picking me up, right?

Lux's response comes immediately, and I smile, automatically relaxing.

Lux: You doubt me?

Sailor: Never.

Lux: Exactly. I just need to grab my sister. See you in a few.

Exiting out of the text thread, my thumb hovers over the

screen for a second before I release a shaky breath and tap on Uncle B's.

Nothing. Not a single response.

My chest tightens.

What did you expect? I practically growl at myself, trying to stifle the white hot anger that licks up my spine and sears my throat as I scroll back through the most recent messages I've sent.

Sailor: Hey, Uncle B! I graduate this year!

Sailor: It's May 25th. Will you come?

Sailor: I'd really like for you to be there.

Sailor: I mean...could you come since Mom can't?

Sailor: You can even bring Hank!

Sailor: Okay...well the ceremony starts at 2PM. It'll be in our school's auditorium. Here's the address!

A series of texts over the course of the year, from sharing my worries over Mom's collapse to my time here at the group home. All of them left unanswered despite the little *read* notification below each message. I lock the screen.

Maybe he'll show.

I've tried holding onto the ghost of him since he walked out on me and Mom three years ago. That was a hard night. Sometimes the nights that came after were even harder. But once I could feel the beating of my own heart again, and Lux could pull a smile from me, I snuck into Mom's phone and wrote down Uncle B's number.

Mom might have been willing to give up on him, but I wasn't.

Not yet.

THIRTEEN

A KNOCK RATTLES my bedroom door. "Sailor?"

Laid out on the floor, I blink profusely until the world comes back into focus.

The knocking comes again, followed by Kelly's voice. "Sailor? You in there?"

"Yeah." The word barely passes my dry lips, and I realize I'm seriously thirsty. *What time is it?* I clear my throat and try again. "Come in."

The door opens, and Kelly comes into the room, not a single hesitation in his steps as he takes a seat on the edge of the bed. Resting his arms on his legs, he leans forward to peer down at me. "What are you doing?"

I tilt my head, eyes trained on the spinning ceiling fan. "Sometimes all a girl wants to do is lie on the floor."

Kelly considers that, then says, "There's usually music coming from this room." He isn't wrong. I've had music playing quietly day and night since I arrived two weeks ago. After staying in the group home, the silence is too loud to bear, especially with my thoughts. But today, the room has been filled with my shallow breaths for the last couple of hours since I took up residency down here.

"I didn't really feel like listening to anything."

He hums. "How are you sleeping?"

I'm not. Not really. "Fine."

"Uh-huh." A pause. "Nice skates. You didn't have those when you moved in."

God, he's trying so hard. I bite back a sigh. "Cova gave them to me." A light flickers on somewhere in the recesses of my mind, a glow of warmth that softens me a little. It's hard not to when I think about Cova. "We've been skating around town." She's shown me *"the Cove,"* as she affectionately refers to it, through her eyes. Our time together, a quiet, unsuspecting, lifeline that's kept my head above water every time I began to feel as if I were drowning.

Whether I was that easy to read or she needed it too, Cova would randomly grab for my hand, keeping me present and steady and *grounded*. The noise in my head had a way of quieting around her, and it must've been the same for her as she would randomly hold my hand a little tighter, our outings extending well into the day.

"I thought that was you I spotted the other day," Kelly says. "You seemed to be enjoying yourself." He sounds cautiously hopeful, but there's an underlying question there. Dragging my gaze from the ceiling, I look over at him. His green eyes are shadowed with concern as they search my face.

"It's kind of hard not to like them," I admit. "Cova and the guys, I mean."

"Is that a bad thing?"

I roll my head lazily until I'm looking back up at the ceiling. *Yeah, it probably is.* I don't answer out loud. Let him come up with his own conclusions. He's read me pretty well so far, but that's Kelly for you.

Maybe he should hit Dani and Theo up for a job.

Except I can't help but feel guilty at wanting to be seen—to be heard—by someone other than him.

Brody flashes through my mind, so similar in looks to mom

that I suck in a sharp breath, my chest tightening. *I just want him to fight for me.*

"Sailor...you know it's okay to let people in, right?" *That's where you're wrong.* Something must show on my face because he looks suddenly heartbroken. "Sailor..."

"It hurts too much." I whisper thickly.

He doesn't say anything immediately. "Yeah," he says finally. "It can." A tear falls fast and hot down the side of my face and into my curls. If he notices, at least he's nice enough not to point it out. "But you'll hurt yourself more by shutting everyone out. The reality is that there will be those in life who want to fight for you and others who won't. There's one thing, though, you can't forget."

I take the bait. "What's that?"

"That you have to decide if you're willing to fight for them, too." Kelly lets that sink in for a moment. "You have one of those chances now. If you're ready for it." I look over at him, brows furrowing. He nods toward the door. "You have a visitor."

Lux. There's no one else here in Siren's Cove that would be paying me a visit and ring true to Kelly's words. When I don't immediately move, Kelly rises to his feet and heads for the door. "He's out back."

I guess he's decided it's finally time for that talk.

Remember to breathe, Mom's voice says in my head. I pull in a deep, shaky breath, *one*, *two*, *three*, *four*, and release.

Again.

I do it again, and again, until the room stops spinning and I can feel the solid floor beneath me.

Slowly, I get to my feet. My curls fall around my face and down my back. I take a moment to wipe at my eyes, making sure the tears are gone.

My heartbeat echoes in my ears with every step I take through the house. My childhood flashes through my mind like a highlight reel, and Lux is in so many frames it hurts. Not once did I ever think there'd be a time in my life filled with the absence of him. I finger my necklace, pausing when I catch sight of him through the sliding glass doors.

Lux is sitting on the porch steps, elbows resting on his knees, but his head is dropped forward, one hand clasped over the other. My eyes sweep over his broad frame, and for a moment the ghost of the child he once was takes his place. Gosh, he'd been such a cute kid. Eyes that twinkled and dimples that'd appear when he smiled. Sometimes one would make an appearance when he was mad enough. I loved the sight of them. I'd make a game of poking his dimples, especially when he would be a little too serious. It was always the quickest way to make him smile. He'd bat at my hand, his face slightly reddening, but he'd grin nonetheless.

Even after all the tears and hurt and anger, the memory still makes me smile.

I miss it. I miss *us*. I miss how easy things used to be.

But could we ever get back to that?

Thinking over what Kelly said, my mind still isn't made up as I finally step outside. Lux stills, the only indicator he's aware of my presence. I hold my breath as I take a seat beside him, releasing it in a woosh at the stricken look across his face as I peak up at him.

He swallows visibly. "Hey."

"Hi. Kelly said you wanted to talk."

Lux is quiet for a long moment, and then he says, "I figured it was time we put everything out on the table." He watches me, almost guarded.

"Fine." I nod my head in agreement. "Let's start with you leaving. Not even saying goodbye."

"It's not that simple."

I clench my hands into fists, my nails biting into my palms. "Sounds like an excuse Brody would give." Lux flinches, and as fast as it came, all the fight leaves me. Fighting with Lux has never felt right. I wrap my arms around myself, as if it'll help hold me together. "You owe me an explanation."

Lux closes his eyes. "I know. It's just...it's not a pretty story, Sailor."

"Neither is mine." He winces, but I push forward. "God, Lux. Just tell me." The tattoos, the scars, the guarded expression he wears like a second skin—the shadows in his eyes. I can't find the boy I once knew underneath it all. "What *happened* to you?"

Pain laces his face. When he finally speaks, the words turn all my blood to ice. "Gia killed herself."

I rear back, my mouth falling open. Of everything I'd tried to come up with, trying to fill in the blanks of Lux's life, I never could have imagined that. "She—she what?"

How could she? But more importantly, *How could I not know?*

His eyes swim with tears, and he stares at his hands. "The day of our eighth grade graduation...Sail, baby, Mom and I had every intention of coming to get you. But, I..."

But he never did. I'd sat outside the group home, everyone else having gone on ahead in the van at my insistence that I was catching a ride with a friend. I'd waited for the better part of the day, watching the street for a white little car that would never come.

I close the space between us before I realize what I'm doing, taking one of his hands in mine. "You what, Lux?" I ask softly.

"I found her." His voice breaks. "Gia. She'd downed a bottle of pills."

My heart cracks wide open, tears silently rolling down my face, but I swallow my sorrow for the time being. I can mourn the girl I once knew later. This moment isn't about me. "Lux--" I squeeze my eyes shut. His large hands cup my face, wiping away my tears. They only come faster in the wake of *him* trying to take care of *me*. I should be comforting him.

Something tugs at my memory. "Those girls she was friends with...?"

"Yeah. Some friends they were." I can't blame him for the bite in his words. "She was never herself when it came to them. I was too young—she was older, so I don't know if there was already something there before…" His eyes sort of glaze over, lost in a memory I wish I could take from him. "But what I do know is that her trying to keep up with them didn't do her any favors."

He takes a deep breath. "I didn't even know we were leaving town until we were gone. To be fair, I don't think my mom did either."

"How'd you end up here? In Siren's Cove, of all places?"

Lux shrugs. "Your mom always talked so fondly about this place. Guess mine thought it might be the one thing to help her. A fresh start, somewhere that didn't feel so…so haunted by what we lost."

Mom had loved this place, but I think it had a lot to do with the people in it. When Brody first moved here, and everything was new and exciting, she'd come out to visit. Trying to repair a relationship with her little brother. She was good at hiding things, but sometimes she couldn't help but wear her guilt when it came to Brody. Maybe that's why she allowed him so much leeway when it came to his inconsistency in our lives.

She even matched up Brody and Kelly as roommates, a move that seemed to benefit everyone for a time. She had her best friend looking out for her little brother, and the guys had each other in helping split the bills. A perfect setup for both men. I'm sure, for Kelly, it was nice knowing there would always be a home, and people, for him to come back to after deployment. And for Brody, it meant he didn't have to carry the weight of adulthood all on his own. *Cheating full responsibility, once again.*

Lux's hands flex against my face, pulling me out of my head. "But my mom's grief was too much for her. She started slipping away, and as much as I tried holding us together, she…" He lets out a shuddering breath. "She took her life exactly a year after Gia did."

I jerk in his hold, shocked, as I try to reconcile the idea of Lux's warm, gentle mother committing suicide. She was so devoted to her kids. It's one of the things my mom loved about her. I can't make it make sense. My mom would have moved mountains to stay with me. *How could Lux's mom leave him behind?*

A sob rips through me, and I throw my arms around his neck. His arms immediately close around my waist, clinging to me as much as I am him. Holding him tight to me, I try to channel all my love for the boy I had grown up with into it, hoping beyond anything that he feels every ounce even as my body shakes with my cries.

In all the time I've agonized over what could've happened that day, ready to jump down his throat if I ever got the chance to see him again, I could have never come up with this. How often have I cursed him? I had never really been able to find any justifiable reason for his sudden disappearance. I was only thirteen, my world was already unraveling, and his sudden absence contributed to my spiral with grief. The one person I thought I'd have forever to lean on, gone. It made everything that came after so much harder.

But at least I had Priya, constantly doing everything she could to keep me feeling stable as my life crumbled around me. Who had been there for Lux?

"I'm so sorry," I whisper against his shoulder. "Lux, I'm so sorry. You must have been so..."

Scared. Heartbroken. Lonely. Everything I'd felt, everything I'd hated him for making me feel.

"I never wanted to hurt you, Sail," Lux whispers. Instead of scoffing like I would have an hour ago, all I can think is, *I know.* I think deep down, I always knew. Lux would never have hurt me on purpose. That's why none of this ever made sense to me.

It's also why it hurt so much.

Burying my face in the side of his neck, he pulls me in even closer. I let him, feeling every dip and plane of his body along the length of mine. I shudder. "I've been so angry with you."

His arms tighten. "I know."

"But I don't want to be. Not anymore. Not when..." *God, how could I have been so stupid?* How could I not have known that something horrible must have happened to pull him so suddenly and completely out of my life? Had I been so caught up with my own grief and fear and confusion that I couldn't even consider that he hadn't disappeared by choice?

How could I have been so selfish?

"Sailor, it's okay. Hey, it's okay. Come here." Lux gently lifts me from beside him and places me on the step below him, between his legs. My back meets his chest and I grab a hold of his arms as they wrap back around me, clinging to him as I fight to keep the loss of his mom and sister from sweeping over me in a rushing tide. *Has he been alone all this time?* My chest tightens at the thought.

"Where—?" I swallow past the lump in my throat. *I don't know if I can ask—if I can handle his answer.* "Did you have...I mean, after..."

Thankfully, he knows exactly what I'm trying to ask. "I started off here, actually. With Kelly and Brody."

"My room was right across the hall." I remember now. He mentioned it the day we went to the beach.

"Even before I lost Mom, I was getting into trouble," Lux explains. "Fighting, mostly. I needed something that made me feel like I had some control." *The scars.* Milo's warning to Nico wasn't just a joke afterall. *Oh, Lux.* "Kelly had already been intervening, so when I found myself with nowhere to go, he didn't hesitate to take me in."

"And Brody was okay with that?"

I feel his nod against my hair. "He remembered me, and that you and I had been best friends. I think he wanted to do something right by you, by being there for me." I bite my bottom lip. *I don't understand. It doesn't make sense.* But that seems to be the theme of this conversation. Which reminds me...

"Why didn't you tell me?" My words come out soft, scared of what he may say that I'm not even sure if he can make out the question. Is it too late to take it back? "You had my number. Did...did you think I wouldn't understand?"

His arms tighten around me. "I wanted to. *God*, I wanted to, so bad, Sail. But..."

"But what, Lux?" I encourage, even as my stomach ties itself in knots at the thought of what he may say next.

"At first I was just...overwhelmed," Lux admits. "I was confused and angry and sad. And you were going through so much, I didn't want to add to it. I promised myself that when I did reach out, I'd be in a better place. I lost myself in my grief and anger—anger at Gia, at my mom, at being taken away from you. I was scared of who I became—where I thought I was headed. I didn't..." He swallows audibly. "I didn't want you to be scared of me, too." All the air leaves me in a *woosh*, and I have to bite back a sob as he continues, "I always planned on coming back to you, Sail. I just...never felt good enough to do it."

A tear falls down my face, fast and hot at his admission. "Lux..."

"I've lost so much," he says quietly. "But I'm hoping I haven't lost everything."

It sounds more like a question, and my heart hurts for him. For us. Kelly's words roll through me. *You have one of those chances now.*

"You could never really lose me, Lux." No matter how angry I've been with him, it was always because of how much I missed him. In the storm of everything, all I wanted was my best friend.

"Don't make that promise if you can't hold on to it," he says. I stare out over the backyard, unsure how to respond to that. "I can see it, Sailor. You're losing yourself to the things eating you alive. Just like I was."

Of course he noticed. He always noticed more than anyone else.

"I'm..." I swallow hard. My voice, when I finally manage to talk, comes out in a trembling whisper. "I'm having a really hard time, Lux."

"Talk to me." He implores. "I'm not asking. I'm *begging*." When I don't say anything immediately, he unwraps his arms from around me and my chest tightens at the absence of his warmth. Lux gets to his feet, and for a fleeting second I think he's leaving.

A wave of nearly debilitating anxiety settles almost immediately as he comes around to face me, kneeling, before taking a hold of my hands in his. He flips them over so they're facing palms up. Crescent moon indents from my nails stare back at us, some scabbed over, some freshly red. There are matching patches like this on my thighs. On my upper arms. On my waist, too. "Please. I won't survive losing you, too."

I curl my hands closed again, my palms stinging as my nails fit back into their familiar grooves.

Can't he see? *I'm already lost.*

FOURTEEN

"YOU'RE UP EARLY."

My hand jerks, hot water sloshing over the side of my cup. I grit my teeth, not because of the tea I just made, but from the headache that automatically starts to form at the sound of Brody's voice.

When sleep never came last night, I got up for the day with every intention of watching the sun rise here on the back porch. *Alone.*

Apparently, that's too much to ask.

Brody takes a seat beside me with his own mug. A mix of coffee beans and something stronger carries on the next breeze and my eyes narrow at the cup in his hand. "Isn't it a little early to be drinking?"

Brody clears his throat, his hand flexing around the handle. "It's a good cure for a hangover." *Of course it is.* Drowning out alcohol with more alcohol—what could possibly go wrong? "Couldn't sleep?"

My brows furrow, and I turn to him with a frown. "What are you doing?" He hums in question, but doesn't say anything. "What's with the small talk?"

He shifts beside me. "I'm just trying to talk to you."

"Now."

"What?"

"You're trying to talk to me *now.*" And about what? The weather? I set my cup down beside me, the tea forgotten. "Why now? You've had years." Before you walked out, I don't say. Before Mom died. Before *now.*

"I..." He swallows hard, and tries again. "I was young."

My body locks up. "No. *I* was young." My heart begins to race. "*You* were an adult, even if you didn't feel like one." Every beat pounds against my ribcage, so loud I can hardly make out my next words as I whisper, "I was just a kid, Brody. I loved you so much, and you just...didn't care enough to stay."

Brody stares down at his mug. I refrain from grabbing it out of his hand and hurling it against the side of the house. "Did you mean what you said?" He says finally. "The day we were out here? When I said I love you, and you..."

"Every word."

Silence fills the space between us, long enough that I don't think he'll say anything else. But then, in a small, uncertain voice, he asks, "Do you hate me?"

Pain sears my throat, tears filling my eyes. "I hate that I love you," I admit quietly. Despite everything. And I may just hate *that* most of all.

"I don't..." He swallows audibly. "I want to be better. To fix this. But I'm...I'm not really sure what you want from me."

I close my eyes and ask the question burning in my chest. "Did you know?" He makes a questioning sound. "The night you left, when you said you wanted more time." He sucks in a sharp breath. My eyes snap open and his gaze clashes with mine. Neither of us look away. "You wanted more time, because she was dying."

He looks down at his mug. "Yes."

She knew. *He* knew.

And he still left. And she never told me.

A roar erupts in my ears, my body tense. My muscles press

against my skin, my body flush with so much heat it feels like I'm on fire. I swallow my scream.

"I didn't want her to die." His voice cracks on the last word. I blink. He hunches over his coffee, eyes staring blankly out at the horizon. "I couldn't...Finley was...Your mom was all I had."

My brows furrow. "Growing up?" Brody gives a swift nod of his head. "What about your parents?" I never knew much about my grandparents other than that Mom had nothing to do with them, so neither did I. As far as I know, they've never tried to reach out. They certainly never came up as an option with Priya.

"What about them?" Brody practically chugs the rest of his coffee. When he's done, he sets it down, his fingers shaking slightly as he draws out a cigarette. The flick of the lighter is loud in the silence between us. He takes a long drag, releasing it on a humorless chuckle. I wave my hand to and fro at the cloud of nicotine that drifts my way, my throat tingling with the need to cough. I narrow my eyes. "Our dad was always too busy chasing tail and the bottom of a bottle to be bothered with us."

Brody rubs at the back of his neck and takes another drag, this time longer than the last. "She...she accused me of being just like him."

I don't say anything, and he clears his throat. "Anyway, Finley basically raised me, until she left. Then my mom took over. Kind of."

"You have different moms?"

Brody looks over at me, brows drawn. "Yeah." He tilts his head. "Your mom really didn't tell you about them?" I shake my head. She didn't, and now I'm sort of starting to understand why. It's not like I've ever really thought about them much, but...

"Do they know about me?"

Something flashes across his face, his bright blue eyes darkening. It's there and gone on the next drag of his cigarette. "Yeah, they know."

I stand up, walk a few feet away to gather my next thought, and some fresh air, before turning around to face him.

"Do they know Mom...?" *Died.* I can't say it.

"I don't know." There's a world of unspoken words there, but unlike him, I know when someone doesn't want me to push. Brody looks out across the backyard, until the cigarette burns down to the nub. Pulling out another, he lights it, takes a drag. "Listen, I...Fourth of July is coming up. We usually grill out, shoot off some fireworks on the beach. Sometimes we take Hank's boat out for the day. I wanted to get your opinion. See if there was anything—anything special you wanted to do."

I try not to roll my eyes at his obvious change of subject, because I know an olive branch when I see one. *He's trying*, I tell myself. *Isn't this what I wanted?*

Taking a chance, I say, "I don't celebrate the Fourth of July."

"What?" There's honest disbelief in his tone as he turns to me. "Really? Since when?"

I sigh and take a seat back on the steps. "Mom encouraged me to explore the range of my identity. Then I'd decide how to express them." Being given that space, that support, in exploring my cultures and connecting with them on my own terms, has helped to relieve some of the pressure of being mixed-race. The strain of always trying to be forced in a box, of being deemed *not enough*, and the invasive questions of "what are you" and "where are you *really* from" as people strip me apart for their own understanding, only to keep minimizing my worth, is often hard to carry.

I feel as if I constantly have to justify my existence. Not just to others, but to myself. *That* thought pains me more than anything. But maybe, someday, I'll be comfortable in my own skin. Deem myself worthy of being exactly who I am—no explanations needed. I am who I am.

"Okay, so...what does that mean?" Brody grasps for understanding, his brows furrowing.

I smile a little to myself at his confusion, but give him props overall for even entertaining this conversation. "Have you ever heard of Juneteenth?" He shakes his head. "It commemorates the day that the people who were still enslaved after the Civil War were finally told that they were free–two years *after* the Emancipation Proclamation. It's a big holiday in the Black community." I watch his face closely, but he just looks curious, not defensive or argumentative, and a tiny amount of the tension I've been holding leaves my shoulders. "I choose to honor that day."

"How do you celebrate?"

I shrug my shoulders. "The same way you could on the Fourth of July, just for a different reason." A party with red, white, and blue but instead of fifty stars and a handful of stripes, it holds one large star and two stripes, barbeque on the grill, music blaring, and red velvet cake and strawberry soda to boost the festivities. "There's no one way to celebrate. But anyway, we already missed it this year."

He doesn't say anything right away, and I feel my discomfort creeping back in. *Maybe I should just head back inside.* The thought of being confined to these four walls will drive me mad. I need to be outside today. The breeze tousling my curls, the lull of the waves, the sun kissing my skin. It makes me *feel* something. Something other than all this pain and grief and the sensation of drowning.

"I didn't realize," he says at last.

"How could you? You would've had to stick around to know about anything I actually care about." I rise to my feet, starting down the steps, then pause and look back at him. Curls fall into my eyes and I push them away. Olive branch or not, it's not enough to heal the rift between us. "I know you lost your sister, but I lost my mom, and I had to deal with that alone. I'm not ready to forgive you for that."

I walk away as he lights his third cigarette, my release of breath a lot lighter than the heavy sigh he lets out behind me.

"SUNSHINE!"

The nickname pulls me from my head. The sun is well over the horizon now, but I can't remember having seen it rise. *What time is it?* Griffin plops down in front of me, head tilting to the side as he takes me in. "What are you doing out here?"

I look past his shoulder, waving a hand at the water. "It's peaceful."

"The lull of the tides," he says sagely, dipping his head in understanding. "It's good for the soul."

"Yeah?"

"It helps quiet the noise." My eyes flick back to Griffin at the vulnerability in his voice. Whatever shadows flicker across his face are fleeting, and he smiles once more. "Heard you and Lux finally talked."

"Is that why you're here?" Wait. "How did you...?"

"Lux lives with us," Griffin explains. "I overheard him talking to Banks."

"He lives with you?"

"What's one more boy for my parents, huh?" He wags his brows at me, and I can't help a laugh. Poor Dani. Her grocery bills must be insane. "When Kelly knew you were officially moving down, him and my mom thought it'd be a good idea to move Lux." *Oh.* My face heats, and he grins. "Don't sweat it. He was practically living with us as it was. We've kind of just always been *the* house everyone ends up at."

After meeting his parents, I can understand why. But then... "Why the shrine in the hallway here?"

"Honestly?" Griffin shrugs. "I think we've all crashed here at some point or another. Kelly and Brody had been really involved in giving back to the community when we were coming up. Well, Kelly mostly, but Brody stepped up to be our surfing coach." I blink. Brody had stepped up to do *what*? "But you know how people say a picture is worth a thousand words?" I nod, and he shrugs. "Maybe it's true, but photos never give you the full picture."

"Why do you say that?" There's obviously more to the story.

"Because I was there. We all were." Griffin looks down at his hands, as if searching for his next words. His shoulders slightly hunch in on themselves as he draws his legs up, resting his arms across his knees as he leans forward. "Its always felt like Brody's been trying to outrun something." Outrun it. Drown it in the bottom of a bottle. But at the same time, giving a pile of teenage boys a place to land. Teaching them to surf. *Giving back*. God, is Brody ever going to make sense to me? "My surf accident didn't help him any."

"Your accident?"

Griffin really shrinks in on himself, suddenly no longer able to meet my eyes. The chuckle that leaves his lips is cold, and I almost don't recognize the guy in front of me. "I'm sure you've noticed the scar."

Not as much as I notice the way you hide it, I want to say.

"Sure, I've noticed." Griffin tenses, and I press forward. "But it's not what I see when I look at you."

His head snaps up, eyes searching mine. "It's not?"

I smile. "No, it isn't."

He bites on his bottom lip. "Sail, it's a little hard not to notice."

"I didn't say I didn't notice. But, it's just another part of you." I shrug. "I think it'd be a real shame for the world to miss out on you because you're too busy hiding."

"You think I'm hiding?"

"Yeah. I do." Behind the outlandish jokes and charm is a boy trying to overcompensate for a blemish that doesn't take away from his looks, but adds to it—and it breaks my heart.

"Any advice?"

I shrug. "Lean into who you are. Completely and unapologetically. If someone's bothered, let them be. That's not a reflection of you and has everything to do with them. You should never feel uncomfortable in your own skin."

Maybe I'm a hypocrite, but this isn't about me.

Griffin looks at me, thoughtful. "Those are some wise words, my little sail boat."

I giggle. Okay, that was a cute one. "I'm not just saying it to say it."

That large grin he wears like armor falls to something softer, more genuine. "I know."

As long as we understand each other. I nudge him. "So, what are you doing here?"

"Honestly?" His full lips purse until they're pouting, and he flops down, his head resting in my lap. "Cova's been sharing pics of you two hanging out, and we decided it's only right that it's our turn with you."

I look back the way he came. "Who else is with you?"

"Milo."

My chest lightens. Peering down at him, I can't help but play with a strand of his curls. "Griffin, are you jealous?"

He huffs. "Absolutely."

I laugh, my head tipping back with the force of it. It's so light, so free from everything that's been weighing me down. A few tears leak from my eyes, and I wipe at them as quickly as possible. I don't remember the last time I laughed like that, and the realization makes me sad.

"You should do that more." His voice is filled with slight awe.

"What?"

"Laugh."

He smiles at whatever look I give him, until we're both interrupted by Milo's shout. "No, no, I got it! You just stay right where you are, Griffin. Wouldn't want to bother you!"

My head whips around. Milo is making his way toward us, carrying a few paddles, or at least trying to. I shove at Griffin's shoulder. With a grunt, he rolls off of me and gets to his feet.

"Excuse me for bonding with my bestie here," Griffin jokes. He holds a hand out to me, and I take it, letting him pull me to my feet, and I turn to Milo.

"Do you need help?"

"Griffin and I got it." Milo glares playfully past me dropping the boards at his feet.

"You look like you have a plan," I say, a little apprehensively.

"Paddleboarding." Griffin supplies. I don't need to look back at him to know he's smiling. I can hear it in his tone. "What do you say, Sail?"

I nod back towards the house. "Let me just throw on a suit."

Milo grins. "Sounds good. We'll set up."

When I return, a spring to my step, the guys are setting down a small cooler, their arms full of towels. "Want me to take something?" There's three boards laying out on the sand, closer to the water, paddles at their sides.

"You've already taken my heart," Griffin grins devilishly, his eyes glinting.

Milo shakes his head. "Ignore him. He doesn't know how to turn off the charm."

"It's a Marshall thing," Griffin gloats.

"I'm sure it is." I smirk. "You must get it from your dad."

Griffin snaps his gaze up to look at me, his face contorting with horror I think is only slightly faked. "Sailor! Are you trying to tell me you have a crush on my dad?"

"I mean..." I can barely hold in my laugh as I continue the ruse, shrugging my shoulders and fluttering my eyelashes with fake dreaminess. "How can you not?"

"Oh my gosh." Griffin groans. He bends forward, wrapping one arm around his stomach and bracing the other on his knee. "I think I'm gonna be sick."

Unable to hold it in any longer, I laugh. Griffin immediately straightens up, eyes wide, mouth open. "Got you!" I manage between wheezing breaths.

Griffin sighs in relief. "Oh, thank god. For a minute I thought I lost you to my dad."

I giggle. "As if."

Standing to his full height, Griffin practically puffs out his chest. "So what you're saying is, no one could ever come between us."

"Yeah, sure."

Milo groans. "Please don't encourage him."

Griffin scoffs. "Milo's just jealous."

"Jealous?" Milo questions as he drops his pile of towels next to the cooler. "You might get a girl on the hook, but someone's got to be able to reel her in."

Griffin turns to his friend, hands on his hips. "Oh, and what, that's you?"

Milo shrugs his shoulders coyly, an impish grin on his face that plays right into his baby face looks. "You said it, not me."

I shake my head, biting back a smile. "I'm sure neither of you have any trouble with the ladies." I mean, honestly. The two of them on their own? Devastating. But add in Banks and Lux, all of them pooling their charm together? Catastrophic to any poor, unsuspecting girls who risk even glancing their way. They're all so alluring, from their looks to their personalities, and full of such quiet confidence that it makes them dangerous.

And they're quickly becoming my problem. Keeping the lines from blurring was a lot easier before getting to know them. I promised to play nice, not to make friends.

"Why Sail, are you saying I'm pretty?" Griffin looks over at me, wide-eyed and playfully innocent as he bats his eyelashes, imitating my fake-innocent charm.

Rolling my eyes, I gesture to the both of them with no shame. "I think you've seen yourselves in a mirror." Griffin smiles so widely that it pulls at the scar across his face. Like I said, it only adds to his looks.

"And they tried to say this is a face only a mother could love." The joke, laced with tension, makes me pause. I search Griffin's face, anger sweeping through me fast.

"Who said that?" My jaw clenches, asking almost accusingly.

"Banks, mostly."

"Ah, yes, well, I hear that's what older brothers are for," I point out, hoping I'm right. "You know, to keep you humble." From what I know of the brothers, I can't see Banks truly meaning that. At least, I hope he doesn't mean it. Sometimes guys are so oblivious.

Milo barks out a laugh. "Humble? That word isn't in Griff's vocabulary, Sail."

"I don't know about that," I muse. "I think you guys don't give him enough credit."

Griffin throws an arm around my shoulders, pulling me to his side. "I knew Sail would see me."

Slowly, I bring my arm up around his waist and look up at him. "Yeah, Griff, I see you." His eyes brighten, and he holds me a little tighter. I can only hope he holds my words just as close. When I glance over at Milo, something flashes across his eyes so quickly I'm almost uncertain there was anything there at all as he smiles at the two of us before quickly turning away.

Scars are something we all carry. Some are just more obvious than others. Milo's? I'm not sure if they're carried or buried. I just hope Cova and the guys know. That someone's there for him.

Speaking of...

"Hey." I clear my throat. "Do you guys know Cova's boyfriend? Rhian, I think?"

The guys pause, exchanging a long look, and that's answer enough.

"We're not fans," Milo finally supplies. "He graduated from our high school two years ago."

"Did something happen?" Griffin asks.

I don't want to involve them. Cova's words halt me in my tracks. Do I have any right to get involved? She was clear on where she stands. But at what cost?

"Sailor?" Griffin presses.

The use of my full name from him jolts me. I grimace. "I'm just...not a fan either."

Milo searches my face. "I'll talk to her." I open my mouth, swiftly closing it when he adds, "Without mentioning you, don't worry." I breathe a little easier at that. "Cova has a knack for keeping things to herself." He gives me a wry look. "Runs in the family."

My heart twists. "Milo—"

Milo claps his hands together, cutting me off. "Okay, let's hit the water!" He heads for the boards without waiting for an answer. I fiddle with my necklace as I stare after him, Griffin lightly pulling me with him to follow.

When Milo turns back to face us, his easy going smile is back in place, but I swear I see a few cracks. "Come on," he says. "Let's get you comfortable standing on the board."

Unable to say no, I follow them down to the waves.

FIFTEEN

FIVE MONTHS AGO

MONTHS.

The doctors had said I would have a couple of more months with her. But in the span of a week, since I wrapped up sophomore year, it became clear they were wrong. Months turned into weeks, and then, too soon, the estimate became just a matter of days.

Days.

I wrestle with myself to believe it. I blame it all on the trick of the mind. There's no way Mom isn't getting better. She's so strong—*was*—she *was* so strong. She beat the odds the first time. Why can't she beat them again?

Almost a year to the day since Mom collapsed, Priya finally brought me back home. For a little while, life almost seemed normal again, the consistent visits from Priya and a medical aide on the days Mom didn't feel quite so herself the only real difference. The biggest change, and hardest thing to adjust to? The absence of Lux. But at least Mom had been home. We'd been together.

Remission. That's what the doctors called it, when she came home.

Until the cancer came back, stronger than ever.

And now, two years later, here I am, back at Safe Harbor and drowning in denial, staring at the machines helping Mom to stay alive for just a little while longer.

Swallowing harshly, I release a shaky breath.

The doctors now say I have days left with her. To say my goodbyes, to hold her hand for one last time. Pinching the mermaid tail in between my fingers so hard it bites into my skin, a gift from Mom when we both returned home, I zip it back and forth across the chain as my right leg bounces vigorously up and down. I sit on the edge of the hard plastic seat outside Mom's hospital room as the doctor speaks with Priya, their faces drawn and tight.

I can't do this.

I push off the seat, so fast it knocks back into the wall. I cut around the corner, rushing down the hall to the exit I've taken more times than I can count since the EMTs rushed Mom back here several days ago.

I shove into the stairwell and rip my phone from my back pocket. My hand shakes as I scroll through my contacts for a number I haven't used in years. I had wrestled with deleting it altogether, but I've never been able to cut the cord.

Before I can overthink it, I hit the number. It rings.

And rings, and rings, and rings.

I grind my teeth together as every ring echoes through me, clanging through the big empty hole he cracked open in my chest the day I begged him not to go and he walked out anyways. That hole has only grown over the years with every ***Who is this?*** when he's actually answered my text messages.

As if it weren't freaking obvious.

"Hey, this is Brody! You know what to do."

Voicemail.

My head pounds as I grind my teeth. "Brody, it's Sailor. Um, Mom isn't...she isn't doing so well. She's um...we're actually at the hospital, and..." I release a heavy breath and sag against the wall next to the door. "And it's not looking too good." My words are quiet as I admit, "She's not going to make it out of here this time." The phone shakes at my ear, and I let out another heavy breath, trying to keep calm. "Mom needs you." In a much quieter voice, I add, "I need you. Here. With me." I drop the phone at my side for a second, trying and failing to keep the tears at bay. My head falls back against the wall and I blink furiously several times before bringing the phone back up to my ear. "*Please*, Brody. Please come."

A plea so similar from years ago. For a moment I'm back in the hallway of our home, watching the door close behind Brody, tears rolling fast and hot over my cheeks just like they are now. Yanking the phone from my ear, I end the call.

A strangled scream rips from a deep guttural place in the back of my throat, and I slide down the wall, wanting to pull at my hair or throw the damn phone. I drop it in my lap instead, bringing my hands up to my face and pressing the palms of my hands into my eyes.

What am I going to do?

The door creaks open and I stiffen.

"Sailor?"

Priya. I squeeze my eyes shut. Maybe if I don't acknowledge her, she'll go away. Maybe if I don't acknowledge her, this won't be real. Maybe I'll get more time. Time to spend with Mom, to find a way to heal her with some new state-of-the-art clinical trial, since pumping chemo into her veins didn't help.

"Sailor."

Silence.

Priya steps into the stairwell, the door clicking shut behind her.

"We can sit here together for as long as you'd like," she says softly, like she's talking to a frightened animal she's trying to stop from running into traffic. "But...I don't think you'll be all too happy with yourself if you don't go sit with your mom."

I release a shaky breath, slowly bringing my hands down from my face. I try to ground myself, my eyes trained steadily on the wall across from me. *Deep breath.* A fist tightens around my heart. How often has Mom coaxed me through life with those exact words? My bottom lip trembles, but I fight against the tidal wave of emotions, inhaling long and deep, counting to four and then letting the breath go.

Again.

I do it again. And again. And again. And again. Until the tears are at bay.

Slipping my phone back into my pocket, I shake out my hands and let Priya pull me gently up to my feet. I turn for the door, ignoring the roar in my head and the way my body screams to not take another step forward.

For Mom, I can do this.

I walk back into the unit, and head for her room.

I can do this.

I can do this.

I can do this.

I can't do this.

I stop short, right outside her room.

"The hardest step is going to be your next one," Priya says quietly from behind me, and I never wished more than to be able to turn around and meet a pair of stormy gray-blue eyes instead, to have Lux's reassurance that whatever comes next, we'll face it together. *It was always meant to be that way.* It was always meant to be us. "And it's exactly why you need to take it."

If I had known when I took that step that there were so many harder ones yet to come, I might have breathed a little easier as I said my last goodbye.

SIXTEEN

I SINK LOWER into my seat, shoulders curling in under the weight of Dani's eyes. She'd arrived at the house this morning, all cheerful smiles and too-observant eyes. *A check-in*, is what she said with a sharp smile. Kelly places a mug in front of me, steam rolling off it, and I can't help but smile a little as the scent of cinnamon overwhelms me. I mentioned liking chai with oat milk and it appeared in the kitchen not too long after that.

"I'll leave you two to talk," Kelly murmurs. He's dressed for a workout, on his way to meet up with some army buddies at the gym. Suddenly, my body aches to loosen tension with the feel of weights in my hands, to push myself to my absolute limits as I sweat it out. The release of endorphins, an absolute rush of euphoria I've savored during the years I played volleyball. Working out was something I could control, and it often helped me sleep when nothing else could. *I miss it.*

I miss me.

"So, chai? Is that a favorite drink of yours?"

I blink, the mug coming back into focus before me. Dani. Right.

"Yeah." When she says nothing, allowing the silence to settle between us, I find myself explaining, "I enjoy it iced too." Stupid. That has nothing to do with why she's here.

Dani laughs. It's a nice laugh, musical and friendly. "Around here, you need most drinks that way." I snicker, because she isn't wrong. The Florida summer heat will have you chasing down an iced drink faster than the sun can melt the ice. "So, I take it you and Kelly have been getting along?"

My hand curls around the cup. "Always."

"What about Brody?"

My lips twist at the mention of his name. "Brody…" I struggle to find something to say. The other morning on the back porch flashes through my mind. "It's complicated."

"Many things can be during a period of transition." A period of transition or not, things with Brody have always been complicated. "Hopefully the support group can provide some relief with that."

"I liked it. Group, I mean." I bring the mug to my lips and pause to continue. "Everyone's pretty supportive of each other."

"I'm glad to hear that." She pauses. "How about Brody? Do you feel supported by him?" Again with the questions! Why are we so focused on Brody?

"Brody…has his own stuff to figure out." I've thought a lot about it after he and I talked. If Mom was taking care of him like he says, with parents like he had, then he's clearly got his own past to haunt him. "I think he's…trying?"

Dani hums thoughtfully, narrowing her eyes slightly as she takes me in. "That may be so, but he's been assigned as your caregiver. That includes ensuring your wellbeing, not just putting a roof over your head. Or being a signature on a form while his friend does the heavy lifting." I wince. She folds her hands on the table, giving me another of those too-perceptive looks. "Tell me, Sailor, are you sleeping well?"

"Sleeping?" I parrot.

"And what about your appetite?"

I shift uncomfortably in my seat. "It's fine." As fine as it can be. Not much to fix there.

My eyes catch on the time programmed into the stovetop across the kitchen and I shoot to my feet. Saved by the bell. Or at least, the stove. "Crap, I, um, I actually have to go. I've got my first shift down at the shop today. Could we, um, finish this later?" I don't wait for her to answer, moving swiftly around the kitchen as I dump my mug and put it in the dishwasher, all the while ignoring Dani's gaze, heavy on my back. Ducking my head, I sweep out of the room. "I'll call you to reschedule!"

I fiddle with my necklace the entire way to the shop, feeling only a little bad about the way I left Dani sitting in the kitchen. It's not like she was alone—Brody was in the house, doing who knows what. Maybe she can have one of those talks with him.

God knows he could use it.

"You know," Banks says, startling me out of my thoughts and back to the tutorial he's attempting to give me on the cash register, "to do the job, you do have to actually pay attention while being taught."

I flush, starting to apologize, but suddenly, there's heat at my back. "Give it a rest," Lux says. "She's having a rough day." Upon arriving to the shop, of course Lux was the first to spot me. He took one look at my face, the tightness in my jaw, the way I kept blinking profusely, and wrapped his arms around me, providing me a chance to ground myself. The last thing I would need is to break out in tears while on shift.

"No, he's right." I wave Lux off. If I start using *having a rough day* as an excuse, I'll never do anything again. "Sorry. You were saying?"

I make myself pay attention as Banks continues showing me the ropes of running the store. We start with walking through opening and closing, to all the things to handle during a shift. He's thorough in demonstrating ringing up and restocking items, along with making returns, and jotting down supplies the shop may need to order on a clipboard that hangs on the wall just inside the backroom. It's surprisingly well-organized, considering who owns the place.

What I found to be most interesting? That Top Fin takes custom surfboard orders. "You *all* make them?" My head draws back, taking in the room once more, this time much slower.

The back room is far more organized than I would have expected. Several tables are set up in a row on the furthest side of the room, surfboards hanging above the workspaces and stools pushed underneath. One tabletop has an array of paint splatters, paint cans littering on and around the table.

I wonder which of them is the artist.

Several two-tier racks are placed against the wall next to the exit door, all holding rows of clothes. There are stacks of bins, neatly labeled and tucked beside the racks along the wall to my left, a kitchenette with a mini fridge along the wall of the doorframe that leads back out to the shop. The counter space holds a sink, microwave and coffee maker, and that's about it. There's not a single dish in sight.

Huh.

"The forms for custom boards are under the register counter, " Banks explains, leading me back the way we came. "We can go over that the next time you come in. Sometimes folks bring in their own boards to be designed."

"And that's a different form?"

Banks nods his head as we emerge back out into the shop floor. "Yeah, we'll go over that one too. For now, do you feel okay holding down the desk?" I nod, faking more confidence than I feel as I hop up onto the stool behind the counter, grateful that at least they don't subscribe to the retail rule of *if you can lean, you can clean*. Leaving me with instructions to call him over if I have any questions, Banks joins Lux in restocking items and changing out displays.

There's a folder on the counter, the local high school logo stamped on the front. I tilt my head, peeking inside. One pocket holds a list of potential classes and electives for the upcoming school year. The other side is stuffed with college pamphlets and trade schools.

"Seniors had to pick up packets. Time to think about senior year, and our futures." The folder closes as it slips from my fingers. I look up to find Lux standing on the other side of the counter, watching me.

I decide not to apologize for going through his stuff. "Have you thought about it? Your future?"

He holds my gaze for a moment longer before looking off into the distance. "Not much." Lux swallows thickly, his eyes suddenly snapping back to me with a force that I feel down to my toes. They curl on their own accord and I can't help but hold my next breath. "Everything I thought about is right in front of me."

I open my mouth, but nothing comes out.

"Hey, Sailor? You have a minute?" Lux straightens up at the sound of Nico's voice. He stands at the other end of the counter, eyes solely on me. He looks hopeful, but all I can see is the bookstore, him just standing there while Cova's boyfriend backed her into the shelves. My teeth grind together.

"I don't." I answer firmly and Banks pauses in what he's doing.

"*Por favor, sirena.*" Nico pleads, voice low.

Lux searches my face, his jaw now flexing with tension. I know every part of him wants to intervene, come to my defense.

"Trying to spare you a black eye," Milo had said, only half-joking. *"Lux on the other hand..."*

Nico doesn't move from his spot. Maybe I should just talk to him, pardon the shop from a fight breaking out.

"Sailor." Hearing my actual name from Nico's lips jolts me enough to move into action. Shoving off the stool, I keep the counter between us for *his* safety as I meet him at the other end. *Depending on what he says, I may just throttle him.*

With a sigh, I cross my arms. "What do you want, Nico?"

"I just needed you to know..." He glances from me, to Lux, to

Banks, and then back to me. "That day, at the bookstore, it wasn't—"

I cut him off. "Please don't tell me it wasn't what it looked like."

He winces, looking off beyond me before meeting my eyes again. "It's complicated."

I scoff, already turning away from him. "Sure it is." Mindful of the guys in the store, I lower my voice as I call over my shoulder, "I just hope the women in your life never find themselves on the same end as Cova."

"I hope so, too." I pause at his admission, and then continue walking away.

I don't bother looking back to see if he leaves.

For the rest of the shift, I keep to myself. Lost in my own head. I'm more than a little disappointed by Nico, and I don't know why. It's not like I know him. The world doesn't often hear the cries of a girl asking for help.

So why does it surprise me at all that someone doesn't hear one girl's cries, even as it's being so obviously observed? Why couldn't he stand up for her?

Lux raps his knuckles against the counter to get my attention. "Shift's over," he says. "Come on. We're out of here."

Brody walks past us, face pinched with tension and a cigarette pack clutched in a near white-knuckled grip. Guess his check-in with Dani went well. A small smile tugs at my lips. Lux watches me knowingly, a glint in his eyes. A dry chuckle leaves his lips. "Come on, trouble."

Falling in step behind me, Lux curls his hand around my hip, steering me towards the Jeep. He opens the passenger door for me, and I get in without hesitation, Banks at the wheel.

Lux slides into the back seat behind me, and we're off. When we don't take the familiar route towards the house, I peek over at Banks.

"Where are we going?"

He grins, more to himself I think than to me as he teases. "Guess you should've asked that before you got in the car."

That small smile that had been tugging at my lips spread into a full one, and it remains on my face when we arrive at our destination. *The Jukebox.* The outside of the restaurant is a replica of its namesake, a towering pink jukebox with bands on the outer edge painted in neon blue and yellow. A patio area off to one side of the restaurant holds generous shade with collections of palm trees and erected colorful umbrellas at every table.

I've been here once already, with Cova. She started off as a hostess and worked her way up to a waitress, all of the employees adorned in fifties retro garb with a few brave enough to roll around on skates.

We push through the swinging doors, stepping onto black and white checkered flooring. Neon blue booths with chrome accents line the outer walls, matching bar stools drilled into the floor and wrapping around the large counter before us in the middle of the room. A real jukebox sits in an open space that looks like it's for dancing. Neon and vintage signs adorn the pink walls, and as I scan the room, I catch sight of Milo and Griffin tucked away in a corner booth, Griffin waving his hand around wildly in the air as if to ensure we spot them.

"They wanted to meet us for lunch," Lux explains as we make our way over.

"More like insisted," Banks grunts.

"Buttercup, I saved you a seat!" Griffin pats the spot between himself and Milo before jumping out of the u-shaped booth so that I can slide in. One wall is entirely made up of windows that look out over the main strip of town. If I look hard enough, I can make out the tip of the surf shop.

"How generous of you," Lux mutters.

Griffin whirls on him. "I'm sure my bestie has had enough of you two for the day. She's just too nice to say so."

"No I'm not," I say, at the same time that Lux chuckles, "No, she isn't."

"Well, *I've* had enough of you two hogging her for the day," Griffin concludes, as if that's all that needs to be said.

Banks steps past Lux, giving Griffin a brotherly shove before sliding into the booth. "Chill out. We brought her, didn't we?"

As everyone settles in, I grab a menu from the middle of the table, thankful that the diner serves breakfast all day. You can never go wrong with breakfast—ever.

Griffin leans into my side, sharing my menu. "The waffles are always a good choice."

Banks gives his brother a look stuck somewhere between affection and disgust. "I don't even know how you could possibly taste the waffles underneath all the crap you load on top of them."

I browse the menu for the waffles, taking in the list of toppings. I glance sideways at Griffin. "The chocolate drizzle supreme?"

He beams. "With extra whip cream and drizzle." *Figures.* I try to picture stuffing my face with the monstrous sugar tower he paints, and cringe.

As if reading my mind, Lux shakes his head. "Trust me. It's not worth the stomachache."

A hand flies to Griffin's chest as he inhales sharply. "It's always worth it. Always."

Okay, no. Loaded waffles are out. I continue browsing the menu as the guys joke around, never moving to grab a menu themselves. Guess you don't need to if you come here often enough. Milo points out a few different options he thinks I might like, Griffin chiming in every once in a while although I don't know how he could be paying attention to our quiet conversation when he's partaking in another, much louder one with his brother and Lux.

Cova's arrival, smooth and graceful on her skates and with a tray of water glasses perfectly balanced on one hand, interrupts the boys before they can start throwing sugar packets at each other. She rolls her eyes at them and turns to me, setting glasses of water in front of each of us before placing the pitcher in the center of the table. "Sail, have you decided on what you want, babe?"

"You're not gonna ask what we want?" Banks asks, at the same time Griffin whines, "Hey, when did we upgrade nicknames?"

Cova shoots Griffin a wink. "It's a girl thing." Then she cuts a glare in Banks direction, the tension thick enough that my eyes dance between the two. *Um, am I missing something? I definitely think I'm missing something.* "And *you* guys have had the same order since I started working here. I already put it in with the kitchen."

Banks slightly narrows his eyes. Challenge accepted. "Maybe we're going to surprise you, *babe*."

Milo knocks his knee into Banks's under the table as Cova scowls. "What part of *it's a girl thing* don't you understand?"

Griffin scoffs, though I'm not sure if he's genuinely pouting or just coming to Banks's defense. "Sounds a little sexist to me."

I pat Griffin's arm lightly. "It's okay Griff, you can be my babe, too." He sits up straight, his grin lighting up his whole face and tugging at something in my chest.

Lux pokes his head up over the top of the tower he's been building from the coffee creamers, peering at us with obviously fake suspicion. "Oh, can he?"

Cova rolls her eyes. "So typical. You guys can never let me have something for myself."

"What, like Sail?" Milo jumps into the banter, as if he had been waiting for this moment. "We had her first."

"Yeah," Griffin chimes in, picking up the sugar packet he'd abandoned at Cova's arrival and tossing it at him. Milo bats it out of the air, and Banks rolls his eyes, reaching to move the container out of his reach.

I've been transported back to kindergarten. I can't believe I've been trusting these people with my life during paddleboarding lessons.

Lux clears his throat, a gleam in his eyes as he stretches out in the booth. "Technically, I had her first."

"Exactly! You had her all to yourself, and now it's our turn." Griffin taps a finger to his temple. "Boy math." *What?*

Banks eyes his brother. "No, that's just *your* math."

Griffin shrugs. "It adds up to me."

"Yeah," Banks agrees wryly. "And that's why you're repeating your trig class again this year."

Lux turns to fully face Griffin, eyes sparkling just like they did when we were kids. Lux has never been able to turn down even a suggestion of a competition. "What makes you think I'm giving her up?"

"Lux," I say. *This is ridiculous.* How did we go from Cova trying to take my order, to them arguing over sharing me like a toy truck at a birthday party?

Griffin smirks as he turns to mirror Lux, his chin high. "What makes you think *you*—–"

I slap a hand over Griffin's mouth before he can finish his posturing. Taking everyone in, I shake my head. "You all are children, you know that?"

"Yeah." Milo agrees as he shrugs his shoulders, a smile on his face as he admits, "We can't help ourselves sometimes."

"Especially when we see something we want," Banks adds.

My jaw almost drops at the intensity in his voice after the playfulness of the last few minutes, but he isn't even looking at me. He only has eyes for Cova, who holds his gaze with a look of... what? Defiance? I can't quite place it. *There's definitely something going on there*, but I've gotten to know Cova well enough to know she won't want me to call attention to it. Instead, I turn back to the pile of kindergarteners at the table.

"I'm not some toy you all can fight over," I say firmly. "Learn how to share."

"I guess we could take turns," Griffin mumbles against my hand before I pull away only to lightly shove him.

"Again, that's regarding toys."

"I don't know," Griffin says in a sing-song voice. "*Sharing is caring* works for a lot of things."

"Like food," Milo adds.

"You guys have never shared your food," Cova says dryly.

"That's because we're growing boys." Griffin pats his stomach delicately.

"Anyways," Cova drags out the word as she looks at me. "What will it be for you?"

"Oh, um..." *What should I get?* I look to Lux before I realize what I'm doing.

"She'll have the trifecta with pancakes, bacon, and eggs scrambled with a cup of fruit on the side," Lux rattles off without hesitation. Cova's slightly wide-eyed gaze shoots over to me, her eyebrows rising. I flush under her attention but give a swift nod to confirm, breathing a sigh of relief when she says nothing.

"The usual for the rest of you?" Cova questions instead. She glances at Banks. "Or are you going to *surprise* me?" Banks lifts his hands in apparent defeat. Cova waits for the guys to nod in consent before she skates off. The ruffle of her poodle skirt has barely disappeared through the kitchen doors before the guys are back to throwing jabs at one another, sugar packets and coffee creamer flying across the table. Banks swiftly confiscates it all, much to Griffin's dismay as he tries to explain in a rush that he needs his ammunition, pouting when the table is cleared.

Unable to help myself, I tap his knee under the table and hand him a sugar packet I caught as a bystander during the earlier war.

Before any of us can register Griffin launching his next attack, the sugar packet smacks Banks in the face. I laugh, so fully and unexpectedly that I can't catch my next breath. My head tilts back, stomach tightening with giggles, and for a moment I feel like I'm floating, as the others laugh around me, too.

SEVENTEEN

BRODY'S BEEN weird since his check-in with Dani last week. I don't think I've seen Hank come around to the house once, and he's been keeping to himself, quiet and strangely withdrawn. The only sign of his presence has been the empty beer bottles on the counter and the ever-increasing number of cigarette butts in the ashtray.

I wonder if Brody's trying to smoke his way into an early grave. I don't know if the thought makes me sick, or shamefully relieved.

At least in his absence I've managed to find an appetite, mostly. It could also be due to the fact that Lux comes around at least once a day if we're not on shift together to ensure I've eaten. I try not to think about the fact that Lux knowing how to cook is just another reminder of how much he's been left to take care of himself. He insists he enjoys the task of being in the kitchen, and the way his eyes softened as I ate what he put in front of me didn't leave any room for argument. I've never blushed so much over a meal. But every one with him has left me ducking my head as he carefully watches me.

Like now, his elbows on the table and hands clasped in front of his face. "What's going on in that head of yours?"

I swallow thickly. "Nothing."

He hums. "If you say so."

I narrow my eyes at him. "Actually, I was wondering when you'd be leaving."

Lux flashes me a sharp smile, his dimple appearing briefly. "Sick of me already?"

I grab my cup and bring the straw to my lips, eyes arched up in the universal gesture of, *what do you think?* He chuckles to himself as he sits back into his seat, watching me from under hooded eyelids, his eyes more gray than blue. Something stirs in the lower part of my stomach and I look away first, nearly breathing a sigh of relief at the sight of Brody appearing from the hallway. Who would've thought I'd look forward to seeing him?

"Morning," Brody mumbles.

Lux and I look at each other before he responds, "Um, it's afternoon."

Like, late afternoon.

Brody blinks, peeking out the large bay window that sits above the kitchen sink. "Well, shit." He laughs to himself, rubbing a hand across the back of his neck. "I guess it is."

I fumble for my necklace, my nails biting into the palm of my skin the moment I curl my hand around the charm. Lux's attention drops to my necklace, eyes flashing with concern. Last night was the first support group session Brody attended. This time, Kelly hung around in the parking lot waiting for us—probably to ensure Brody didn't bail. I wish he would've gone in with him, like a parent who sits with their kid on the first day of kindergarten, so at least one of us knows what happened in there—what he could have possibly said.

If he even spoke at all.

The entire ride back to the house, Brody was strung tight with tension. I sat still, holding my breath, waiting. For what? I couldn't be sure. I don't know if Kelly could be either. He kept eyeing Brody, even once we got into the house. But whether he was unable to cope with his session or the weary weight of our eyes, Brody just grabbed a six pack and headed down to the beach. Any fleeting hope I may have had—hope I didn't even know had stirred up in me at him being there—went out like a light.

Shuffling around the kitchen, starting a pot of coffee, Brody gives a brief glance over his shoulder and we lock eyes. He immediately looks away. "I, um, was thinking we could have a beach day. Play some volleyball."

Something tugs in my chest. Did he remember I used to be on a team, or did someone have to tell him?

"Looking to get served by your niece?" Lux jokes, watching me carefully even as he responds to Brody, who laughs.

"Let's see what she's got."

"*She* is sitting right here." I pipe in. Cautiously, I ask, "Who's coming?" Hank? His little girl?

"I'll leave it up to you guys." I release a breath at Brody's answer. "Though, Kelly's Army buddies want in."

Lux smirks. "Kids versus adults? Hope none of you are sore losers."

"Who's a sore loser?" I jump a little in my seat at Kelly's question, twisting around as he comes into the kitchen. "You better watch those fighting words before someone makes you eat them, Armstrong."

As Lux relays the conversation, Kelly bantering back with his usual easy humor, I watch Brody move around the kitchen, forgoing the food he looks at in the fridge and in the cabinets. Guess I'm not the only one having a hard time eating. I press my lips tightly together as he pours a shot of whiskey into his cup of coffee and slips out of the house without another word, heading for one of the chairs around the firepit in the far corner of the backyard.

It's on the tip of my tongue to ask Kelly if Brody's okay, if he knows what's going on with him. But something holds me back. I swallow it all, down, down, down, until my stomach aches.

That ache stays constant all through the rest of the day, tying itself up into tighter and tighter knots. But it's not until the conversation I overhear later that evening that it flips over into true, gut-churning nausea.

"I'm worried about you man. *Your niece* is worried about you."

I stop short at the sound of Kelly's voice, hovering in the shadows of the hallway. It would take only one of them moving away from the kitchen to spot me.

Brody chuckles dryly. "I wouldn't be so sure of that." Before Kelly can respond, he pushes on, "Do you know what she said? She said that she hates that she loves me."

"Sailor?" Kelly sounds almost...hopeful? "You talked to her?"

"Why do you seem so surprised?" I stiffen at the sneer in Brody's voice, grabbing hold of my necklace. I don't release my next breath until I feel the charm biting into my skin.

Kelly doesn't back down. "You mean, for a guy who thought he could flake out on his niece, even after being assigned custody *and* having her delivered practically to your doorstep?"

I press my back against the wall, needing something to anchor me at the brutal honesty of his words.

"You don't know what you're talking about."

"I do know. Just like I know how you've been in and out of Sailor's life like some sort of revolving door whenever it suited you. So why would you be so surprised by her words? Is that really your issue right now?"

My legs give out and I slide down the wall, knees drawn to my chest as I sit there in the hallway, listening.

"Step off," Brody warns.

"What? Are your feelings hurt?" I've never heard Kelly sound like this before. Sharp and goading and almost mean. "Well, tough it out. You have someone depending on you now."

A chair screeches in protest, and I flinch. "She shouldn't be."

"Whether she wants to or not, she is." Kelly raises his voice slightly and I hug my knees tighter. "Finley chose you—despite everything—to look after that girl."

"I can't—I can't do it," Brody admits quietly.

I feel like all the air has been sucked out of the house at his admission. I bite my bottom lip to stop it from wobbling.

The chill of Kelly's next question raises the hair on the back of my neck. "Can't, or won't?"

Tears come fast, hot, and completely unforgiving when Brody doesn't answer. I don't have to see his face to know that he's at a loss for words, his mouth more than likely open with no remark in sight.

He never could find the right words to say when it matters most.

"You know, don't you." Brody's quiet claim is so similar to my own the day we were out on the back porch.

Did you know?

"Know what?"

"Why she chose me." It's not a question.

There's a beat of silence. "I do."

"She chose wrong."

I shut my eyes but a tear still escapes, rolling down my face.

"Brody, you need to pull yourself together." The edge is gone from Kelly's voice now. He sounds like he does when he talks to me: Gentle, but firm. No room to run. "You have the *ultimate* responsibility now. You may be hurting, but so is Sailor. She needs you."

"She doesn't even want me."

"What she wants is for you not to hurt her anymore."

"You think I've hurt her?"

"You know you have. And more than that, I think you're both drowning. You just can't seem to pick your head up long enough to see it."

"You don't know what the hell you're talking about."

"Don't I?" Kelly challenges. "You're drinking more—which is saying something—and you're blowing through these damn packs of cigarettes like you've got nine lives." Something hits the kitchen cabinets before smacking against the countertops. "If you're so determined to put yourself into an early grave, have the decency not to do it when you're all the girl has left."

"Then why don't you take her? You were so determined to help raise her when Finley found out she was pregnant to begin with." With each word, Brody gets louder. "You wanted to swoop in and be the hero!"

"I didn't want to be a hero, I wanted to be with your sister!"

"Well it seems that she had other plans. And just like now, they don't involve you." Tension runs thick through the house. I choke on it in an attempt to catch my next breath, holding in my tears a losing battle as they rush down my face. "Doesn't matter anyways. She's not staying."

"What do you mean? Who isn't staying?"

"Sailor."

I clutch at the back of my legs, hard, my nails digging into the skin as I try to hold myself together.

"Why wouldn't she be staying?"

"Why would she be?" Brody throws back at him.

My chest tightens. I don't know what to think. I don't know what to *feel*.

"Brody—"

"I talked with Dani, and—"

Whatever else he says gets lost as I shove myself up to my feet, grabbing a hold of the wall as I stumble over them. A roar starts in my ears and spreads through my head as I find my footing and stumble to the front door. The doorknob slips through my hands, once, twice. On the third try, I wretch it open. I think someone calls out to me, but I don't look back. I can't.

I need to get out of here.

Panic bubbles up in my throat, my chest tightening until I can't grasp my next breath. I shoot off from the house, no destination in mind but to get as far, far away as possible.

"She chose wrong."

"She's not staying."

"Why wouldn't she be staying?"

"Why would she be?"

The memory of their conversation nips at the heels of my feet. But it's the honesty in every bite of Brody's words that pulls me under.

EIGHTEEN

"SO WERE you planning on just sitting here, watching all the fun?"

I startle as Griffin plops down beside me in the sand. A second later, Milo settles on my other side, the three of us staring out at the pier.

The carnival is in full swing, but I don't even remember getting here to the beach. It wasn't until the tears dried that I noticed the neon lights adorning the rides and various vendors. The twinkling music has long since become a steady hum in the background.

My hands flex around my knees as I hunch over them. "How did you guys find me?"

"It's where I like to come, too," Griffin admits.

"And Kelly asked us to help look for you," Milo adds.

Kelly. Not Brody.

"She's not staying."

Of course he wouldn't be looking for me.

I hold my breath, waiting for the guys to ask questions, but they don't. Instead, Griffin draws his own knees close to his chest, wrapping his arms around them, mirroring my posture. He turns his head towards me and rests his cheek against his knees. "Don't be sad, Sail."

Something tugs behind my ribs. My mouth jerks up a little, a weak laugh punching out of my chest, but I hardly feel it.

We sit there quietly for I don't know how long, before someone crouches in front of me, picking up one of my bare feet and wiping the sand off. I peek up, watching quietly as Lux, once satisfied with his sand removal, slips on my sock and then my sneaker before doing the same with my other foot. His shoulders are tense, and a muscle ticks in his jaw as he clenches it tightly.

In my haste to leave, I had forgotten shoes.

"Kelly asked us to help look for you."

There was nothing quiet about the way I left. Kelly must've realized I was still in the house. That I'd heard everything they said.

Only when my sneakers are securely laced does Lux finally look up to meet my gaze.

"Thanks," I whisper.

His jaw flexes as he leans forward, tapping the top of my shoe. "Thought you'd get far without them?"

I swallow thickly. "I wasn't running away."

His eyes flash, and then harden as he stares at me. "No?"

I shake my head, blinking quickly to keep the tears at bay. I tap at my chest, hoping he'll understand. "I just...couldn't breathe."

Milo tilts his head. "Anxiety or panic attacks?"

Without taking his eyes off me, Lux answers. "Panic." He searches my face. "Something happened after I left."

"I think they thought I left with you." I admit quietly. He looks off across the beach, eyes unseeing as he works through something in his mind. We sit quietly, giving him a moment. I don't think any of us would even know what to say. I know there's nothing in particular about the conversation I overheard that I'd like to share.

"But don't you worry your little head about our girl here!"

Griffin pipes up suddenly. "We basically read her the riot act when we found her." Leaning into me, Griffin taps the back of my hand lightly. "Bad Sail," he scolds.

I laugh suddenly, not having expected it. A smirk tugs at Lux's lips as he takes us in.

"Yeah, I'm sure you two really ripped her a new one."

I nod, fixing a serious expression on my face. "Oh, you have no idea. They were very..."

"Firm," Milo supplies, at the same time Griffin says, "Macho."

"Yep, that," I confirm, trying my best not to smile. "I am very chastised. And now I know better."

Griffin sits up straight, chest puffed out, as he eyes Lux. "And you're welcome."

With an arched eyebrow, Lux fixes Griffin with a stare that would have most guys folding under the pressure. I bite down on my bottom lip, trying in vain not to be the first to break as we all wait with bated breath. Without a single warning, Lux lunges at Griffin, wrapping an arm around his neck and pulling him under his arm. I scoot to the side, dodging flailing limbs as they scramble in the sand.

"Absolute children," I huff, a smile spreading across my face.

Milo slings an arm around my shoulders. "You have no idea."

Banks walks up to us, eyeing his little brother and best friend wrestling around in the sand. "What did Griffin do?"

Griffin tries to hold off Lux, straining to push him back. With a quick glare up at Banks, Griffin whines. "*Hey!* I'm the victim here!"

"For once, he's not lying," Milo defends.

Griffin beams. "Thanks bud—argh!" Lux overpowers him, wrapping an arm around Griffin's head and dragging a fist rapidly across the top of his head. "Oof! Not fair."

A twinkle of lights on the pier grab my attention, and Banks looks over his shoulder, following my gaze. Looking back at me, he nods his head towards the pier. "Well, come on then."

Milo nods. "Good idea." Pushing up to his feet, he holds out his hands for me to grab, pulling me up once I take them.

"Whaaaat?" Griffin whines. The question comes out muffled, his face stuffed between Lux's arm and side. "Whassa good idea?"

I tilt my head. "Sorry? What was that?"

Milo chuckles. "Pretty sure he's asking what's the good idea." Griffin loudly mumbles something, throwing a thumbs up in the air to let us know Milo assumed right. "We're gonna head up to the pier."

Griffin wiggles in Lux's grip, though I'm not sure he would have freed himself if not for Lux deciding to let him go. Popping up, face flushed, Griffin wheezes, "I wanna go, too!" Lux claps him on the shoulder, keeping him grounded as he tries to get his breathing under control. Griffin looks sideways at him. "Sometimes I don't think you know your own strength."

"Aww." Lux reaches out, pinching Griffin's face with his other hand. "The baby."

Shoving him off, Griffin gets to his feet, wiping sand off. "I'm not the baby, Milo is!"

"Really?" I ask, eyes a little wide. The other guys laugh while Griffin pouts at me.

"Yes, really."

"By only three months," Milo scoffs lightly.

Pressing my lips together as firmly as possible, I quickly turn to Milo before my smile can break through. "So, the pier?"

Milo grins largely enough for the both of us, but it's Banks that responds, throwing down a challenge. "As long as you don't mind losing."

I straighten up. "Are you willing to bet on that?"

Banks shrugs, almost indifferently, as his eyes skim our surroundings. "Pick the bet."

I narrow my eyes. *Game on.*

The next several hours are a blur as we bounce around from game to game, taking breaks often for a ride or treat in between. I think bumper cars with the guys are, by far, my favorite followed closely by beating Banks three points to two in a tense water race game. Though I wasn't looking for it, the respect in his eyes made me feel almost proud.

Spying the funnel cake cart, I proclaim, "I'm ready for my winnings!" Milo clears his throat and I correct myself. "I mean, *we* are ready for our winnings."

"Pay up big bro!" Griffin slaps his back and just barely manages to dodge the swipe of his brother's hand.

Banks huffs but digs out his wallet. "I don't know why you're so nice to these fools." Claiming my win wasn't going to be all that sweet if I reaped all the benefits without the others, so I made sure the stakes included the group—much to Griffin's delight.

I smile. "These 'fools' are your friends."

With a quick shake of his head, Banks argues, "Doesn't count when I'm related to one of them. I had no say."

"Aww," Griffin chimes in. "You have plenty of say, bro."

"Yeah, we just don't listen," Milo adds. The two of them burst into laughter.

"Just be glad she didn't take Griff up on his suggestion," Lux points out.

Griffin collects himself, lifting his chin. "I think Banks being my servant for a whole week was a great idea."

"Yeah, if you want me to spit in your food," Banks retorts.

Milo looks sideways at him. "Given that some thought, have you Banks?"

"Yeah, but he'd never actually do it," Griffin defends. A wicked grin tugs at his brother's lips, and Griffin's step falters. "Right, Banks?"

Banks winks at me, and starts for the funnel cakes, Griffin hot on his heels. "Banks? Right? *Right?*"

We all chuckle as we follow after the brothers, Griffin's voice rising in distress as the four of us collect my—*our*—winnings.

I moan over the sugary sweetness of the powdered funnel cake, Lux eyeing me out of the corner of his eye. A flush works its way across my face and down my neck, and I tuck into my treat, trying for all the world to ignore the weight of his gaze and the flicker of heat in his eyes.

Griffin loses himself in the piled sugar rush decorating his funnel cake, an array of caramelized strawberries and ice cream. Having effectively distracted him from giving his brother the third degree, Griffin finds the nearest picnic bench and promptly falls into his plate. We sit in comfortable silence, the noise of the fair wrapping us in its embrace.

It's nice. Unexpected, but nice.

"Next ride?" Griffin drums his hands against the table when he finally comes up for air. A smear of ice cream decorates his face, and I giggle. Milo snorts, but makes no move to help out his friend.

"*What?*" Griffin whines, eyes wide as he looks between the two of us. "What is it?"

Banks clicks his tongue in a way that unexpectedly reminds me of Dani, taking a napkin from under his plate and reaching over to wipe off the ice cream on his brother's face. "I swear, we can't take you anywhere." Griffin pouts a little before perking up once more, getting back on course about our next ride.

With everyone in agreement, we get rid of our trash and start off as a group.

Or we were, until I'm lightly tugged back, away from the others. Someone's finger curls in the belt loop of my shorts, and I look up into Lux's face.

"Come on," he says.

My brows furrow. "Where are we going?"

Redness spreads over his ears and he ducks his head. "Ferris wheel."

"Oh?" I reply, tone dripping with sarcasm. "I don't remember you asking me." Lux's jaw flexes under my gaze, and I press my lips tightly together so as not to grin.

"Don't be a brat," he warns. Unable to help myself, I pop up on the soles of my feet and poke the side of his face, right where I know his dimple to be. His lips immediately tug upwards, just a little.

He bats my hand away. "Sailor."

"Lux," I mock back.

With his finger still locked in my belt loop, he tugs me around to face him and steps into my space, ducking his head this time to meet my eyes. I suck in a sharp breath at the intensity in his gaze. "Will you get on the Ferris wheel with me?" He swallows thickly, his voice dropping lower, and a stirring of butterflies starts in my stomach. "Please?"

Trying to rid myself of his spell I suddenly feel under, I take a step back, only as far as he'll allow me to. With a shrug of my shoulders, I smile sweetly. "Since you said please."

Reaching out with his other hand, he tugs playfully at one of my loose curls. "Always a brat."

We walk quietly to the Ferris wheel and get in line. I shiver at the wind coming off the water and Lux steps back, grabbing at the back of his hoodie with one hand and pulling it off over his head. His tee underneath, rides up, showing off some muscle and I quickly look away. "Sailor?"

His tone is teasing. I pointedly look up at the lights of the ride instead of at him. "Hmm?"

He chuckles, hands finding my waist and turning me back toward him. With a dip of his head, he searches my face from under his long lashes, a smirk slowly tugging at his lips. "See something you liked?" He winks and I huff some incoherent protest as he starts sliding the hoodie over my head.

As soon as my head peaks through the hole, I glare at him. "You're so full of yourself."

He continues smirking, silently working my arms through each sleeve and letting the fabric fall around me. It hits just above my knees and I stop short of snuggling into the warmth left by his body heat. *He would never let me live it down.*

The intoxicating spice of his cologne reaches my nose and I

discreetly try to draw in a deeper breath. The flash of his dimples tells me that I was, in fact, not discreet at all. Not even a little.

Honestly, so what? I'm just a girl. Sue me.

We make it to the front of the line and the operator ushers us into our cabin. Once the door clicks behind us and we take our seats, it starts its slow journey up. I grab hold of my necklace, zipping the charm back and forth across the chain.

Lux breaks the silence. "I'm glad to see you're eating."

I drag my eyes up. Lux has an arm slung on the back of his seat as he leans back on the bench across from me, legs spread out.

"I'm trying," I admit quietly.

He turns to me, and I get swept up into the intensity of his gaze as he softly pleas. "Tell me about it?" I know he's asking about more than just my recent eating habits. About all the things I keep close to the vest, that I've tried, in desperate vain, to bury.

"I don't think we have that kind of time." I feebly gesture to the Ferris wheel.

Lux leans forward, his arms resting on his legs, his face hardening with determination. "We have all the time in the world, Sail. We don't get off this ride until you're ready." Something stirs in my stomach at his words. I feel like he's talking about way more than the actual ride we're currently on.

"Talk to me," he encourages, and for a moment it's like we're in the backyard all over again.

"Talk to me."

"I'm not asking. I'm begging.*"*

"I won't survive it, losing you."

I swallow thickly at the memory of Lux and the guys coming to find me tonight, how they did their best to cheer me up, how they've drawn me into their circle even though I've tried to remain on the outside.

I never had a chance. Not really. Not with them—or with Cova. With them, I don't feel so lost.

Something shifts in my chest and my next breath comes easier. Letting go of the necklace, I fist the sleeves gently instead.

"Talk to me."

With a shaking voice, I do. Like the rise and fall of a tide, I lay out the bad and not-so-bad times of the years we were apart. From my time at Safe Harbor to the countless hours spent in hospitals at Mom's side. I don't know how long we stay on the Ferris wheel, but we're never ushered off. Around and around we go, Lux hanging on to my every word. His jaw clenches on and off, especially when he realizes he hasn't been the only one who's gotten into fights.

His hands ball into fists and I lean forward, taking one of them in mine. "It's okay, Lux. Really, I'm okay."

"It shouldn't have had to be like that," he says through gritted teeth.

I shrug my shoulders, running my thumb across the ink on his knuckles. "But it was." Keeping my eyes trained on his hand in mine, I continue, "We don't get to control the cards we're dealt in life. But...I think it's how we play our hand that counts."

His other hand appears in front of my face, his pointer finger hooking under my chin and lifting my gaze to meet his.

"How are you willing to play your hand now?"

"I don't know." I whisper.

His eyes search mine. Lips parting, to say what, I don't know, because Griffin's voice rings out, pulling us out of our little bubble. "Luuuuuuux!"

I pull away, swinging around to find Griffin waving his arms wildly above his head from below. Milo appears at his side, tugging at his shirt, but Griffin bats him away. Cupping his hands around his mouth, Griffin shouts up. "It's time to share, Jellybean!"

Ducking in my seat as people look between Griffin and the Ferris wheel, I slap a hand over my mouth as I giggle. Lux shakes his head, running a hand through his hair, and something tugs in my chest at his familiar curls peeking through. My fingers itch to reach out.

"That smile of yours is the only thing that saves him, I swear,"

Lux mutters. He grows serious. "It looks good on you, Sail." I glance at him, raising my eyebrows, and he gestures at my face. "The smile. And the friendships."

I grin, unable to keep from teasing—from letting myself enjoy, just for a moment, the way things between us feel almost as easy as they used to. "*Especially* the friendship with Griffin, right?"

Lux rolls his eyes, even as he smiles. "Yeah, *especially* that."

NINETEEN

PEEKING through the window of Sweet Nothing, I can just make out the ombre colored braids sitting atop of Cova's head. She lounges in one of the bean bag chairs, tucked away in a corner with her head deep in a book. Smiling softly to myself, I head for the door, the bell chiming overhead as I step inside.

Weaving through the shelves, Cova picks her head up, as if sensing me. Her lips curl up, light dancing in her brown eyes. "Hey, *babe*."

I laugh along with her, taking the empty bean bag chair beside her. "You live to ruffle those guys' feathers, don't you?" I question.

Cova winks at me. "What's the point of hanging out with them if I can't?"

"They do make it easy," I agree.

"Too easy."

"*But*," I draw out. "It would seem that someone likes giving as good as he gets."

Cova's brows shoot up her face, and props her chin up with the cup of her hand. "Hmm. Really?"

I grin at her, thinking back to how quick Banks was to dig underneath her skin at the diner. "Really."

"That's interesting." Cova's eyes suddenly narrow on me and I straighten up. "Nearly as interesting as someone ordering for you."

Mirroring her pose with the cup of my own hand, propping my chin up as my elbow digs into my thigh, I hum. "Hmm."

"One could even say it's as interesting as a ride on the Ferris wheel." My mouth pops open at her words, and her smile cuts sharply across her face, eyes lighting up. She winks. "Small town, babe. News travels fast. Now, spill."

I shrug my shoulder and sit back, hands falling into my lap. "There's not much to spill."

"But there's something?" She prompts.

"Lux and I..." I search for the right words. "We're just trying to find our way back to one another. As friends."

"Friends." Cova repeats skeptically. I nod. "*Right.*" She drags the word out, a smirk tugging at her lips.

"Cova!" I giggle. "I'm serious."

"And I totally hear you." Cova presses her lips together tightly. "I've just never seen someone look at their friend the way he looks at you."

"Interesting," I say, because two can play at that game. "The same could be said for you and Banks."

Cova's mouth drops open, her cheeks flushing red.

Willing to spare her the sudden awkwardness, I catch her up on the conversation I overheard between Brody and Kelly, and how the guys found me on the beach. How, no matter how much I want to insist that Lux and I are just friends, I'm confused by the feelings I have in the face of being around him after years apart, especially now that we've both grown up. I've done my best to fight off the butterflies that flutter in my stomach, and tried to ignore some of the things he's said since we've reconnected. I mean, what is he thinking?

I conclude with the Ferris wheel, and when I finally finish, Cova lets out a low whistle.

"Damn. That's a lot to unpack." She studies me. "How are you feeling after overhearing Brody?"

I look off across the aisles, just rows and rows of books. Stories to lose yourself in, but stories to find yourself in, too. "Honestly? It hurt. A lot. I shouldn't be surprised by anything he said, but I am. I'm also confused." Cova tilts her head, and I continue. "I'd always known there was more to the story where my Mom and Brody were concerned, like their childhood and all, but I mean, I hadn't even known they don't share the same mom until this summer." Not that it means all that much to me. But if I didn't know that, what else don't I know about my Mom? *Does it even matter?* I knew the most important parts of her.

What is learning about the roots to this messed up family tree going to do for me?

Cova leans in, nodding every so often as I tell her about the conversation with Brody on the back porch, her eyes slightly widening.

"Do they know about me?"

"Yeah, they know."

I think Mom did the right thing, not sharing any of this with me.

We sit silently for a moment, neither of us rushing to say anything as the weight of my words sink between us.

Finally, Cova says quietly, "Sometimes, the people we're related to aren't worth knowing."

Something shifts in me, a puzzle piece I hadn't known was missing settling into place at her words. I had never given too much thought to having grandparents or cousins. It had always just been Mom and I...and sometimes Brody. It had always been enough for me.

My Mom was enough for me.

She had filled such a large space in my life, and what she didn't cover, Lux did. Now, I wonder how much that may have been her trying to compensate for what I didn't have. But how would I have known I was "missing" anything if I never felt it was gone in the first place? The hole in my life now is because she's gone. Nothing more, nothing less.

Unshed tears fill my eyes as I agree with Cova. "No, they're not."

"Good." She squeezes my hand. "Now, let's talk about what's *really* important."

I look at her warily. "What's that?"

"Lux giving you his hoodie!" I blink until the tears disappear. Cova beams brightly and I can't help but laugh. "Tell me—in exact detail—how that went down. Don't leave anything out!"

I don't.

Cova shakes her head when I finish. "I don't understand where guys learn to do that move! But even so, why is it so hot?"

"Right?"

She sighs. "The way they take off shirts and hoodies should be illegal."

"What should be illegal?"

Rhian's voice makes us both jump, and all the color drains from Cova's face as he steps out from behind a bookshelf.

"Rhian!" Cova's voice is high, almost alarmed, so different from her usual soft, easy tone. She scrambles to her feet and I do the same, watching in fascinated horror as her entire face transforms into a fake imitation of her usual beaming smile. "Hey! I wasn't expecting to see you!"

He moves into her space, a hand resting on her hip as he leans in for a kiss. She meets him halfway and he nips at her lips. She sucks in a sharp breath, barely covering a wince. Slowly, he pulls back and looks over at me. "I hope you're not trying to take my girl from me." Cova lightly hits his chest and he snaps his other hand up, grabbing a hold of it, his knuckles slightly whitening. Cova grimaces.

My brows furrow. "What?" Take her? "I'm not into girls."

He smirks, shooting Cova a sneer. "That makes one of you."

"Rhian!" Cova hisses.

I narrow my eyes. "Your point?"

Rhian shrugs nonchalantly, a wicked smirk tugging at his lips. "Was made. Come on, Cova." Tugging on Cova's hand, he starts toward the door with her in tow. She wrestles against his hold, trying to tug her hand free of his.

"Rhian, wait. At least let me get my stuff," Cova begs. "Please."

I grind my teeth together.

This is not my fight.

This is not my fight.

This. Is. Not. My. Fight.

I practically vibrate with the need to pull Cova away from him. To fight for her.

He lets her go, and Cova crouches down to grab her bag, shoulders hunched as she shoves a few things back in. When she rises, she doesn't meet my eyes, but stops at my side as she turns back to Rhian. "Just so you know, no matter what Brody says, you *are* wanted here. More than you know."

"Cova..." I start quietly, but I have no idea what to say. Not with Rhian watching us.

She smiles, but it doesn't meet her eyes. "See you around."

Rhian tugs her to his side and throws an arm around her shoulders as they leave the store, neither of them sparing me a backwards glance. Cova leans into him and I ball my hands into fists, my nails biting into my skin. I inhale, *one, two, three, four* and release the breath.

Again.

I do it again and again, until I feel like I'm no longer going to scream or go running after Cova. I've barely stepped out of the bookstore before a familiar voice calls my name.

"Sailor!"

You've got to be kidding me.

Maybe I can duck back into the shop. Or I could just keep my head down and continue walking, act like I didn't hear him. As quickly as the idea comes, it goes, Hank catching up to me in several strides with a beaming smile.

"Just the girl I was looking for!"

What could he possibly want from me?

"I scored some concert tickets for tomorrow evening and I was hoping for a guys night out with Brody," he says, chatting like we're old friends. A sinking feeling starts in the pit of my stomach as I connect the dots before he even asks, "I was hoping you might watch Evie for me."

I stare at him. Why is he asking me and not one of the guys? I know they've watched her before. Doesn't she have a little friend's house she can run off to? I can't *possibly* be his first choice.

I can't even imagine that I'd be his last, and yet, here he stands, grinning like we're old friends. Like we know each other at all simply because I'm his best friend's niece.

My extended silence must eventually make it clear that I'm not interested in making this easy for him. "Listen, I know it's a big ask. But, could you? It's only a few hours."

Can I? Yes. Do I want to? It's a fast and hard no. *Will* I? Ugh.

"I can drop her off at the house," he adds quickly, like he can sense my resolve starting to crumble. "She's got a ton of toys there, so keeping her occupied shouldn't be an issue. It's really just, you know, dinner and bedtime. And she's a really easy kid, I swear."

I grab at my necklace, my nails digging into the palm of my hand. It keeps me grounded as I try to remain calm in the face of the man I've spent years blaming for so many of Brody's mistakes.

"Yeah, sure, no problem."

Wait. What am I saying? It's a big problem!

Hank beams at me before I can take it back. "That's great. I'll bring Evie over tomorrow...say, four?" I try not to cringe. *That early in the evening?* What time does she go to bed, anyway?

"Yep." I rush out the one worded answer in hopes of ending this conversation.

"Amazing. See you then!"

I smile tightly as I cut around him, needing as much distance as I can get between us.

Prying my hand from its death grip on my necklace, I draw my phone out of my back pocket and text the first person I can think of to ask for help, my fingers trembling so terribly that it takes me several times just to type out three words.

Sailor: I need you.

TWENTY

MY LEG BOUNCES rapidly as I sit on the couch, pulling at the sleeves of my sweatshirt until they cover half of my hands. I've sent a flurry of texts to Cova, but I've yet to hear a word from her.

That worries me more than I'd like to admit. Is she okay? Should I say something—really say something—to the guys? I know Cova doesn't want to involve them, and I've done all I can to respect her wishes. Breaking her trust might cost me her friendship. But keeping it might cost her safety.

Someone plops down beside me on the couch, poking my cheek. "You're thinking too hard," Lux says.

I bat his hand away. "Just have some things on my mind." He watches me silently, amusement alight in his eyes, making them shine more blue in the moment, and I sigh. "Thanks for coming."

He leans back and raises his arms so that they rest on the back of the couch. "You needed me." As if it's that simple. Lux hooks a thumb over his shoulder. "I hope you don't mind, but I brought the cavalry with me."

I tilt my head to peek past him. The guys come through the front door, all big smiles and unrestrained energy. Griffin, predictably, practically bounces his way inside.

"Cupcake!" He clears the two steps into the living room and

promptly throws himself down on my other side. "Did you miss me?"

I raise my eyebrows at Lux. "Did you bring them, or did they just tag along?"

Throwing his arm around my shoulders, Griffin answers first. "We couldn't let you two have all the fun."

"Plus, we've watched Evie plenty of times," Milo explains from somewhere over my shoulder.

"But fair warning." Banks's tone makes me look up in alarm, but the smile twitching at the edges of his mouth gives him away. "She's got quite the little crush on us. So don't take it too hard if you're not given any attention."

I roll my eyes. "Oh, please. What is she, like, four?"

"Almost five," Milo says, like that makes a difference.

"Have you ever tried sharing attention with a four-year-old?" Banks asks, almost incredulously.

Lux smirks, looking over my head. "Griff's tried, and his feelings get hurt every time."

"I'm still technically a kid too!" Griffin pouts. "Who said I shouldn't be given attention? What, because I'm a teenager? It's unfair!"

Leaning into him, I pinch his cheek. "Aww, is somebody jealous?" Red creeps across his face, and he tries ducking his head. "Griff, she probably can't even wipe her butt correctly. A little more attention is probably warranted."

"Bold of you to assume he doesn't need the same sort of attention," Banks says dryly.

Griffin glares over his shoulder. "I know how to use the bathroom."

"Of course you do, buddy," Banks agrees mockingly.

Griffin shoots up from the couch, jumping over the back and tackling Banks down to the ground. I stare, genuinely shocked at how smoothly Griffin cleared the couch to make that happen.

"Yeah, the moments where he's suddenly graceful still catch us off-guard too." I drag my eyes away from the two brothers wrestling around the kitchen to Milo, who winks. I smile in response, but it's quickly wiped off my face at the sight of Brody appearing from the hallway.

"I thought I heard you guys." He glances at the Marshalls, shaking his head with a look of fond amusement that takes me back to being six so quickly I get a headrush. When was the last time I saw that expression?

Lux's hand brushes my shoulder, his thumb rubbing smoothly back and forth. There's a chorus of "Hey Brody" from the guys, but I just feel tense. I haven't spoken to him or Kelly since I overheard their conversation the other day.

"I ordered a bunch of pizzas for you guys," Brody says. The guys murmur their thanks and I keep focus on Lux's thumb. Back and forth, back and forth, back and forth. After a moment, Brody swallows visibly and looks at me. "And...thanks again for watching Evie, Sailor."

I didn't do it for you. Instead of biting out the words, I give him a stiff nod. I need to do this, for me. My issues aren't with her, not really. I'm not so messed up that I'm going to take my feelings out on a four-year-old.

The front door opens, followed closely by the squeal of a little girl who has no idea that she's an accessory to my heartache. "Uncle B!"

I flinch. *That will never not hurt.*

Lux gently squeezes my shoulder, but I still reach for my necklace, needing the bite of the charm to ground me. *I can do this.*

There's a rush of air that slams into me, and Lux's legs lightly knock against mine, a little whisper pulling me from my thoughts. "Luck, will you play dolls with me?"

Evie leans on his legs, a pair of big blue eyes peering up at him, accompanied by a hopeful pout and a cloud of blonde curls.

Griffin leans over the back of the couch to whisper conspiratorially in my ear. "She has a hard time saying, 'Lux' but refuses to just call him 'Lucky.' Stubborn little thing."

Okay, that's kind of cute.

"Evie, this is my friend Sailor," Lux tells her. "Can she play with us?"

Tilting her head, Evie blinks up at me. "You wanna play dolls with me and Luck?"

"I'd love to play dolls with you and Luck." I smirk at Lux as his cheeks go slightly pink. Griffin chokes on a laugh, pulling back quickly before Lux can retaliate.

Milo appears with a bright pink doll carrier and Evie bounces on the balls of her feet at the sight, barely able to contain her squeal as he lays down the case on the coffee table.

"Thanks again." Hank calls out as he moves for the door. "We'll be back later tonight. Love you, Evie-girl!"

Evie drops the dolls she was in the middle of pulling out, her head popping up at the sound of her dad's voice.

"Daddy! *Wait!*"

Her cry rocks me to my core, *hard*, and for a moment I'm back in the hallway of my childhood home. Instead of Hank standing at the front door with Brody, it's my Mom, and I'm the one shouting. *"No! Wait!"*

I suck in a sharp breath, jerking out of Lux's hold as ice slides down my spine. *What the heck.* I blink profusely, willing the past to stay exactly there. My nails bite into the palm of my hand, and I press my feet as firmly as I can into the ground.

I am not there.

I am not there.

I am not there.

I am not there.

It becomes hard to breathe. All I can do is stare, waiting for Hank to turn away just like Brody did. Waiting to watch Evie fall apart, just like me.

But instead, a huge grin softens Hank's face as he bends down and holds out his arms, and somehow, that's so much worse. My chest tightens and my vision blurs as Evie runs across the room, Banks quick to help her up the steps from the living room. She throws herself into Hank's waiting arms with the surety of a kid who's never been dropped, and he holds her tightly, tickling her relentlessly and covering her face with a bunch of kisses. Evie shrieks with glee and I look away, fixating on the chairs out back around the firepit.

Fresh air sounds good right about now. With fresh air, I can maybe find my next breath.

"Sail." Lux coaxes gently, for my ears only. I barely hear it over the pounding of my heart, but I'm still able to come up for air, just enough to look at him. Like I'm resurfacing from under water after holding my breath for so long.

"I—I'm—" *What? Okay? Fine?* I won't lie to him. To me. "I just need a minute," I whisper.

When the giggles turn into piercing squeals, I can't help but turn back around. Brody and Hank are gone, but Griffin carries a still-smiling Evie back over to us. His usual bright grin is in place, but his eyes quickly cut to me, scanning my face, before returning his attention to the little girl in his arms. "So! What are our Barbies up to today?"

He puts Evie back on her feet. They both settle on the floor in front of the coffee table as Milo finishes pulling the last of the dolls out. Evie taps her pointer finger to her lips, her head tilting side to side. "Umm, a fashion show!"

Griffin nods, reaching for a doll. "Sweet, my doll is going to be one of a kind."

Banks snorts. "How fitting."

"Hey!" Evie turns to Griffin, eyes narrowed as she throws her hands on her hips. He freezes, arm outstretched, the doll in hand. "*I* pick the dolls."

"Yeah, Griff," Milo taunts from over Evie's head, sitting on her other side. "She picks the dolls."

Griffin drops his doll and holds his hands up in surrender. "Right. I forgot. My bad, Evie-girl."

Sitting up a little taller, Evie beams up at him, giggling. "It's okay, Griff. We all make mistakes."

Milo gently nudges her. "Evie, why don't you choose each of us a doll?"

Lux leans forward, joining the conversation. "And could you grab an extra one for Sailor?" Evie's lashes flutter as she looks at me from underneath them, lips a little pursed. I wait for her approval and only once she nods her head, holding out a doll like a peace offering, do I take a deep breath and sit down on the floor to play.

"SAY?" Evie wraps her little arms around my neck, leaning into me. My arm automatically wraps around her waist, a softie for the nickname she dropped on me five minutes into playing dolls. *Damn her.* Why do I have to be such a sucker for cute kids?

Doesn't she understand that I'm trying not to like her?

Brushing some of her blonde ringlets back from her face, I answer. "Hmm. What is it, sweet girl?" The term of endearment just falls from my lips, and I can't even be upset. It's fitting for her. Evie is probably the most well-behaved little kid I've ever met, and she's been stuck to my side since I helped style her doll's hair, staring at me like I've hung the moon. It's like the guys barely exist, and I've never seen Griffin look so offended.

I wonder if she's ever had an older girl to look up to, with all the boys around.

She giggles, sticking her face in my curls to whisper in my ear. "Can we play dress up?"

I glance briefly at the guys sitting around the table with the dolls Evie gave them, a grin tugging at my lips. Now *there's* an idea.

Milo watches us both closely, narrowing his eyes. "What are you two up to?"

This gets the rest of the guys attention, but before anyone else can ask questions, I get to my feet and take hold of Evie's little hand.

"Come on!" I usher her out the living room as quick as her little feet can carry her, both of us giggling as the guys call after us. "I think the guys would *love* to dress up with us. What do you think?"

I peek down at her to find a large smile on her face. "Yeah!"

I place a finger to my lips, like we share a secret, and Evie's shoulders shoot up to her ears as she hunches in on herself, a mock serious expression on her face as she lifts her own finger to her lips.

"Sailor?" Milo calls worriedly.

"We'll be right back!" I shout over my shoulder, a discerning grumble of uncertainty being the resounding response from the guys. The smile slowly falls from my face as we venture down the hallway, Evie's hand becoming a heavy weight in mine.

I usually try my best not to venture to this side of the house, where Brody and Kelly's bedrooms are—one orderly and neat, bedsheets so tightly tucked at the corners you could bounce a quarter off it while the other is a disarray of clothing trailing across the floor, the bedsheets spilling halfway off the bed. There wasn't a doubt in my mind whose room was which the first time I peeked into both open doors, an open office space acting as a buffer between them.

But Evie seems to know exactly where we're going, pulling me along until she stops before the linen closet. Mustering up some courage, I throw my shoulders back and pull the door open. Bins of what are clearly Evie's things sit on two of the five shelves, storing everything from toys to extra clothes. A bright pink trunk that matches her doll carrier sits at the bottom of the closet, overflowing with the dress up clothes she wants to get into.

How many times have I ignored these brightly-colored bins? The first time I opened this door in search of towels, I stumbled back, chest tight, tears clouding my vision as they rolled hot and fast down my face. I had gripped the doorframe, hunched over as I tried to grasp a breath that wouldn't come.

I can't help but wonder once more if Brody bought her all of this.

Not wanting to spoil what's turning out to be a good night by spiraling, I quickly grab the trunk and kick the door closed, ensuring Evie's out of the way. She starts ahead of me, back to the living room and I pick up my pace. If nothing else, sacrificing the guys to a four-year-old looking to play dress up will pull me right back into a good mood.

I'm grinning like a cat who caught the canary by the time we make it back into the living room. The guys groan good-naturedly as they take in the trunk, rolling their eyes as they flop back on the floor.

"Should've known," Banks mutters, throwing his arm over his eyes as if that'll make the costumes disappear. Lux runs a hand down his face exasperatedly as he half heartedly protests with a string of mumbled *no*s. Obviously used to their small bouts of protest, Evie giggles weaving through the guys until she's at Banks's side.

He peeks from under his arm. His eyes soften considerably as she tilts her head to the side and I can't help but melt at the sight. Evie Benson definitely has these four wrapped around her little finger, and I can't even find it in myself to be mad about it. Honestly, watching her and Lux together has certainly resurrected those butterflies in my stomach.

"You'll play dress up with me," she says, all wide eyes and wobbling lips. "Right?"

Banks purses his lips as he hums like he's actually debating it. She starts pleading in earnest, grabbing the arm he's thrown across his face. He lasts all of ten seconds before he's sitting up, pulling her into his side. "Alright, Evie-girl. Pick out some costumes."

Griffin raises his hand in the air. "Can I call dibs on the crown this time?"

Twenty minutes later, the guys are all adorned with feather boas, tiaras, and clip on earrings. Evie's placing the finishing touches of play makeup on Griffin that she insisted was needed for all of the guys when the doorbell rings. I quickly send off a collection of photos I snap of the guys in their various fairytale states to Cova, letting her know that she's more than welcomed to come join in on the fun before pocketing my phone.

"That's probably the pizza," Banks says. "I'll get it." He shuffles toward the door, the elastic bands of the wings around his shoulders hanging on for dear life. I follow quietly after him in case he needs a hand, trying to contain my smile.

A delivery guy stands at the door, pulling out several pizza boxes from his carrier. He blinks repeatedly at Banks, who lifts his chin with a pointed sniff. "You act like you've never seen a pixie before!" He huffs, tossing his feather boa with a flourish over his shoulder and I burst out laughing, falling into the wall beside me as I try to keep myself upright.

Oh my gosh. Best night ever.

Collecting the pizzas, Banks closes the front door, pausing at my side as he looks down at me. "Someone please come and collect Sailor before she hurts herself."

"Alright, wheezy." A strong arm curves around my waist and I'm lifted in the air. I cling to Lux's arm as I try to wrestle my laughter into submission.

Evie takes the two of us in. "You two should get married!"

We all freeze, and I blink almost owlishly at her, the laughter immediately drying up. Lux's arm flexes around my waist, and I run my hand back and forth across his arm before I realize what I'm doing. I tap him, a silent request for him to let me go, and he immediately loosens his grip.

"Um, sorry, kiddo." I shrug in a *what can you do* sort of manner. Lux stands so close behind me that I feel him immediately tense. "We're too young."

Evie shakes her head. "Not for *real*, silly."

Oh. *Of course.* I flush, feeling like an idiot.

Banks watches on amusingly, his eyes bouncing over my head and back to me like some sort of ping pong match. He enjoys the tension between Lux and I a little too much. I refrain from flipping him off with wide little eyes still watching me. Griffin and Milo quickly distract her while we move into the kitchen. My eyes flit up to meet Lux's every few seconds. For his part, he just stands on the other side of the counter, watching me.

"What?" I ask finally, unable to take it any longer.

A smirk pulls at his lips. "So, the only reason we can't get married is that we're too young, huh?"

"Shut up." I mumble. "I didn't even say that."

Placing his arms on the countertop, the veins pronounced, he leans forward. "Mmm, but you were thinking about it."

I keep my eyes solely on the plates and napkins I'm collecting while Banks lays out each pizza box. My heart races in my chest and I can feel my face get hot.

With the weight of his eyes still trained on me, I let out a dramatic huff. "Hardly," I say firmly.

Lux grins, leaning away from me, but from the look in his eyes, I don't think he'll drop this one anytime soon.

TWENTY-ONE

I STIR at the sound of chuckling. “I see you guys have been replaced.”

“We never stood a chance.”

Warmth engulfs my side and my brows pull together at the breath fanning across my neck. My eyes flutter open to a head full of blonde hair, and my arm flexes around the small body snuggled on top of mine, Evie’s little hands fisted in my sweatshirt. *What time is it?*

The last thing I remember is the six of us winding down for a movie, my head in Milo’s lap and feet tucked into Lux’s while the other two constructed a blanket fort. Milo had quietly assured me that they had her and that’s about all I needed to drift off.

I look up, finding a pair of gray-blue eyes already watching me, an arm thrown over the back of the couch and the other tossed over my legs. A flutter stirs in my stomach and I quickly look away.

“Thanks again for watching her.” Hank crouches down beside us. “I hope she wasn’t too much trouble.”

I smile softly, surprising myself a little. “Not at all.” I pry her little fists off my hoodie as Hank scoops her up into his arms with a care that catches me off-guard. I’ve never really thought of Hank as being a gentle guy, but his face is soft and fond as he settles Evie against his shoulder. She curls into him in her sleep, tucking her face into his neck.

Somehow, the worst part of all of this might be the realization that Hank's not actually a total jerk after all.

"You good to take her?" Banks asks as I sit up, stretching out the crick in my neck. "One of us can give you a lift."

"Nah, I'm good, thanks," Hank assures him. "Only one of us had a little too much to drink." As if it were the introduction he was waiting for, Brody stumbles into the house. I tense, watching him carefully. "Have a good night."

"Catch you later bro!" Brody practically shouts as Hank slaps his shoulder, shushing him good-naturedly in passing. As if just seeing Evie, Brody's shoulders bunch up around his ears and he throws a finger up to his lips, missing it by a mile as he hits his cheek instead. "Shhh."

"I should go to bed," I say quietly. Of all the many shades of Brody, a drunk one is definitely not my favorite

Lux gives me an understanding nod. "We'll clean up here."

"Crew!" I take a step back as Brody fixes his sights on me. Griffin rushes forward, grabbing hold of Brody before he can take a nosedive down the two steps into the living room.

He should have just let him take the fall. *Maybe it would knock some sense into him.*

"I'm going to bed, Brody," I announce over my shoulder, aiming for the other end of the couch so that I don't have to pass him directly.

"Crew—Crew, wait." Brody hiccups. I try to ignore him, but it's like a battering ram to my heart with each slip of the nickname from his lips. A pull to the past that I've been trying to put behind me. "Crew."

I whirl around, chest heaving. "Stop *calling* me that!" There's movement out of the corner of my eye but I ignore it in favor of glaring at Brody, the tension in the room so thick I feel like I'm choking on it. Leave it to Brody to ruin the night—and here I thought babysitting his "favorite niece" was going to be my biggest issue of the evening.

Brody pulls up short, blinking furiously at me as he holds onto Griffin's shoulder for balance. I really wish Griffin wasn't in the crossfire of a Lehmann standoff. *The guys shouldn't be here for this. I* don't even want to be here for this. "Don't be like that, Cre—Sailor. Sorry. *Sailor.*"

My name comes out slurred, and my voice shakes as I retort. "Be like what? Why do you even care?" He flinches, but I keep pushing. "I'm not even staying, right? So what does any of it matter?"

Griffin startles, his head drawing back as if I physically hit him. "You're...what?"

The wounded look marring Griffin's face is enough to make me feel like I kicked a little puppy. Deflecting, I throw it back on Brody. "Take it up with him. *He's the one* who doesn't want me here."

My eyes snap to movement beyond the guys. Kelly stands in the hall, eyebrows drawn and forehead creased with worry. He must've returned from his own night out while I was asleep.

Brody shakes his head. "No. That's n-not what—"

"It's not, *what*?" I cut him off. "It's not what it sounded like?" I scoff. "I *heard you*, Brody."

There's a moment of silence. No one says a word, no one moves. It's like the entire room is at a standstill, holding a collective breath before the other shoe drops.

"Why don't you call me Uncle anymore?"

Is he *joking?* "Why don't I call you—?" My hands curl into fists at my sides as I begin to tremble, the adrenaline shooting through me so fast I can barely get my next words out. "*That's* what you're focused on?" Keeping my eyes on him, I take several steps back with a shake of my head. "You are unbelievable."

His eyes widen considerably, a little glazed as if he's not really here with us. Then he lurches forward, panicked, hand reaching for me. I jerk away. "Don't touch me."

"Wait! No! Sailor." Something tickles at the back of my mind, like I've been a part of this song and dance before. There's shouts of protests from the guys as Brody manages to grab a hold of me, his hand clamping around my upper arm, drawing me in for a hug. He's a lot stronger than I give him credit for. I try to pull myself away from him, twisting side to side in an attempt to break his hold, but he doesn't give. Instead, he mumbles, over and over, "I'm sorry. Don't leave me. Please."

I try to make out what else he says into my shoulder as he curls himself around me, and we stagger back a little. My nose scrunches at the stench of nicotine, the alcohol on his breath nearly as overwhelming as the words coming out of his mouth.

"I'm sorry. I'm so sorry. Don't leave me. Please. Please, Fin. I promise—" His voice cracks and I stiffen.

Fin? He's talking about Mom? No, he's talking as if *I'm* Mom. Suddenly, I'm a little kid again, peeking through my bedroom door, watching Mom face off with Brody, trying to get him to choose us.

"Just go, Brody."

And he had. Even as I called out to him, begging him not to leave. His pleas are an echo of my own all those years ago, and just like then, they fall on deaf ears. Except *I* now stand on the other side. *Oh how the tables have turned.*

"Brody," Lux tries to coax.

Banks jumps in. "Let go of her, man."

"Finley, I swear—"

"Brody!" I growl, struggling against him. "Stop it! I'm not her! I'm not Mom!"

Hands shoot out from behind Brody, curling around his arms and effectively breaking his hold on me. Brody's hands grasp for purchase as he stumbles and I choke as I'm yanked violently forward, nearly falling to my knees. Someone catches me around the waist and my hand flies up to my neck as I cough profusely.

"Knock it off, Brody!" Kelly orders through gritted teeth as he pulls Brody further away from me, but the broken chain glinting in Brody's hand like a beacon catches my eye and a roar starts in my ears.

My fingers skim my neck, feeling for what I know to already be gone. My chest heaves so rapidly I feel like I may pass out.

"Sailor?" Milo gently calls for my attention. "What is it?"

"M—my..." I try to swallow past the large lump in my throat. "My—" A sob tears through me, my eyes wildly sweeping the floor for the mermaid tail. Trying one last time, I manage to get the words out, "My necklace."

"Shit," Lux curses from behind me.

"Don't worry, Sail, we'll fix it," Griffin tries assuring me, but before his words can wash over me, Brody opens his mouth.

"Crew, it's just a necklace. Relax."

The noise in my ears becomes so loud I can hear nothing else as my vision reddens. A roar rips from my lips and I throw myself forward, trying to break from Lux's hold, but he doesn't budge. White-hot tears fall fast from my eyes and I push my hands down hard on Lux's arm in a desperate attempt to free myself so I can get to Brody.

Just let me hit him!

It's finally too much, and the scream bursts out of me. "*It's not just a necklace! That was from Mom!*" The smile disappears from Brody's face. "I told you not to touch me—to let go—and you couldn't even listen. If you had just listened..." I wrestle with the onslaught of anger swallowing me whole as I hiccup through the pain searing my throat. "But if it's not what you want, then who cares what anyone else is saying, right?" I cling to Lux's arm, using him to anchor me instead as the storm beats wildly in my chest. "Always the Brody show, to hell with everyone else!"

"That's—"

I cut him off, turning around in Lux's hold and beating at his chest. "Let go of me." I plead desperately, my voice breaking. *I need someone to listen to me.*

Lux's jaw flexes and I cry. "Lux, *please.*"

Ever so slowly, he drops his arms from around me. I rip myself away, knocking into him as I go around the couch from the other end so that I don't have to pass Brody. I grasp at my neck as I stumble for my room, a sob tearing from my lips as I come up empty, the way I knew it would be.

It's gone.

"Sailor!" It's Griffin's voice, but I already know the others are going to follow.

I whirl around. They're staring after me, shuffling in place like they can't decide on whether or not to give me space or make sure I don't run. I don't want to hurt them, but I can't handle being pitied right now. "I just need some space. *Please.*"

I need to get out of here. Just for a little while. Put as much distance as I can between myself and here. My mind races, and I grasp the frame of the bedroom doorway as my head spins. I suck in sharp breaths, but I can't seem to get enough air into my lungs, pain searing my chest. I...I can't breathe.

"Hey, hey," Lux murmurs, suddenly standing before me. He cups my face, bending down so that we're eye to eye.

I thought I told him to leave me alone.

"Sailor." Lux firmly calls for my attention but I'm lost to the onslaught of emotions, the current dragging me out to sea so quickly I gasp for my next breath. "Can you hear me?"

"It's going to be alright. We got you, Sail." *Milo?* A hand holds tight to one of mine, placing it against a firm chest. "Just breathe with me, yeah?"

"Get her something to lean on." *Banks?* "Quick, before she passes out."

There's an onslaught of heated voices and a bunch of shuffling shadows in my otherwise blurring vision, and I flinch. I'm shuffled backwards until a wall meets my back, and I'm carefully guided down to the floor, my knees at my chest.

"Sail, baby, I need you to breathe," Lux says, desperation in his voice.

"Lux, give her and Milo some space," Banks murmurs. "He's got this."

"I can't leave her." The anguish in Lux's voice startles me enough that I try to focus on the steady beat of the heart below my hand and take in a shuddering breath.

"You're not. None of us are." *Griffin*, sounding gentler than I've ever heard him, all his humor replaced by a softness so like his mom's that it almost sets me off again. "We're all right here."

I gulp in another breath. This one almost doesn't hurt.

"There you go," Milo whispers. He squeezes my fingers. "There's nothing that hasn't happened tonight that can't be fixed, Sail. We got you. You're safe. Just let go."

Let go.

I take in another breath, and another, the tears only rushing down my face harder.

Let go.

I don't know if I can.

Before the tide of panic can take over, I focus on a more glaring matter. "I...I thought I to-told you all to le-leave me alone." I choke out quietly.

"Hate to break it to you, Sail, but we're not that easy to get rid of," Banks says dryly from where he's crouched next to Lux, one hand firmly on his shoulder.

Bones weary, I let my eyes drift close. "Hmm, I would've thought being easy was your thing, Marshall." The guys all laugh, Griffin the loudest. The ghost of a small smile tugs at my lips.

"Very funny," Banks says, but I can hear the smile in his voice. The room falls quiet as I continue keeping pace with Milo's steady breaths, my nails practically digging into his chest, clinging to the lifeline he's thrown me.

But no matter how much I fight to tread water, I still feel like I'm drowning.

PART 2

FOOL ME TWICE

TWENTY-TWO

HEAT LIKE I'VE never known encases me from all sides.

I shift to free myself from the raging inferno. At least, I try to. A body pressing into my back keeps me from moving more than a few inches, and I make a face before peeling my eyes open.

Sunlight filters in through the half opened window, spilling across the tattooed arm banded around my waist. My eyes trace the obvious veins running underneath the deep olive skin. The *VIDA* inked across the knuckles laced with mine confirm just who's sharing the bed with me.

A flush creeps across my cheeks.

Lux's arm flexes around my waist when I slowly try to withdraw my hand from his, pulling me tightly into him as he curls around me. His face burrows into the back of my neck and I try not to flinch at the sudden ticklish sensation, my heart beating wildly in my chest. *What the hell?* I must've never regained my breath after that panic attack and passed out. Yeah, that's exactly it. I'm dreaming—this is all a dream. In reality, I'm still on the floor with Milo, and he's trying to coax me back to consciousness or something.

Lux's breath ghosts across my skin, leaving goosebumps in its wake, and I squirm, the butterflies in my stomach in a frenzy. Okay, so I am very much awake.

A grunt leaves his lips and I still, holding my breath. When nothing else happens, I begin squirming again, trying to break free from his arms.

"If there's one nice bone in your body, you'll stop moving," Lux grumbles. My breath hitches as his hand glides across my stomach and down to my hip to grip me firmly, keeping me as still as possible.

Definitely not a dream.

"I—" Licking my lips, I try again. Grasping for one coherent word, I blurt, "Sorry." Cringing inwardly, I squeeze my eyes shut for one pounding beat of my heart before they flutter open again.

"Oh, good!" I jolt at Griffin's voice. "You guys are up!"

"Barely," comes a mumbled response from somewhere below me.

"Well, I know someone who may be," Banks points out, tone light and amused. A pillow flies over my head, hitting him–hopefully right in the face–if the grunt filled laugh is any indicator from the floor. Lux had perfectly aimed for his target all without jostling me. I tense all the same, and Lux's thumb instantly begins rubbing in smooth circles against the patch of bare skin from where my sweatshirt has ridden up in the night.

Nope. That's enough of that. I shoot up in bed, only to flinch at the immediate pounding in my skull. Blinking furiously, I rub at my eyes before cataloging the room's occupants, taking in the sleeping arrangements that apparently took place at some point in the night. Griffin grins at me from the couch across the room, one of my books resting on his chest. Milo is on the floor in a makeshift pile of bedding, one arm thrown over his face. Banks is on his other side, holding the offending pillow.

"You know, there's a perfectly good bedroom across the hall." I swallow thickly, trying to clear the morning rasp in my voice. The hand still holding me jerks. Without thought, I place my own hand over his. We both still and I immediately yank my hand away.

Right. Okay. Anyways...

I scoot toward the side of the bed and peer down at Milo. "Why were you sleeping on the floor?"

"We didn't want to leave you." Something loosens in my chest at Milo's admission, and I take what feels like my first real breath since last night's fiasco. I look away from the guys, a tear sliding down my face. I wipe it away as quickly as I can, hoping none of them saw it.

They stayed.

"You should've," I whisper. "I didn't need—"

"Don't," Lux says firmly. I don't turn back to look at him. "Don't do that."

A knock on the bedroom door silences our pending argument, tension strumming through the room.

Griffin unfurls to his feet, standing tall as his eyes fix on the door intently, as if he can see through it. Banks rises as well, moving so that he stands between me and the door.

"Sailor?" Hearing Kelly's voice instead of Brody's makes me relax at least a little, until I remember the state of my room.

And the people in it.

Eyes wide, I push up from the bed and move around the Marshall brothers to open the door, trying to angle myself so that at least there's not a clear line of sight to the bed. *Crap. Is Lux still laying there?*

"Um. Hey, Kelly."

Kelly grunts, eyes sweeping across the guys—and my now fortunately empty bed—before pulling back to focus on me. Where I thought I'd find a reprimand, all I find is a searching gaze. "You okay, kid? That was...a pretty rough night."

Tightening my grip on the doorknob, I look past him at the wall. "I think you and I both know the answer to that."

"I know you overheard me and Brody talking." Tension lines his face, a flicker of guilt in his eyes. I frown. "I'm sorry." He releases a shaky breath. "I should've talked to you sooner. I was trying to give you some space, but I see now that I shouldn't have."

I shake my head. "I needed that space. There was no way I was ready to talk about it." I'm still not. "But it doesn't matter. It won't change anything."

Not with Brody. One way or another, we would've found ourselves here.

"Doesn't mean I'm not sorry for it."

Memories from last night flood through me, and I swallow hard. The panic on Brody's face. The desperate pleas. His voice breaking.

"I think I'm the one who's sorry," I whisper.

"Sailor—"

I cut him off. "He thought I was Mom."

Kelly's face shutters, tears swimming in his eyes as he swallows hard. I tense, my body locking up momentarily before I force myself to relax. I've never seen Kelly waver. Tension fills the otherwise silent room, like we're all holding our breath. Then, finally, Kelly admits, "He did."

We stare at each other, a silent understanding passing between us.

I'm not okay. But Brody isn't, either.

Finally, Kelly musters what looks like an attempt at his usual smile. He stands to his full height, looking past me into the room. "I was going to start on breakfast, if you guys want to come help me."

Banks chuckles. "Yeah, alright, we hear you loud and clear."

Heat engulfs my face, and I look away as Banks starts corralling the guys out of the room.

Kelly stands off to the side, letting the guys pass him one at a time, and my embarrassment is quickly replaced with amusement at the guys ducking their heads, shoulders curved forward as if they can hide themselves. Only Banks looks amused more than chastised, bumping shoulders with Kelly as he passes. *I might have to sic Kelly on them more often. I can have a lot of fun with this.*

Except Lux clears his throat, and I freeze. "You guys go ahead. I just need to talk to Sail for a minute." Kelly stares at him with an unreadable expression, and Lux adds, a little too quickly, "With the door left open, of course."

I guess receiving a pass on a closed door is only for the nights your uncle traumatizes you.

Griffin immediately reappears, popping up behind Kelly as he fixes us with a faux-stern look. "That's right! No funny business you two." He does the universal sign of *I'm watching you*, two fingers pointing to his eyes and then at us before he walks backward, disappearing down the hallway. A small smile tugs at my lips.

And then they're gone, and it's just me and Lux.

Again.

"Hey." Lux murmurs, his hand brushing against mine. I turn to him, staring down at his inked hand rather than meeting his eyes. "Sailor."

I swallow. "I'm tired, Lux."

"I know." He hooks a finger underneath my chin, and lifts my gaze to meet his. "I just wanted to say I'm proud of you."

I blink. "For what?"

"Not running." For staying. For fighting at even a small chance of making any of this work.

He doesn't have to say it. It's written across the softening of his face.

I shrug my shoulders, looking past him as I remember our conversation on the Ferris wheel. "You asked how I'm willing to play my hand. This is me playing it."

By some mercy, the rest of the day goes smoothly, sparing me from a test of whether I'm bluffing or not. But the easy momentum falters when Milo and I head straight from our shift at the shop to our support group after locking up, and I nearly stumble over my own two feet at the sight of Brody taking a seat in the front room.

What is he doing here?

Did Kelly drag him here or did he come on his own?

Does Kelly even know that he's here?

"Sail?" Milo calls for my attention, and I don't think it's his first time calling my name, his brows drawn with worry as he steps directly in front of me.

"Hmm?" I force a smile I don't feel at all.

Milo looks over at the occupants in the room then back to me. "You gonna be okay?"

Trying to shake myself out of my thoughts, I keep the smile in place. "Yeah, of course. Why wouldn't I be?"

Milo doesn't say anything, just takes my hand and gently guides me down the hall to our group. My head spins with every step.

If Brody doesn't even want me living with him, why is he here?

Was coming here his idea?

I mean, Kelly had called Brody out for trying to flake on me. So what could he possibly be doing here? Is there a course on how to let your niece down gently? Are they going to help him get rid of me? Even Brody thinks Mom made the wrong decision in appointing him my guardian.

But she had to have had a reason—a good one.

I can't find it, and apparently neither can Brody, but there must have been one.

Right?

My thoughts spiral around and around all through our group session. I don't hear a single word anyone says. My hand brushes my collarbone and jerks back at the lack of metal. Instead of tears biting at my eyes like they have all day anytime my hand comes up empty, my body stiffens as I zone back into the meeting in time to hear the lilt of a familiar accented voice starting to talk about a younger cousin getting into trouble.

Staring at Nico as he speaks, all I can see is the ghost of his friend over his shoulder, my thoughts racing in frustrated confusion.

How can he be so nice here, but be friends with someone like that?

Why doesn't he do anything about it?

And then, guiltily, *Why don't* I *do anything about it?*

Anger bubbles inside of me, my chest tightening the more and more I hound myself with questions I can't answer. The things I can't fix.

As soon as Theo wraps up our session, I'm out of my seat and across the circle, in Nico's face as much as I can considering I'm nearly a foot shorter than him. He throws up his hands in alarm. "Woah, *sirena. Dime.* What's going on? You've been staring daggers at me all night."

"How could you?" I hiss.

His brows shoot up his forehead, eyes a little wide. "What?"

"How could you be friends with someone like *him*?"

Nico's eyes narrow just a little as he pieces together what I'm talking about. "Did he do something to you?"

I scoff. "Me? What about Cova? Does she not matter?" He looks away, dropping his gaze. I keep pushing. "You've seen the way he treats her."

Something hard and defiant shines in the amber of his eyes as they snap up to meet mine. "So have you."

"Sailor." Milo calls softly from somewhere behind me, his hand taking hold of mine. "Come on."

His voice is gentle, but the note of command in it is firm. I let him tug me away, but I keep glaring at Nico until I'm forced to turn away to watch where I'm walking. My body shakes with tension, coiled and ready to lash out. Tears roll hot and fast down my face. I wish I'd let Roni teach me how to fight back at the group home the one time she'd been in a good enough mood to try bonding. I really want to punch something.

Or someone.

I try to focus on the steady warmth of Milo's hand, but it's not until I feel the unsteady ground of sand underneath my feet and register the light and sound of the fair that I realize where we are. Stopping in almost the same spot as where he and Griffin found me, Milo lets go of my hand as he takes a seat.

I look out across the beach. There's a group of college-aged kids sitting around a fire pit in the distance. An older couple strolls hand-in-hand down the beach, carrying their shoes in their free hands. The water laps across the shore, spreading wide and fast before being called back out to sea. It's peaceful. I could lose myself to it.

"You're good for her, you know." Milo's words pull me back to the here and now, the tightness in my chest still there but lighter at his observation. "Cova, I mean."

Silently, I sink down next to him. *I don't know what to say.*

"Something happened with Rhian, didn't it?" Anger licks down my spine at Milo's question and I nearly rear back. *Am I mad at Milo?* If he knows about his cousin's relationship—how she's being treated—why isn't he doing anything?

"You once said you're not a fan of him." I say slowly, watching him closely to try and read his face. "So why…?"

I wrestle with my question. It's not Milo that I'm actually mad at—or even Nico, really. It's the entire situation. But I've been here a month, and I'm ready to tear Rhian's face off. So why the hell haven't the people who have known Cova for years done something to help her?

"I wish she'd never gotten wrapped up in him. That she'd never met him at all. He was different, at first. Not at all like the dude he is now. Or, who knows, maybe he was like this all along but played well enough at hiding behind a mask none of us could see behind until it was too late." Milo's baby face hardens into something nearly unrecognizable as he bites out the words. He releases a heavy sigh, like he carries the weight of the world on his shoulders, the tension bleeding from him as fast as it came. He tugs at one of his dreads that falls into his face. "But I can't force her to walk away from him. I've tried talking to her and she's never been ready. She has to want to do that for herself."

"What if she's scared to?" I ask quietly, heart racing as I think back to the times I've seen Rhian hovering over her, grabbing her, threatening her. I think about what Theo said at group last week, when one of the other girls was talking about living in a domestic violence shelter with her mom, about how the most dangerous time for people in abusive relationships is when they try to leave.

"I really don't know, Sail," He admits softly. I hook my arm through his, and he leans against me. "All we can do is be there to support her when she's ready."

A little help can go a long way. That's what Priya had said to me when I was trying to find my footing at the group home. It's how I found a sense of purpose in such an unsteady part of my life.

Milo nudges me, and I meet his tired smile with one of my own. "And from the sound of things, you'll be ready as soon as she is."

I duck my head. "Seeing Brody tonight at the center...it really triggered me."

"And you lashed out," Milo guesses.

I sigh. "It's just...Nico's seen what I have. I don't understand how he could be friends with someone like that."

Milo shrugs. "Do you believe there can be more to a story than what you see?"

I think about Griffin hiding his insecurities behind his smiles, about Lux hiding all that grief behind his tough exterior, about Brody hiding something I don't even know how to define under false bravado and bottles and bottles of liquor. I begrudgingly admit, "Yes."

"Then for as much compassion as you hold for Cova, try to do the same for Nico. We don't know the battles he faces or the kind of friend Rhian is for him." Milo looks out at the waves. "For every person we meet, there's a different version of us that they could tell. It doesn't mean it defines us or that those closest to us would agree with the version of us they hear from someone else. There's so much gray muddled in what many would argue is a black or white world."

I'm not even sure if Rhian knows how to be a friend to someone. But he must be able to, right? It's not like I know Nico all that well, but what I do know, there's no way he would be friends with someone like that if there wasn't more to the story.

Right?

Milo's right. About so much of it. Hell, all of it.

I mean, don't I show the same level of compassion for Milo and the guys even though I question why they haven't helped Cova? And whose to say they haven't? Maybe they've tried. But Cova's not the kind of person you push into doing something they're not ready for. It's bound to push her in the opposite direction, and in this case, it would be closer to Rhian.

And that's the last thing any of us want.

I sigh. "You're wise beyond your years, Milo."

He smiles, but it doesn't reach his eyes, and that tightness in my chest returns.

TWENTY-THREE

THE MORNING after my talk with Milo, I realize who should actually be on the other end of my anger regarding my own life.

As if summoned by the thought alone, Brody trudges into the kitchen where Kelly and I are eating breakfast—well, he's eating, I'm mostly pushing things around on my plate. He heads right for the coffee pot and pours himself a cup before opening the cabinet directly above the little coffee station, pulling out a now-familiar bottle of whiskey, and I snap.

"So, did you show up to your support group to get some tips on how to kick me out?"

Brody jerks, a mix of coffee and whiskey sloshing over his hand. Kelly puts down his fork, breakfast forgotten. I lean back in the booth of the kitchen nook, eyes steady on Brody as he curses softly, making quick work of cleaning up the mess before turning to, surprisingly, meet my stare.

"I, um, actually have been meaning to talk to you." His voice is soft and hesitant.

I'm sure he has. I refrain, just barely, from rolling my eyes. "About what, you breaking my necklace?"

Brody swallows thickly, taking a deep gulp from his mug

before answering. *Liquid courage*, I guess. "I didn't know it was from your mom."

I tilt my head to the side. "Would it have made a difference?"

He stares down at his cup. "I guess not." As if finding an ounce of courage, he picks his head up, rolling his shoulders back as he meets my stare more purposefully than he has since I was probably six years old. I sit up just a little taller. "I'm sorry."

I open my mouth and immediately snap it shut. "You're... *what*?"

"Since you've gotten here, I haven't done any of this right," Brody says. *What's happening right now? Am I being pranked? This is a joke, right? Yeah, a joke. It has to be. Better yet, I never actually woke up this morning.* This is one, very unfunny, dream because that warmth starting to kindle in my chest kind of feels like hope, and it can't be. *I refuse.*

Hope with Brody is the act of throwing myself on a sword time and time again, and I refuse to bleed for him anymore.

"Done any of what right, exactly?" I push, unwilling to sweep everything under the rug. Kelly remains quiet, giving us the space to work through this—whatever it is—while still being a silent referee if it calls for it.

Brody runs a hand through his hair, a few of his blonde locks falling back into his face. The same floppy waves as Mom's, and I feel a sudden pang of grief. "This kinship placement. You being here. Supporting you." He struggles to find his words. "I'm meant to be your guardian and I've done a real shitty job of it."

"It's not much different from how you've handled being my uncle." *I will not pull punches.* Not with him. Not after everything he's done.

Brody flinches, but he remains standing. "You're right."

I blink rapidly. *Come again?* "I don't understand." I look between him and Kelly, whose raised eyebrow tells me he's as surprised as I am. "What's changed?"

Brody frowns. "What do you mean?"

"I mean, why the sudden apologies? It sounds like..." I press my lips firmly together, unable to finish the sentence. *It sounds like you're saying you want to do better. That you want me here.*

"Sailor, I..." Brody takes a deep breath. "I want to be the person you deserve."

I shake my head. "I don't trust you," I whisper.

Not him. Not this moment. *None* of it.

"I know I have some things to work on—"

I laugh, cutting him off, but I don't feel an ounce of humor in any of this. *Some things to work on?* Understatement of the century. "I can't do this right now. I need to go." I push out of the breakfast nook, unable to look either man in the face. "I've got to help Griffin and Banks open the shop this morning."

"Sailor, wait," Brody starts, but Kelly cuts in.

"Let her go." His words are firm, and I breathe a little easier as I slip out of the house. The Jeep is already sitting idle in the driveway, and the tension bleeds from me when I open the passenger door to find Lux in the driver's seat. His sharp eyes cut from me to the house and back, taking in whatever's happening on my face and clearly drawing some conclusions.

"What happened?"

I shake my head. "I don't even know."

For once, he doesn't ask questions, just leaves it at that and pulls away from the house. Wrapped in the intoxicating spice that's Lux's cologne, I sink into my seat, my muscles loosening.

Just when I think I've finally gotten to the point where Brody can't surprise me, he goes and completely snatches the rug out from underneath me. What's his endgame here? He can't be for real about wanting to make up for everything. Where would he even start?

How would he start?

Putting an end to the drinking could be the biggest way. Even when I was little, I could tell that the alcohol was a big part of what messed him up—*still* messes him up. But somehow, I think that would be a hard no for him. He might be willing to put in some effort, try to make some changes, but when it actually means putting his money where his mouth is, I just can't see that happening.

But then...I didn't think him apologizing would ever happen either. But it did.

My mind drifts back to the other night the guys and I babysat Evie. Brody being drunk, the way he thought I was Mom, the panic in his voice. His actions may have been the riptide that yanked me under water, but Brody's really the one who's drowning.

I think he has been for a long time now, even before Mom died. Maybe even before she got sick.

"Sugarplum!" Griffin's cheerful greeting as he pulls my door open startles me back to reality as I realize the Jeep has stopped outside the shop. *Have we been sitting out here long?* "What are you thinking so hard about? You're gonna get wrinkles."

Unable to help it, I smile at him. "Just wondering how slow Lux could possibly drive when he knows you and I are on shift today."

Griffin helps me out of the Jeep, glaring playfully over his shoulder at Lux who rolls his eyes. Firmly shutting the door, as if he has the final word, Griffin sniffs. "He's always trying to keep us apart. It's like he doesn't understand how best friends work."

"Oh, I know how it works," Lux calls through the window. "I'm just not sure how much I like it between you two."

"Wow." Griffin clicks his tongue. "You hear that, Honey Bunches of Oats?" Honey Bunches of—*what?* "Green's not your color, Lux." My head tilts back, the sun kissing my face as I laugh, all of this morning's troubles falling away. They look absolutely *ridiculous*, arguing through the rolled up window.

Arms band around me and my feet leave the ground. A squeal escapes my lips. "Griffin!" I throw my arms around his neck, clinging tightly as he takes off for the shop.

I'm still laughing as we make our way into the shop, Banks raising his eyebrows as my flailing legs nearly take out a rack of wetsuits. "I don't even want to know what's happening right now, but can you try to do whatever it is without messing up the merchandise?"

"Sorry," I say sheepishly, trying to tuck my legs away from the racks.

Griffin pointedly turns his nose up at the both of us, looking off to the side as he sniffles. "Whatever color that is, it's not looking good on you bro."

"What?" Banks shakes his head. "You know what, never mind, I don't want to know."

I pat at Griffin's chest. "You can let me down now."

The sound of giggling from a group of girls around our age entering the shop is probably the only reason Griffin doesn't argue as he places me on my feet. He heads back the way we came, probably to see if they need help finding anything.

"I'm gonna get started on an order," Banks hooks his thumb over his shoulder, gesturing to the back room where they make the custom boards. "You good to watch the register?"

I nod, tucking myself behind the counter and settling in.

Griffin's voice carries through the shop, entwined with the music playing through the shop's speakers, but I can't make out what he says. By the sounds of constant giggling, things must be going well, for him or the store, who knows. I hope it's for him.

One girl—pretty, with chestnut brown hair that hangs past her shoulders—is practically glued to Griffin's side as they move through the racks. She seems to cling to his every word, not really paying attention to the array of items he shows her, though she probably only asked to get his attention. I can hear her friends exactly where they left them, and I wonder if they showed up to look around or shop for something else. By the constant appearance of curious heads peeking up over the racks from the front of the shop, my guess is they came here for their friend who only has eyes for Griffin.

As if hearing my thoughts, the girl's voice carries over as she and Griffin stop at one end of the counter. "I saw you out on the beach the other morning, surfing."

"Yeah?" Griffin sounds almost bashful, ducking his head a little. "Well, um, maybe you should join me sometime."

Even sitting at the other end of the counter, I can see her eyes light up. "Yeah?"

From the corner of my eye, I watch Griffin stand up a little straighter, tucking some of his hair behind his ear. I spot the moment she sees his scar, her eyes widening before cutting away, locking eyes with me. I turn to fully face her, eyes slightly narrowing.

Go on. Say something. I dare you.

She winces, dragging her eyes from my hardened stare, but unable to look at Griffin, either. Her eyes flit all around the store. "Oh, um, actually, I need to go."

Without waiting for a response, she ducks her head and scampers off back towards her friends, hissing whispers of "What's wrong?" and "What happened?" drifting across the store as they hustle toward the exit.

Griffin stays exactly where she left him, his back to me, arms hanging at his sides. He hangs his head, shoulders slumping, and I don't even think, my feet carrying me to him in a matter of seconds. I step directly in front of him, heart breaking at the vacant look painted across his face, the shadows in his eyes.

"Griffin?" I call gently, but he doesn't respond. "Griffin."

Still, nothing.

Moving in closer, the front end of our shoes meeting toe to toe, I reach out, cupping his face. Slowly, I lift his gaze to mine, and blood roars in my ears with the need to go after the girl who doesn't even realize how miserably she's broken the spirit of the most liveliest person I've ever had the privilege of knowing.

I swallow hard, pain searing my throat. I need to be here for Griffin. "Hey," I say, careful to keep my voice soft. "Don't let this moment define you. You're more than your scar, Griffin. You know that, and more importantly, the people who matter most to you know it, too. If she can't see that, she doesn't deserve you."

Griffin blinks slowly, and I press my lips firmly together,

hoping what I said wakes him up from this heartache. If I could, I'd take on his pain.

"But my scar *does* define me." Griffin says thickly, voice choked with emotion. Tears burn my eyes. "You just *saw* it for yourself."

"Maybe for those who are shallow, but those aren't the people that will ever matter to you, Griff," I promise. "And honestly? That's their loss."

"Theirs?" He echoes, voice still too hollow for my liking and the strings cutting into my heart tug a little hard.

"Absolutely." A light flickers somewhere in his brown eyes, and I latch onto that small glimmer of hope. "I know that in these moments it may be hard to remember, but you're beautiful exactly as you are. I won't ever let you forget it."

"Promise?"

I draw my hand away from his face, holding up my pinky finger between us. A small smile tugs at his lips, the light in his eyes burning brighter, and he raises a hand to hook his pinky with mine.

"Honestly, Griffin, you're so charming that if I wasn't in love with Lux, you'd have been my first choice." The words slip out without my thinking, and I freeze, eyes widening.

What did I just say?

Oh my gosh.

I slam my eyes shut.

I was just trying to make him feel better. It needed to be dramatic enough to get through to him—to distract him. Yeah, that's exactly it. Griffin will believe that, right? *Right?*

My heart thunders in my chest, the roar of blood in my ears so loud that if Griffin does say anything, I'm not sure I'll actually hear it.

Finally, he drops his forehead against mine, and I suck in a sharp breath, waiting.

Please, please, please, please let it go.

We never have to mention this moment, like, ever, again.

"Don't worry, my little tater tot." Griffin assures me quietly. It's the use of one of his cheesy nicknames that almost makes my slip-up worth it. *He's going to be okay.* "It's our little secret." He drops a swift kiss to my nose and pulls back. My eyes flutter open to find that small smile still on his lips. I release a shaky breath. "And thanks."

The tears I've been blinking back finally spill over my face, my smile entirely watery as I throw my arms around him. He's quick to hug me back, and it's then I realize how entirely grateful I am to have not pushed him away. *Who knew us becoming friends would save the both of us.* "You're welcome, honey bun."

Griffin lets out a startled bark of laughter, tightening his arms around me for another hard squeeze before he pulls back to look down at me, his natural sparkle back in his eyes and that familiar, mischievous grin back on his face. "What I *will* be telling Lux, obviously, is that I'm your number one man."

Oh yeah, he's definitely going to be okay.

I'm glad he's back—or at least, he's trying.

A sad Griffin is not a Griffin meant to walk this world. It isn't right. I'll do all I can to make sure he continues smiling, and joking.

"Obviously," I agree. "Who could have doubted it?"

Griffin walks off with a last squeeze of my hands. I watch him go for a moment before turning back towards the counter, only to stop short at the sight of Banks in the doorway, a towel in hand as if he'd paused in what he was doing. How long has he been standing there? Based on the crease in his forehead, long enough to piece together most of what happened. After a few seconds, Banks nods at me with silent gratitude, and that string that tightly tugged at my heart loosens.

I think we're all gonna be okay.

TWENTY-FOUR

"SO," I ask Dani as we make our way out into the waves, "do you typically paddleboard with your patients?"

Dani shrugs her shoulders, an impressive move considering she's stretched out across her own board. "I meet my *clients* where they're at." Letting her hand glide through the water, she flashes me a grin that's so like Griffin's I find myself smiling back automatically. "Plus, something about the ocean can really calm a person."

Make them open up, is what she doesn't say, but it's resting there between us.

Maybe she thinks that at least if we're in the ocean, it'll be a lot harder to run off. This is our first time together since I originally walked out on her with the excuse of needing to make it to the shop. The check-in that apparently solidified for Brody I wouldn't be staying with him.

Although he's still claiming that he's changed his mind.

He's adamant about making this work, and that unsettles me almost more than his drinking.

I'm not surprised that Dani switched up tactics with her check-ins. What *does* surprise me is that she waited until our next scheduled appointment, two weeks later. When she showed up at the shop this morning with a wetsuit and a board under her arm, I was curious enough to commit and see this check-in through.

I stop moving through the water and sit up, securing my paddle before looking off across the expanse of the pure blue sea. It stretches into the horizon. Endless. Its depth never to be fully uncovered. The waves bop me up and down on my board. "Yeah, I guess it can." Dani doesn't say anything, giving me the space to find my next words, if any. Finally, I ask the question that's been on my mind for days. "Have you spoken to Brody?"

Dani tilts her head, giving me a sidelong glance. "About?"

The corner of my lips tug up a little as I huff. "Wanting to make this work."

"This, as in...?" Dani prompts.

My eyes drop down to the board underneath me. "Me. Living here. Permanently."

"What do you think about that?"

I shake my head. "I don't know."A trembling breath leaves my lips. "It scares me, I guess."

Dani searches my face. "What about it scares you, Sailor?"

My gaze drifts past her, skimming across the water, back to the sand. It's easier to say this when I don't have to look someone in the eye. "All my life, despite knowing better, I always believed in Brody. I always had *hope*."

"Because you love him."

"Yeah." Except loving someone doesn't mean you have to hold on to them. The more I tried to hold onto him—or at least the idea of him and what I wanted him to be—the more I found my heart wrapped in barbed wire. I've bled so much over him, hurt so much because of him. I don't want to hurt anymore. "And you know what they say. Fool me once, shame on you, but fool me twice..."

"You should never feel shame for having faith."

"I feel ashamed for believing in a man who has never shown me anything differently than what he has all my life. For still wanting to believe in him anyways—even when it hurts." I tighten my grip on my board. "And *that* makes me a fool."

Dani's brows furrow, like she's searching for the right thing to say. I wait. Finally, she says, "If you've held onto the chance of Brody showing up for you how you've wanted all these years, why push him away now?"

Because pushing him away is how I keep myself safe. "Because he *had* all of these years." I swallow thickly. "So what's changed that he's suddenly so ready to try and give our relationship a shot?"

"Have you asked him?"

I nod.

"And?"

"And...nothing." Slowly, I rise to my feet on the board, paddle in hand. Heat floods my body and it has nothing to do with the sun shining on us.

I focus on breathing as I push through the water, leaving all thoughts of Brody, for the time being, behind. If I give it too much thought, I think I may just scream.

"If you've held onto the chance of Brody showing up for you how you've wanted all these years, why push him away now?"

Yeah, screaming sounds good. Like it might heal something in me.

It's not until Dani and I pull our equipment back onto the beach that she says anything else. "Other than things with Brody, how's life in the Cove been for you?"

The guys and Cova come to mind, and I can't help but smile. "It's good."

"Friends, a job—all things considered, you're adjusting well," Dani agrees. "Senior year is around the corner. Have you given much thought to what you want to do after high school?"

Picking up one of the towels we dropped earlier on our way into the water, I take a moment to dry myself off as much as I can in the wetsuit as I think over a response. "Not really." After all, I'm not even sure where I'll *be* for my senior year.

"I want you to start giving it some thought," Dani presses gently. "Having a goal to focus on can provide you with some purpose. I'm not saying you have to figure out your entire life, but choosing something that you care about and working toward it intentionally can make a difference. The more meaningful it is to you, Sailor, the better."

Meaningful?

Something tightens in my chest.

What do I want for my life?

Dani jumps in quickly, her hand coming to rest on top of one of mine as my heart rate kicks up. "Sailor, breathe." I release a shaky breath, the pain biting into the palms of my hands kicking in. *Ouch.* Slowly, I unfurl my fists around the towel. "I meant what I said. You don't need to map out your future right this moment. I just want to help you lay a good foundation for whichever path you *do* choose. Okay?"

Unable to speak, I nod my head.

"Priya gave you a journal, right?"

I nod, and almost smile at the memory. When Priya had first been assigned as my caseworker, I had a hard time adjusting. She gave me the journal, telling me it could be an outlet. I never wrote in it. If I used it to voice my fears...my worries...it'd make it real. Like reading it on paper in my own handwriting would solidify something I hoped more than anything wasn't true.

When I saw how personal diaries could end up in the wrong hands at the group home, the way they could be used against someone, it proved further that I'd done the right thing by never taking pen to paper. The other kids couldn't use what they didn't know against me.

But just because I never wrote in it doesn't mean I don't still carry it around with me.

Which is why I guess Dani knows about it.

"Whenever an idea comes to mind, no matter how small or silly it may seem, write it down."

Write it down.

Okay. I nod my head.

How hard can it be?

DANI'S WORDS hover over me like a storm cloud the rest of the day. I dig the journal and a pen from my duffel but leave it beside the bag. It sits there on the bench in front of the bed, the bright teal cover nearly shouting for attention.

I don't know what to write. Where would I even start? Even something like *learn to surf* feels too big. Any kind of thinking beyond the immediate present just feels impossible. *Permanent.*

Mom dying taught me that life is too short. We're not guaranteed a tomorrow. So how can I plan for one?

I hug one of the many decorative little pillows to my chest, curling into the large gray wicker basket chair. If only it would swallow me whole, then I wouldn't have to think about this whole...assignment.

It all seems like an awful lot to try and uncover. I mean, *I'm only sixteen.*

A familiar, intoxicatingly spicy smell fills the air, the warmth of the body that takes a seat beside me helping me to sink a little into the couch. "What are we glaring at?" Lux asks.

Without taking my eyes off the offending item, I say, "Dani wants me to write in the journal."

"Write what?"

I shrug my shoulders, hugging the pillow a little closer. "What I want next."

The words sink between us, heavy and loaded with so much more than just the concept of school. I shift in my seat, knocking my shoulder into his arm, and I suck in a small breath. Lux leans forward, shoulders hunched as his arms rest on his legs.

"You still haven't unpacked your bags," he states quietly.

I blink. *That's not what I thought he'd say.*

"Um, no."

"Is *that* what you want?" Lux questions, the timber of his voice deepening. "To be living out of suitcases?"

I open my mouth, close it and then open it again. "That's not what she meant. She wants me to figure out what I want to do after high school." I know that's not what he's asking, but I don't know how else to really answer him. Pointing out that I'm technically living out of a duffel will not do me any favors at this moment. Somehow, I don't think he'll find it funny.

Lux doesn't take the bait. "And what about senior year?"

I swallow thickly. "What about it? I don't even know if I'm going to be here."

Lux looks at me, his gray eyes darkening as they cut through my defenses. "Brody said he wants you to stick around—"

"Right now," I cut him off. "He wants me to stay *right now*. But it wasn't too long ago he was saying something different to Kelly. And in a week or two, who's to say he won't change his mind again?"

His jaw flexes as he looks away. "It seems to me like you have your mind made up."

"Lux—"

"I don't understand. Do you not even want this?" *Do you not want us?* He doesn't say it, but he doesn't have to. Clasping his hands together, the veins in his arms become more pronounced as they ripple across his olive skin. "Were you ever gonna fight to stay?"

"I never planned on fighting to stay somewhere *I* didn't even want to be. And let's not kid ourselves...I wasn't wanted here either," I point out quietly. "Brody's pulled the rug out from underneath me all my life. When I got here, I promised myself no more surprises—not with him. I wasn't going to let myself get comfortable just to have it all taken away. So, no. I haven't unpacked."

He doesn't respond. Putting aside the pillow, I tuck my legs underneath me and place a hand on his shoulder as I lean into him. The muscles underneath my hand tense, but he doesn't move away. "Lux. What's going on? Talk to me."

At first, he's silent. Then, quietly, he says, "Your room looks exactly like it did the day you arrived. And the bags..."

I know that tone. *He's scared.*

The strings around my heart tug and I move on instinct, pushing up on my knees to wrap my arms around him from behind. I rest my head on his shoulder as I assure him softly. "Our cards have already been dealt, remember? I'm not gonna fold." No matter what happens at the end of summer, Lux, Cova, the guys...that doesn't all just go away. Not anymore. "I won't disappear on you. On any of you. Okay?"

It's something I never would have said at the beginning of the summer, but I know now that I couldn't cut myself off from them anymore than I could cut off my own leg. "You have my number, Lux, and I have yours. Whatever happens this time, neither of us are going to refuse to use them."

Saying it out loud brings an incredible sense of peace to me, washing away the tension I've carried all summer regarding my losing battle with keeping them all at bay. *I never really had a chance.* A smile tugs at my lips.

Honestly, I'm glad I lost that fight.

A deep sigh leaves Lux's lips and his hand comes up to my arms where they're banded around him, grabbing hold of them like a lifeline. "I'm sorry. I freaked a little."

"It's okay." I hug him tighter. "It was your turn."

He chuckles, and somehow, everything's okay again. "Tell me more about this journal assignment," he says, and I do.

TWENTY-FIVE

"SAILOR?"

Brody's voice drifting in from the front of the store makes me look up from the surfboard I'm studying in the back room. The board is a painted vibrant, glossy blue, a shapely white foam line cutting diagonally across the middle. *It looks like the ocean.* The layers of color and shadow are hypnotizing, and the book I planned to read during my fifteen-minute break is still abandoned in my bag.

"Sail!" Brody pokes his head into the room. "There you are."

I huff. "It's Sailor."

I try to keep my body relaxed, but with every footstep that brings Brody closer, I tense. The echo of his apology fills the space between us with every step.

"I'm sorry."

"...I haven't done any of this right."

"I know I have some things to work on—"

Whether he's been working on them or not, I couldn't say. I've tried my best to block him out since he turned up in the kitchen trying to apologize.

Sometimes it's just a little too late. And the wounds from the night I babysat Evie are still too fresh.

He stops at my side, close enough that I can feel his body heat. "Wow, it's coming along great."

I take a step to the side and gesture to the table. "Whose project is it?" It's the closest thing to a greeting I can handle giving him.

"Milo and Griffin." Brody pauses, rubbing a hand across the back of his neck and chuckling. "Well, I think Griff watches more than anything. But he's learning."

I wait for him to say something more, but he just hovers next to me. Finally, I crack. "Was there something you needed?"

Brody clears his throat. "Um, yeah, actually, I have a couple of things I want to run by you. I was thinking we could host a barbeque at the house, with the guys, prior to heading out to Summer Nights and joining the festivities."

My brows furrow. "Summer Nights?"

"It's an annual mid-summer beach party the town puts on every year. Everyone goes."

"And you want to...hang out before the festival?" Just so I understand what he's asking here—what he's expecting.

Brody rubs at the back of his neck again. "Yeah, if that's okay with you. We can throw some meat on the grill and just hang out before joining the town. It's, uh, tonight." I must've missed the announcement—and fliers. *Have* there been any fliers? How did I miss any of it? Or is it an unspoken festival the townsfolk just know it's time to commence?

"And the other thing?" I question. *Let's lay all the cards out on the table at once here.*

"What?"

"You said you had a couple of things to run by me."

"Oh. Yeah." Brody clears his throat and looks up at me from underneath the bill of his hat. "You, um, seem to like paddle-boarding, yeah?"

I nod my head. *Where is this going?*

"What would you say to paddleboarding this weekend?"

"With...you?" I don't understand. He wants to hang out, like, just the two of us? And twice in one week? This must be part of the fine print in having changed his mind to wanting to be my guardian.

I didn't sign up for this.

I can always say no. The word sits on the tip of my tongue.

"Yeah. What do you say?" He looks nervous. Almost hopeful.

No. "Sure." *What am I saying?*

Brody stands a little taller. "Yeah?" *I think I already regret this.* "To paddleboarding?"

I think I nod my head, the weight a little heavy. "To paddleboarding, and Summer Nights."

A huge smile breaks out across Brody's face, softening his features. *Wow. He looks so young.* "Great!" Brody looks like his birthday has come early. "See you tonight, then!"

SUMMER NIGHTS HAS, in fact, been advertised all over town.

I blink at all the fliers and banners hung across the roadways as the guys and I head back to the house after shift, my head still spinning from the conversation with Brody hours before. I don't realize I'm spacing until Milo leans forward from the back seat, resting a hand on my arm. "Everything okay, Sail?"

I fiddle with the sleeves of my hoodie, my hands disappearing in the fabric as I nod my head. "Yeah, I just...Dani kind of gave me homework, I guess you could say, and I've been a little distracted since then."

I don't have it in me to go into what happened with Brody, and it's not like I'm *not* thinking about Dani's assignment. Since she gave me the task of thinking of my future last week, I've been lost to my thoughts more than usual. I've taken the journal everywhere with me, but the pages remain blank. I've picked up the pen several times but have stopped short of taking it across the page. *I just need to give it some time. Something will come to me. Hopefully.*

"Yeah?" Milo prompts. "Want to share with the class?"

I glance at Banks, who has his eyes on the road, one arm propped on the open window. "Um…is it weird for me to tell you?"

Banks looks over at me, cocking an eyebrow. "What, because your case worker is my mom?" I nod, and he shrugs. "Wouldn't be the weirdest part of my day. I promise not to tell her you're procrastinating."

Laughing a little despite myself, I give in and share the assignment with them. It's like opening a faucet, and everything else pours out of me. How I don't have a clue as to what I want to do with my life. That before I found out my Mom was sick, and Lux was still in the picture, anything felt possible. That no matter what I chose to do with my life, I knew those two would be in it, at my side.

But then suddenly, that was no longer the case, and a future without either of them looked bleak. A tunnel with no light at the end.

And maybe now there's some light again, but knowing how easy it is for that light to go out has changed everything.

They take in every word, sitting with me in the Jeep long after we pull into the driveway, listening. At some point, the front door flies open, Griffin bounding down the steps, but he slows at whatever facial expressions he sees on our faces. He takes a seat on the porch steps, waiting like a patient puppy, and I smile softly to myself.

"Well," Banks says when I finally stop talking, "as someone who just graduated this past spring, I couldn't tell you what I want to do with my life right now." Something tugs in my chest, but I refrain from showing anything outwardly that'll make him stop talking. "But I can say that whatever it is, I can picture you all right there with me."

I turn sideways in my seat, batting my lashes. "Aw, Banks, are you saying we're besties?"

Milo laughs from the backseat as Banks rolls his eyes. "You and my brother sound so much alike it's scary."

I grin. "You love it."

He shakes his head. "One Griffin is enough, thanks."

"Agree. It's a good thing I'm not him. I come with my own quirks."

"Oh, I've noticed." Banks throws his car door open and slides out. I give a mock gasp, following after him with Milo hot on my trail.

"What exactly are you implying, Banks Marshall?" I call after him.

He turns, a smirk tugging at his full lips, eyes alight with the mischief I usually only see in his brother. Walking backwards towards the front open door, he raises his hands with a shrug of his shoulders.

"Take it how you want to, Sail—oomph." Banks walks right into Lux who throws an arm around his friend's neck and bends him in half. In a sudden headlock, Banks grabs a hold of Lux's arms, trying to free himself with no luck.

"What was that?" Lux mocks, laughing as he and Banks end up twirling in a few circles as Banks tries, and fails, to find a way to get loose. "Sail will take *what*?"

Griffin hops off the porch, leaning against me, watching the two wrestle around, jokes and muffled grunts passing between them. "Man, it's a good thing Lux stepped in before I did. It would've been embarrassing for Banks if his baby brother had to teach him the same lesson."

Milo raises a brow at Griffin from my other side. "You? Putting Banks in a headlock?"

Griffin scowls. "What are you saying?"

"He's not saying a thing," I assure Griffin, placing a hand on his arm to settle him as I shoot Milo a warning look.

He grins larger and I know any attempt to settle things has completely left the front yard. "All I'm saying is I only ever remember one Marshall ending up in a headlock, and it's never been Banks."

"Oh yeah?" Griffin puffs up his chest, stepping around me and closer to Milo. "The thing about that—" Griffin moves fast, but Milo moves faster, having already anticipated his friend's move. The two end up on the ground, at my feet, wrestling one another with Milo wrapping Griffin up in a headlock.

"No fair, man." Griffin whines. At least, that's what I think he said. Pinned underneath Milo, it's sort of hard to hear him.

With everyone now preoccupied, I shake my head, walking past them all and into the house.

Kelly greets me at the door with a wave. "Hey! Meat's already on the grill." His brows shoot up as he takes in the WrestleMania matches behind me. "Uh..."

"Don't even ask."

"With this crew, it's usually better not to," Kelly agrees, following behind me. We end up in the backyard, a few boxes of soda sitting on the table with bags of ice beside it, like he had been in the middle of setting up.

Remembering my manners, I clear my throat. "What can I do to help?"

For the next ten minutes, I get the drinks squared away and pull out the paper plates and plastic cutlery. I'm putting a trash bag in the outside bin to dispose of the party's waste when the guys join us, some slightly out of breath but all red and pink faced with large smiles on their faces. "Thanks for finally joining us."

"Aw, sorry Sail," Griffin ambles down the steps towards me, hooking his thumb over his shoulder. "Someone had to give these guys a lesson."

"And you think that would be you?" Banks' voice is light with amusement.

"If not me, who?" Griffin challenges.

Before anyone else can end up on the ground in a show of dominance, I rest my head against Griffin's arm, patting his chest. "Thanks for handling them, Griff."

He throws an arm over my shoulders. "Anything for you, dumpling."

"Don't fill his head," Banks says. "It's big enough."

"Food's ready." Kelly calls. *Saved by the bell.*

"Perfect, I'm starving!" Griffin steers us towards the grill, throwing a hand over his stomach.

Milo follows us over. "You're always starving."

Sniffling, Griffin lifts his nose in the air. "I'm glad you've noticed."

"How can we not?" Banks reaches forward and ruffles his little brother's hair. "You ensure it becomes everyone's business."

"So?" Griffin argues over his shoulder, trying in vain to bat the hand away. Banks pulls away with a laugh. "I like to make sure others care."

"No one cares." Lux jokes. *What is this, Pick on Griffin Day?*

Griffin starts to turn around for another standoff but I throw my arm around his waist, leaning into him. "I care, Griff."

He's quiet for a moment. "You know what, Sail? That's all that matters."

"I think you're losing your girl to my brother." Banks mock-whispers behind us. I roll my eyes, trying hard to ignore the flutter in my stomach.

Your girl. He's obviously talking to Lux. *Am I his girl? Do I want to be? Am I even ready for that?*

I lose myself to these questions for the rest of the evening, so much so that I don't realize Brody has joined us until he takes a seat beside me around the firepit the guys lit so we could make s'mores.

He doesn't say anything, though, and I surprise myself by asking, "Did you and Mom do things like this when you were kids?"

"Cookouts, you mean?" I nod, and Brody smiles, a little wistfully. "All the time. It was something our dad actually enjoyed doing as a family." His smile fades, an underlying bite to his words, and my eyes widen a little. *Talk of family is definitely a touchy subject for him.*

He shakes his head like he's trying to dislodge something, pulling his smile back on. "When your mom was still around, our house was *the* house to be at in the neighborhood." Brody points to Kelly, his tone wry and almost fond as he adds, "That's why this one ended up always being around."

Kelly shakes his head. "Well that, and I was getting paid to do yardwork at your place long before you were even born."

The humor falls out of Brody's eyes. "Mmm, the son that was actually wanted." He leans to the side in his chair, pulling out a pack of cigarettes. He digs around in his pocket once more and withdraws a lighter. Holding it tightly in his hand, Brody lightly taps the pack against the arm of the chair, but to my surprise, he doesn't light up.

I tear my eyes away from Brody's hand to meet Kelly's gaze. "You grew up with Mom?"

"Childhood friends, like you and Lux."

I smile to myself. *How cute.* "And you loved her."

Kelly swallows thickly. "For as long as I can remember. Always had." His next words are soft. "Always will." He clears his throat. "What you and Lux have is a gift. Treasure it."

I can feel the weight of Lux's eyes on me, but I can't get myself to look at him. Instead, I remain focused on the two men sharing a glimpse of a past I don't know much of. "What about you, Brody? Who was your best friend growing up?"

Brody stares at the fire, and when he doesn't immediately answer, I look at Kelly, who's watching Brody with a slight frown on his lips. "It was Finley," Brody finally answers.

"You said she basically raised you until...until she left." I try to find the right words to gently ask my next question, conversation around the firepit quieting. "Why *did* she leave?"

As if on autopilot, Brody digs out a cigarette and lights one, dragging in a large inhale.

“Sailor has asthma.” Lux points out, and Brody cusses under his breath but puts it out, his pointer finger tapping against the box before he finally speaks.

“My mom and Fin...didn’t get along.”

“Understatement,” Kelly says. “His mom didn’t like your mom. She was only a few years older than Fin, and whether it was because they were super close in age or because she didn’t want to share the spotlight with the man’s only daughter, she had it out for your mom from day one. Made it unbearable to live in the same house together.” Brody shoots Kelly a look, but doesn’t argue his point. Kelly sighs. “The tipping point was your mom finding out she was pregnant.”

I swallow. “With me?”

Kelly nods his head, shifting in his seat. “Yeah.”

Brody jerks forward in his seat. “That’s enough.”

“She has the right to know,” Kelly says.

“You don’t even know if it’s true,” Brody snaps. The two stare at each other, tension filling the air. I blink, glancing at Lux, and he returns my look blankly, clearly not knowing any more than I do. *What do we do?* I’m not sure what’s even going on.

Kelly narrows his eyes. “Which part do you think they weren’t serious about?”

“Any of it.”

Kelly rocks forward in his seat, hands curling into fists. “You’ve got to be kidding me.”

I clear my throat. “Um, what’s going on?”

“Leave it,” Brody warns Kelly tersely.

Kelly scoffs. “So much for your sister having been your best friend if you’re still willing to feed into the bullshit your folks have been dishing all these years.”

Brody pushes out of his chair so suddenly, I flinch. “You don’t know what you’re talking about.”

“Sail.” Lux calls for my attention softly, a warm hand coming down on my leg. I turn my head to find Lux crouched beside my chair. “How about we get out of here, yeah?”

I can't find any words, not sure what I'm witnessing. So I nod, and let Lux take a hold of my hand, helping me to my feet and guiding me away from the fight brewing between the two men meant to look after me. The only connections I have left to my mom.

She would be so upset at the sight of them right now. I just know it.

The five of us end up in the Jeep with me tucked in between Milo and Griffin in the back. No one says a word as Banks pulls out of the driveway, placing distance between us and the house. *Should we have left them with each other? Will they be okay?*

I'm not even sure who I'm more concerned about.

A hand wraps around my own, prying my fingers from the palm of my hand, and it's only then the pain registers. The light of the setting sun reveals the angry red crescent-shaped marks my nails have left there, and Milo gently rubs his thumb across the indented skin.

"I've never seen them at each other's throats like that." Griffin says quietly, breaking the silence.

"Family secrets on top of family secrets." I sag against him, exhausted. "I'm so sick of it."

"It'll be okay, Sailor." Griffin tries to reassure me, the use of my actual name a shock to my system. "Whatever you learn, it won't change a thing."

It could change everything. And from the sound of things, it could change it for the worse.

Will Brody change his mind again?

Will they send me away?

My lungs feel tight at the thought, and I can't catch my next breath. I pull my hand out of Milo's, rubbing at my chest.

"Hey, hey, hey," someone says gently. "It's okay. Sailor. Hey."

I feel like I've been submerged under water, and I can barely make out the voices around me. Someone takes hold of my hand again, resting it against their chest. I recognize the feel of the calluses on Milo's fingers. The steady beat of his heart thumps under my hand. *Ba-dum. Ba-dum. Ba-dum.*

It's not what Mom used to do, but all the same, it makes me feel safe. Seen.

Loved.

I don't want to be tossed aside.

TWENTY-SIX

A BONFIRE RAGES in the distance, illuminating the shadows of people milling about the beach lined with balloons tied to weighted decor to keep them from floating off. Heavy bass from the speakers thumps steadily, laughter and shouts ringing through the night. A huge sign erected in the sand welcomes everyone to Summer Nights. Jacked up trucks and Jeeps with dropped tail-gates curve around the outskirts of the party, some with large American flags flying.

One of them is flying the confederate flag, and I tense at the sight of it, my spine prickling with familiar apprehension.

"Ignore 'em," Milo murmurs to me. "You'd be surprised to find how many people don't actually know what it really represents."

Having grown up in South Carolina, I understand all too well what he means. It still doesn't make it any easier to stomach.

"Folks always claim Florida to be one big melting pot, but a melting pot doesn't mean acceptance," Milo explains, his eyes skimming the party. The guys walk quietly around us. I swear they're hovering. I assured them multiple times that I'm fine, but Griffin refused to let go of my other hand even after I found my breath. Now, he gently squeezes it as Milo continues. "At least here in the Cove, I'd like to think it does—Cova too."

I hope they're right. However nice people are to our faces, a couple of mixed-race kids coming up in the South are never going to have it that easy. Acceptance or not, we're bound to have some problems.

Griffin tugs on my hand suddenly, pulling me to a stop. A group of dune buggies fly past, seemingly out of nowhere, and I nearly jump out of my skin. "Where the hell did they come from?"

Banks chuckles. "The races are about to start."

"Race?" I perk up.

He eyes me. "Got a need for speed?"

"Growing up, we used to go to the skating rink. If there was a race to be won, Sail was right there." Lux shakes his head, a smile on his lips before he suddenly turns a little serious. "Don't get any ideas."

Griffin looks borderline offended. "Why haven't *we* gone skating?"

I shrug my shoulders. "I skate with Cova."

Griffin turns quickly on the balls of his feet, fully facing me. "We need our own thing."

"Griffin, pudding cup, you *are* my thing." No matter what it is that we end up doing, whether it's just the two of us or as a group, with Griffin, it's always an adventure. He brings an air of lightness to any day we spend together, whether it's at the shop or the beach. Competing in trying to one-up each other on goofy nicknames. With him, and honestly the others standing here with us, I smile. *A lot.* Griffin's the best dose of medicine a girl can get. Put him and the others together? My cheeks often hurt from laughing and my stomach cramps. It's the only kind of pain I want to feel moving forward. It's a better way to know that I'm alive.

And with them, I'm living.

A huge smile rips across Griffin's face, his scar more

pronounced, and I'm reminded of just how handsome he is. Without a word, Griffin sweeps me off my feet into a bear hug, crushing me to him.

"You guys hear that? I'm Sail's *favorite*."

I tap at his side, wanting to be put down. "I didn't say that."

"It's what *I* heard."

"Well then get your ears checked." Lux chimes in.

There's a thump, alarmingly close to my ear, and Griffin lets out a yelp. He puts me down but keeps me close, rubbing at the back of his head and scowling at his brother, who must have been the one to whack him. "You know, one day I may just lay you out."

Banks raise a brow. "Lay me out?" He folds his arms across his chest, muscles flexing. Lux stands at his side, mirroring him, and I run my eyes over the veins in his arms. Swallowing thickly, I tear my gaze away.

"That's what I said." Griffin tugs me in front of him. "And this is perfect, because now things are an even playing field."

Milo stands beside me, gesturing my way. "More like we have the upper hand."

Lux leans forward. "Yeah? And why's that?"

"*Well.*" Griffin drags out the word tauntingly. "With Sail on our side, it's three against two. Plus, you won't possibly retaliate."

I look incredulously over my shoulder at Griffin. "Are you using me as a human shield?"

"You're our protector." Milo winks.

Griffin pats me on the head. "Shh, the adults are talking."

I raise a brow at Milo. *He's kidding, right?* I smirk to myself. "You're right, Griff, I should let you all talk."

Breaking out of his hold, I step to the side. Griffin immediately tries to backpedal, reaching for me with apologies flying from his lips but his brother is quick to take the opportunity handed to him. Banks tackles Griffin, the two ending up rolling around on the ground at my feet. I step back to give them some room, glancing up to find Milo in a headlock, a satisfied grin on Lux's face.

"Oh, how the tables have turned," Lux gloats.

"So not fair." Milo pries at Lux's arm, to no avail.

"You guys did this to yourself." Lux points out. "Surrender now, or—*oof!*" His breath leaves him as Milo suddenly gets the upper hand, slipping out of Lux's hold and swiping his legs out from underneath him. Lux takes a hold of Milo's arm, bringing him down to the sand with him.

I roll my eyes, taking another few steps back to avoid the flailing limbs. *Why do these boys always end up on the ground?*

I glance around, but not many people are paying us any attention. If this summer has taught me anything, it's that these four do this often enough that the people of this town are unfazed. I open my mouth to break them all up, but pause at the sound of a familiar voice, tinged with wry amusement.

"Why do they always end up on the ground?" Cova asks, echoing my thoughts as she stops beside me.

"Beats me." I turn to her, then freeze at the shadow that lines the underside of her jaw. A black-and-blue bruise peeks from underneath the collar of her sweatshirt, too, so dark against her throat that I suddenly feel sick thinking about what could have caused it. Cova glances over at me as if sensing my gaze, eyes widening slightly when she realizes what I'm looking at. Her smile disappears and she straightens up, tugging at her sweatshirt, and like that, the bruise is gone.

Well, that one is. *Is she covered in them?*

"Cova..." I breathe quietly, unable to find my next words. *Are you okay* seems a little inadequate.

"I'm okay." She answers quickly, in a whisper. Her eyes cut to the guys before looking back at me. She mouths her next words, repeating, "I'm okay."

My eyes sting and I blink repeatedly, fighting to keep the tears at bay.

I look away, breathing deeply.

One, two, three, four. I inhale through my nose, holding it for a few seconds before releasing it through my mouth, wrestling with myself to not scream.

Again.

One, two, three, four.

I focus on only this for a couple of minutes, until I no longer feel like I'm going to cry or scream. Cova's hand gently brushes against mine in comfort, and something starts to boil deep within me, heat flushing through my body. *She shouldn't be doing that. I should be comforting her.*

I'm not the one with bruises.

Finally, the guys wave a white flag and help one another to their feet, wiping themselves off. Milo spots his cousin first. "Cova, hey!"

There's a chorus of greetings and hugs, and some of the softness returns to Cova's expression as she brushes sand from his hair.

"You all will never change, will you?" She teases, tugging fondly at one of his dreads. "Just a bunch of puppies."

Griffin grins, face flushed. "Woof," he says cheerfully.

Cova laughs, throwing her head back in genuine mirth. The movement exposes the mark under her jaw, and Banks' eyes narrow, humor disappearing from his expression as he takes a step towards Cova. *He sees it.* The bruise. Or, at least, a part of it. Lux hones in on Cova at the same moment, head tilted as he sweeps his eyes down her form and back up. His hands flex at his side, and a weight seems to lift off my chest. *I'm not the only one who knows. They see it too.*

"Cova," Banks says, voice low. "What the hell—"

"Don't." Her jaw flexes, but the one word leaves no room for argument.

Griffin tries a different approach, reaching out to put a careful hand on her arm. He telegraphs his movements, giving her plenty of time to pull away, and I wonder if he learned that from his mom. "Can we get you anything? For, um. The pain? If it hurts?"

What can we do? It's what we're all really wanting to know, what we need her to tell us.

Cova smiles at him, weak but real. "No, Griff. But...thanks." She makes eye contact with Milo, and neither cousin says a word but the conversation is there in their eyes. Milo's the first to look away, jaw clenched.

Banks opens his mouth, to say what, I haven't a clue, but immediately shuts it as someone calls out to our group.

I turn to see Rhian and Nico strolling over to us across the sand. The guys immediately shift around us, putting Cova and I loosely in the middle of the circle. Rhian's gaze skims over us, a wicked grin on his lips as he focuses on me and Cova. "You two just can't seem to stay away from one another, can you?"

I lift my chin. "Well, we're friends. So that kind of comes with the territory."

Rhian tilts his head, arms crossed over his chest and brings his thumb up to his bottom lip. "Well," he says, "I like to keep a tight leash on things."

"So I've noticed," I snap back. Nico shifts beside Rhian, his eyes on me, but I barely spare him a glance. Thinking about the bruising so close to Cova's throat makes my own tighten with rage. "Maybe try loosening that leash a bit. Before someone chokes."

"Well, you can't be too careful." Rhian holds my stare. "When a pet slips its leash, someone's likely to get hurt."

Lux takes a step forward, clearly ready for a fight, but I push past him until I'm nearly toe to toe with Rhian. "Is that a threat?"

"If the leash isn't tight enough..."

"What? You'll fix it?" I question, raising a brow. Rhian chuckles, wiping his thumb back and forth across his bottom lip. "With that firm hand of yours, right?" His eyes cut sharply over my shoulder, no doubt to where Cova now stands behind me, and I bristle.

"Don't look at her. We're the ones talking."

Rhian glances down at me. "You've got one hell of a mouth on you."

I smile sweetly, tilting my head to the side. "Thanks, I bite as hard as I bark." *Want to test the theory?* I'm begging him to take the bait, no matter how stupid it is.

"Rhian." Nico calls for his friend's attention. "That's enough man, let's go."

Warm spice fills my nose, and I can't help relaxing at Lux's steady presence at my side. "You're gonna wanna listen to your friend there," Lux warns.

"Cova, let's go." Rhian orders. I don't take my eyes off the threat in front of me, but she must hesitate because his nostrils flare. "Cova, now."

Suddenly his hand shoots out, reaching past me and I throw my arm up and out, batting his arm down. Striking out with the palm of my hand, I get Rhian in the throat. He grabs at his neck, trying to suck in a deep breath, face red. My eyes narrow on his hunched form and I swiftly kick him between the legs. He drops at my feet with a wheeze that rivals a wounded animal.

Crouching at his side, my eyes locked on the flames of the bonfire beyond him, I whisper. "Let this be a lesson: you're not entitled to put your hands on anyone. Hopefully you'll think twice next time." I glance sideways at him. "You should probably put some ice on that."

I push to my feet and meet Nico's wide eyes but say nothing. As far as I'm concerned, we have nothing left to say to one another. His face shuts down and he looks away first. Quietly, he helps Rhian up who stumbles away with him like a dog with its tail tucked between its legs.

Now if that isn't sweet justice, I don't know what it is. *I know exactly who could use a leash.* I sneer after them until I'm suddenly turned away.

Dark gray eyes sweep across my face before Lux pulls me into his arms, his body vibrating. I hug him back, pressing my hand into his back to rub soothing circles, reassuring him that I'm okay.

He buries his face into my curls, breathing deeply, and I stand still, letting him hold me for as long as he needs. The alternative, I'm sure, would be to charge after Rhian and rearrange his face. Conflict where I'm involved has never been something Lux stomached well when we were younger, and he always retaliated. Always.

"You're insane," he mumbles into the top of my head. "And you're going to give me a heart attack."

I pat his back. "Someone had to teach him a lesson."

Hopefully we can leave this all right here, with Rhian's pride in the sand.

For Cova, it won't be that easy. Something twists in my stomach.

"So," Griffin says, breaking the silence. "When were you going to tell us you were such a badass?"

The tension cracks and everyone laughs, even me and Lux. He loosens his hold enough that I can turn around in his arms to look at everyone. "You end up in a group home and you learn a thing or two." I shrug my shoulders before meeting Cova's eyes. "I'm sorry."

Tears fill her eyes and she sniffles, lifting her chin. "For what? Being the greatest friend a girl could ask for?" A few tears roll down her face and she swipes at them quickly. "You have nothing to apologize for."

I can see her trying to put on a brave face, but she can't totally hide the tremor in her voice. We may have gotten rid of Rhian for now, but I know it's not over. Still— "I couldn't watch him put his hands on you again."

"I know," she whispers. Milo steps up to his cousin, pulling her into a hug, and she seems so much smaller as she clings to him, all but hunching in on herself. Milo rocks her gently, looking out at the water with his chin resting on top of Cova's head and something tugs in my chest. He seems older than her, shoveling the weight of both their burdens. *That's* what family is supposed to be. I know, without a doubt, that if nothing else, those two will always have each other.

We all have each other, I realize. And I'm part of that *we*.

"Come on," Milo says quietly. "I'll take you home."

"No." Cova pulls away from him, shaking her head. "I don't want to be there right now. I want to hang out with everyone." She hiccups. "Just give me a moment, yeah?"

Lux gestures to the rest of us, and we give them some space, heading for the bonfire, my hand held tightly in his as he keeps close to my side. I almost stop short at the sight of Brody already there, his head tossed back, laughing without a care in the world.

"Hey!" Brody shouts as we get closer, waving a hand animatedly in the air, a beer held tightly in the other. There's a woman in his lap, too, her arm thrown around his neck. So much for the claim of knowing he has some things to work on. "There you guys are! I need to talk to you boys about something."

He waves them over but they hesitate.

"Go on." Banks encourages the other two. "I'll hang back with Sail. You can catch me up later." He and Lux seem to have a silent conversation, before Lux finally nods and peels off with Griffin, leaving me and Banks alone.

Without sharing a word, we start down towards the water, stopping just out of reach of the waves that wash ashore, the party at our back. Cova isn't the only one who needs a moment. The wind rolls off the water, tussling my hair and I tuck some of it behind my ear. Banks shoves his hands into the pockets of his shorts, shoulders tense as he stares off in the distance.

"So," I say finally. "How long have you been in love with Cova?"

He doesn't respond immediately, and then with a deep sigh, he admits, "Since elementary school."

I take in the stars decorating the sky. "Does she know that?"

"Yeah, she knows. She was my first kiss." I smile to myself even as something tightens in my chest when his tone shifts, wistfulness replaced by resignation. "Nothing to be done about it though."

"Isn't there?"

Banks shakes his head. "I don't think that's what she needs. Not from me, at least." I glance at him and he meets my gaze, shadows darkening his hazel eyes. "She doesn't need a knight in shining armor, or someone trying to sweep her off her feet. She needs friends. Good ones. And so, I'll be that for her."

He'd be whatever she wants him to be, I realize. No matter the shape it takes, he loves her enough to put aside his own wants to be exactly what she needs.

She needs friends, good ones.

I'll be that for her.

"We all will," I say, and this time, when he looks down at me, he smiles.

TWENTY-SEVEN

THE GUYS HAVE A SECRET, and they are very, very bad at pretending they don't.

In the past week, I've found them whispering excitedly with their heads together more times than I can count. Whenever they spot me, they get quiet, sometimes slapping one another to shut up as quickly as possible. The other day, Milo tackled Griffin into a rack of bathing suits when he didn't take the hint, slapping a hand over his mouth to stop him from talking. It's a little insane the lengths they're going to in an attempt to keep whatever it is quiet.

At least I've gotten more than a few laughs out of it, even if Griffin and I did have to spend fifteen minutes picking up the scattered merchandise.

When Cova stopped by the shop later, I told her what was going on. She shook her head, eyes skimming the shop for the culprits. "Discretion is not in their vocabulary." She turned to me, a genuine smile on her face, the first one since Summer Nights. "Griffin's the worst one when it comes to surprises. I don't know why he tries."

"*Hey.*" His whine carries from somewhere in the shop.

"True or not?" Cova calls out, daring him to lie.

"I ruined your surprise party *one* time!"

"Four times!" Milo chimes in from the other side of the shop.

"Okay, four times, but that's in, like, all the years we've known each other!"

"Then there was that one Christmas..." Milo adds.

"Alright, alright. I get it." Griffin huffs. "So I get excited for my friends, sue me!"

"Hmm, not a bad idea."

I smile, shaking my head at them before I catch sight of the time. I grab my bag from under the counter, my stomach already tying itself in a knot at the impending quality time with Brody. Cova raises her eyebrows at me. "Hot date?"

I roll my eyes. "Not even close."

Milo appears from in between the racks of clothes and squeezes my arm gently as he passes us. "Try to have some fun, Sail." *Try* being the operative word here.

"I'm supposed to go paddleboarding with Brody," I tell Cova as we walk out of the shop together. Willing to take her mind off things the night of the festival with my own troubles, I catch her up on Brody suddenly wanting to keep me, the whiplash of his sudden urge to be active in my life, the tension between Brody and Kelly, and the obvious family secrets I'm not sure I want to know anything about.

Especially if it has to do with Brody and Mom's parents. I mean, I don't even know those people. They apparently don't want anything to do with me either. Some things are better off just never knowing, and where they're concerned, I'm okay with that. I need to be.

I can't take any more. And anyway, *what will it help to know any of it now? Mom's already gone.*

"Right," Cova says when I run out of words, her colorful ombre braids falling over her shoulders as she nods. "Well, I second Milo's encouraging words, but don't forget that Brody's ability to have any sort of relationship with you is a privilege, not a right." Her soothing tone washes over me, and my muscles loosen.

It is *a privilege.* “He’s your guardian, not your friend. You don’t have to let him in.”

My thoughts must show on my face, because Cova looks off in the distance, chuckling dryly to herself. “I know. Rich words coming from me, right?”

I shift my bag over my shoulder so I can squeeze her hand. “I’m not judging you, Cova.”

A day or two after the festival, I spotted her with Rhian. She’d frozen like a deer in headlights when she saw me. I smiled at her and went on about my day. Not once have I brought it up to her. She doesn’t need to be bombarded with questions or to feel ashamed. It’s her life to live. I can only do what I can as her friend and be there for her as she allows. Banks was right. She needs friends, good friends. I want to continue being that for her, and to her.

And when she’s ready to get out, we’ll be there to help.

“Why not?” Cova turns to look at me, a tear slipping free from one eye. “I judge me.”

I shrug. “You need someone in your corner, not pushing you into one.”

The tears come fast, rushing down her face. She wipes at them furiously. “It’ll really suck if you leave, you know.”

Yeah, I think. *It really will.*

The house greets me with complete silence when I make it back, and I find myself grateful for the space and quiet. Switching my outfit for one more suitable for the water, I start hauling out supplies for the afternoon, making trips back and forth between the beach, the shack in the backyard, and the house. Towels, a cooler full of *non*-alcoholic drinks, boards, paddles—check, check, check, and check.

All that’s missing is Brody.

I bring my hand up over my eyes, squinting. I scan the beach as if it’ll make him suddenly appear, the warmth of the sun beating down on me.

When I don’t immediately spot him, I take a seat underneath

a couple of grouped palm trees, a welcoming cover of shade. I lean back against the nearest trunk and close my eyes.

I don't mean to fall asleep, but the next thing I know, someone is shaking my shoulder.

"Sailor." I scrunch my nose, turning on my side and willing whoever it is to go away.

A hand rests against my hip, lightly rocking me back and forth. "Sail, baby, wake up."

"Lux?" I open my eyes, frowning up at him. He frowns right back from where he's squatting at my side, head cocked and brows furrowed in concern. *I don't understand, what is he doing here?*

I sit up quickly, looking up and down the beach. "Where's..." *Brody.* The clench of Lux's jaw is telling enough, and I know without him having to say it. My shoulders slump. "He forgot," I say numbly. "Didn't he?"

A muscle in Lux's jaw ticks as he nods. "Showed up at the shop to help with inventory."

Like he had nowhere else to be. Lux doesn't have to say it.

With a heavy sigh, I push to my feet. I don't know what I had been expecting. I'd thought a scheduled date in Brody's own backyard was one thing I could actually count on him showing up to. And worse, *this whole stupid thing was his idea!*

Fool me twice, right?

I did this to myself.

Unbelievable.

Lux's face fills my vision, gripping a hold of my chin between his forefinger and thumb. "Look at me," he orders, quietly but firm. "Whatever you're thinking, let it go." I try to look away but he jerks my gaze right back to his. "I mean it, Sail. Whatever's going on in that beautiful head of yours has no place there."

"You have no idea what you're talking about." I push at him, but he doesn't waver. "And you're not the boss of me."

"I know exactly what I'm talking about." I huff, a slight pout on my lips because we both know how true that is. We have too much history for him not to have an advantage. I stop short from stomping my foot at the thought. We might be childhood friends, but that doesn't mean I have to let him turn me back into acting like a little kid. I'd never hear the end of it, if I did. "As for being the boss of you..." He chuckles softly, the low timbre of his voice curling down my spine. "I don't think anyone ever could be."

"Then what do you think you're doing?" I challenge, sucking in a sharp breath when he reaches forward with his free hand to tuck a few wild curls behind my ear. His eyes search my face, all the warmth going with him as he drops his hands and turns away, towards the water. *Where is he—?* I forget my question as he bends down to pick up one of the boards and paddles, the muscles in his back rippling. *When did he ditch his shirt?*

Did he even have one on?

I feel like I would've realized he was shirtless all this time.

Man, where is my head at?

Without looking back, he calls over his shoulder. "You coming?"

I snap my mouth shut, heat warming my cheeks. Silently, I follow him down the beach. Lux sets me up with the board once we're about knee deep in the water. With a wink, he goes back for the other board and I look away.

We don't need to do this.

We should probably just put everything back.

I debate with myself, round and round, until he joins me again, paddle and board floating in the water, at his side. Silently, we rise on our boards and head out further into the waves.

With every stroke, the light bobbing of the ocean and the sun kissing my skin with its warmth, the tension unravels in my chest. Tilting my head up to the sky, I let everything go. Out here on the water, nothing can touch me. A lone tear falls down my face, but for once, it doesn't turn into a flood. Just a simple, quiet release. I smile.

Maybe I needed this after all.

Peeking over at Lux, I watch his eyes track the tear, but he says nothing. We paddle for a while before taking a break, sitting on our boards with our feet dangling in the water.

Finally, I clear my throat. "Thank you."

"You never have to thank me, Sail."

I sniff. "Well, I'm going to."

He laughs, and I stiffen as his hand ghosts across my skin in a gentle caress. Goosebumps rise in the wake of his touch, and I bat his hand away. "Whatever you want, Sail." He clears his throat, turning serious. "Look. Some people won't ever realize when they have a good thing in front of them, you know? It doesn't have anything to do with you."

I look down, the water so clear I can see the white sand at the bottom, our feet lightly kicking back and forth below us. I silently curse Brody, and myself. *I can't believe I let myself get roped into this little outing. I mean, did I really think he was going to show?* "Yeah, well," I say, with more confidence than I really feel. "His loss, I guess,"

Even as the words leave my mouth, I feel myself start dropping back into a spiral again. Because maybe it is Brody's loss, but what about me? What am *I* losing, every time I let myself believe in him again? What do I lose if I give up on him once and for all? What if—

Lux grabs a hold of my board, pulling me towards him. I squeal as I rock sideways, hand flying out to take hold of his arm to steady me. Our boards bump into one another and I worry for a split second we'll both fall off when his hand cups the side of my face and he leans in, his lips meeting mine. The kiss comes gently, with no warning, a caress of his full lips against mine, and I lean into his hand. My fingers curl tightly around his arm, trying to keep myself steady in the wake of kissing my best friend.

Wait.

I push away, sucking in a sharp breath. I feel every part of us where we touch, the sweep of his gaze along my body lighting me up. My toes curl in the water, and I don't know if I want to pull him closer or shove him further away.

What are we doing?

What is he *doing?*

Oh my gosh.

We just...He...

"You're too in your head," he growls, pulling me back towards him, and this time I let myself fall. His lips brush against mine, once, twice. Like he's trying to memorize every curve of my lips. His kiss, warm and inviting, is like the sunrises here in the Cove. A greeting. A promise.

Like I've finally come home.

I don't realize I'm crying until he pulls back, forehead resting against mine as his eyes flit across my face, worry etched into his. "What is it?" He asks, voice thick.

I scramble back, heart racing. "This was a mistake." I grapple for my paddle, hands shaking, and start back to shore. As soon as my board hits the sand, I'm off and scurrying towards the house.

I shouldn't have kissed him back.

I shouldn't have let him kiss me at all.

I don't make it but a few feet across the sand before Lux catches up to me, grabbing my arm and turning me around to face him. Cupping my face in between his hands, his thumbs gently stroke my cheeks. "Sailor, please. Talk to me."

Shaking my head, I try to grab hold of something that'll make sense. Something that I can say that won't hurt him. "We shouldn't have done that." *Well done, Sailor. Why not just rip the boy's heart out and stomp on it.*

"Why not?" When I don't immediately say anything, he tries again. "Come on. All cards on the table, remember?"

Honesty. He's asking for me to be honest with him.

That much, I can give him.

"I'm scared."

"Of what?" The floodgates are thrown open and I can't stop the tears even if I wanted to as they roll fast and hot down my face. "Sail, baby, please just talk to me."

"Kissing you..." I pull in a shaking breath. "It felt right."

His brows draw together as he tries to piece together what I'm getting at. "And that's a bad thing?"

I shake my head. That's not it at all. God, that's not it. "I don't want to lose this. Us. Whatever it is we're building here, together." With every word, they come out quieter and quieter until I'm unsure if he made out anything I just said. But his eyes soften and he moves in impossibly closer, his breath mingling with mine.

"We won't lose this."

"You can't promise that."

He thinks for a moment, and something seems to flicker in his eyes. His spine straightens as he seems to recall something. "What happened to our cards already being dealt? That, no matter what, we're not going to lose this—us? You said you weren't going to fold."

I press my lips firmly together. I did say that. The evening he found me in my room, glaring at the journal after Dani gave me an assignment to figure out what I want to do with my life. I had sworn those words to him when he voiced much of the same worries I have now, except his trigger had been my unpacked bags.

My trigger is Brody, and all this whiplash with his back and forth.

He'd been so adamant about wanting to suddenly keep me, to hang out with me. But the first chance he gets at keeping his word, he drops the ball. Just look at how fast his original plans for us derailed Summer Nights. When Brody joined the festivities down at the beach, he didn't try to hang out with me. He hardly spoke to me. Instead, he lost himself to shoving his tongue down some chick's throat and finding the bottom of every bottle that made its way into his hand. And when neither of those options were enough? He'd pull out that god forsaken cigarette pack, smoking each one all the way down to the nub before going back for another.

"Sailor." At some point, I closed my eyes. Lux's firm voice brings me back. "Look at me." I open my eyes slowly, meeting his steady gaze. "I know Brody's actions have left you feeling really vulnerable and scared. But no matter what happens next, we won't lose this. If you hold onto nothing else, hold onto that."

I hesitate and then nod.

"Promise me."

I swallow thickly. "I promise."

I can bear the weight of any pain to come for a little while longer, as long as Lux, and the others, are on the other side of it all.

I hope.

TWENTY-EIGHT

BETWEEN THE TENSION of Summer Nights and Brody blowing off our plans to paddleboard, I decided to skip on attending the support group this week. It's probably for the best. I wouldn't want to have to kick Nico in between the legs in front of Theo. I don't think I can stomach sitting across from him right now.

I just need some space.

My head is spinning with the events of the summer, and my chest has felt tight even after talking with Lux. We haven't kissed again since the other day out back on the beach. For the most part, everything has stayed the same between us.

Like now, as he sits here in my room working quietly away on his laptop while I read.

"Don't drop that!" Banks' shout rings down the hall loud and clear, cutting through the silence filling the house. Tearing my eyes from the book in hand, I cock my head, listening to the sudden rumble of activity.

"I've *got it*." Griffin shouts back. *What is going on?*

"What are they up to?" I ask, peering over at Lux. He hums but doesn't meet my curious gaze. *This must've been what all their whispering was about.* Grinning, I slip out of bed and throw on one of Lux's hoodies I've claimed. It falls to the tops of my knees, and I clench the sleeves in my hands to keep them from completely disappearing.

"Sail, wait." Lux calls, getting up from the couch, his laptop forgotten, but I ignore him. His arms wrap around my waist from behind and I squeal. "Wait!" *No way.* I grab a hold of the door frame, pulling myself forward. His fingers skim my sides, and I erupt with protests.

"Lux, no!" I giggle.

He doesn't let up, and I kick my feet furiously as they dangle in the air, trying to catch his shins. When that doesn't work, I let go of the door frame, throwing my elbow back. He drops me with a startled grunt, eyeing me as he rubs ruefully at his side. "You're a violent little thing."

Lifting my chin, I sniff, "I don't like to be tickled."

"Okay, killer."

"And don't you forget it!" Turning on the balls of my feet, I start down the hall. Lux chuckles but follows after me, his hands brushing my sides teasingly. I bat his hands away, ready to drop him to his knees if he tries any more funny business.

I stop short at the end of the hall, Lux's hands clamping down on my waist as he knocks into me. Pink and gold balloons line the hall from the door to the living room. The sliding glass doors are completely rolled open, a gold happy birthday banner hanging above the frame and more balloons tied out back. I stare.

"Is..." I swallow past the lump rising in my throat. "Is this for me?"

Breath fans my ear, and a chill rolls down my spine as Lux murmurs, "You didn't think we'd miss celebrating your birthday, did you?"

I mean...in all honesty, I haven't even thought about it. Time has blurred over the last few weeks, and I've barely even looked at a calendar. Summer Nights was the only reminder that we were already well into July, but even then, my birthday still hasn't come to mind. If it had, I still wouldn't have been able to picture *this*. With Mom gone, it's been hard to picture at all.

"So, all the secrecy..."

Lux chuckles. "Yeah, it's been a little hard to keep it under wraps. Griffin's been very excited."

"*Just* Griffin?" I raise my eyebrows at him. "You've all been so obvious that there was something going on."

"If it was so obvious, how come you never figured it out?" Banks teases as he passes by. *Touché.*

"Wait. Is this what Brody called you guys over for? At the festival?" That's when they had started acting strange.

But *Brody*? That makes no sense at all.

"Believe it or not, this was his idea." Lux gestures around us. "'A birthday party his niece won't ever forget,' I think is how he phrased it."

I didn't realize Brody even *knew* my birthday. I mean, there was that one time he showed up to the house when I turned seven, but as I got older—looking back—I realized he had no idea it was my birthday when he got there. When he gave me that money, it was the first and last time I received a gift from him.

Maybe this is Brody's way in making things up to me, for the present or the past. I've got to admit, *this is really nice.* It doesn't excuse everything else, but...it's nice.

"Oh, hey, there you two are!" Brody exclaims as he comes into the room, clapping his hands and rubbing them together. "Perfect, you got the cake—thanks, Griff."

Griffin winks at me. "Happy to."

I smile, bouncing on the balls of my feet. "Brody, this looks so great."

"Yeah?" Brody hesitates. "You think so?"

I soften, just a little. "Yeah, I do."

A huge grin pulls at his face, his bright blue eyes gleaming just like Mom's.

I wish she were here. I never thought I'd have to celebrate a birthday without her.

"Great." Brody beams at me, and for just a moment, I think that maybe, this will be okay.

"Meat is on!" Milo announces as he comes back inside. I spy Kelly out at the grill. With a squeeze to my waist, Lux steps around me and heads outside, Banks following after him. Laughter carries from out back as the two of them join Kelly.

A sudden curse makes me turn to see Griffin and Milo huddling together around the open cake box, staring down at it in wide-eyed horror. I don't think I've ever heard Milo swear. "Uh, guys? Is everything good over there?"

Milo's gaze snaps over to me, guilt written all over his face, before looking away just as quickly. Next to him, Griffin looks like a deer caught in headlights.

What is going on? Did they get the wrong cake? Maybe it's a bachelorette cake or something. I open my mouth to reassure them that they don't need to worry, but the front door opening distracts me.

"Knock, knock!" Cova calls, stepping into the room with a present in her hand. She puts the gift down and comes over to wrap me in a hug. "Hey, birthday girl!"

I hug her back. "Can you believe all of this?"

She pulls away to beam at me. "Right? I almost couldn't believe it when the guys finally told me about it."

I swallow thickly. I'm absolutely not going to cry. "Thanks for coming."

"There's nowhere else I'd want to be tonight, Sail." Her eyes narrow as she looks past me. "What's up with them?"

Looking over my shoulder, I spy Griffin talking to Lux off to the side in the backyard, hands gesturing a little wildly. Lux's body tenses, eyes glancing my way briefly before looking back at Griffin.

Something's wrong.

I shake my head, but my heart starts beating faster. "I'm not sure."

"Um, hey, Sail?" Milo steps up to my side, rubbing at the back of his neck as his eyes flit from me to Cova and back. Cova shifts to fully face her cousin, eyes narrowing as she takes him in. "Can we talk for a second? There's—"

"Ay!" Brody shouts, arms thrown out wide as he looks past us to the door. "There's the birthday girl!"

My head whips around to see Evie beaming in a cute fluffy tutu and tiara atop of her head, Hank right behind her.

My smile falls from my face, a ringing filling my ears as everything just seems to come to a screeching halt.

I must have fallen asleep. Lux and I never actually left my room, and now I'm having a nightmare.

But as Evie runs past us, throwing herself into Brody's arms with an ecstatic shriek of "*Uncle B!*", the pressure that sinks into my chest is all too familiar. I've never been more awake.

Someone tugs on my hand, but I can't move. Hell, *I can't breathe.*

Pain sears my throat. I reach for it instinctively, and nearly keel over as my fingers touch only bare skin, the absence of my necklace worse than ever, because I. Can't. Breathe. I grasp at my neck, unsure what to do. A sob tears from my lips before I can swallow it, a tremble wracking through me.

Someone cuts off my view as they step in front of me. Lux's eyes fill my vision and I suck in a sharp breath, the world rushing back like someone pressed play.

"I got you," Lux murmurs. "I got you, come on."

No. I can't. I can't lean on him. Not now. This was a mistake. Hoping was a mistake. Coming here to Siren's Cove at all *was a mistake.*

My breaths come faster. I thought I could try. I thought I could do this. I thought I could hold onto all that I have with Lux, with the others. But I can't. My hands tremble as I bring them up between us and push him back, eyes trained on the ground. "I—I need a moment. Just give me a moment."

"You won't run?" Lux's eyes are pleading with me and the weight sitting on my chest drops to my stomach.

If I were to run, now would be the time. This would be the reason, the final nail in the coffin, the bated breath I'd been holding all summer because I just knew there was another shoe to drop.

Unable to say a word, I squeeze his hand and walk away. The photos on the wall mock me as I round the corner. Funny. I'd been able to cancel out the noise these framed photos have made for me all summer. Now? They're louder than ever.

I rush down the hall to my room, closing the door as quietly as I can. Heat rolls through me, head to toe, and the moment the door meets the frame, a sob rips through me. My hands fly to my face, and I try in vain to quiet the sounds coming from my mouth. I drop to the floor, my knees biting into the wood as I keel over, a stifled scream tearing through me so hard I swear I tear something in my chest. The trembling consumes me, my shoulders shaking, and I feel like I'm going to be sick.

I thought I was stronger than this. I thought I had become stronger than this over the summer. But it's like I'm that little girl in the hallway all those years ago all over again, the pain suffocating. I'm not sure I can actually bear it, not any longer.

People have always said karma's a bitch, but I really think it's hope.

TWENTY-NINE

I DON'T KNOW how long I sit there on the floor before an eerie calm finally washes over me. I rise to my feet, taking a few steadying breaths and wiping away my tears.

When I open the bedroom door, I pause at the sight of Lux sitting in the hallway, his back pressed against the closed door to the spare room across from mine with his knees drawn to his chest. He looks up at me but remains on the floor, hands clenched into tight fists.

Music spills from down the hall, but I barely hear it over the screaming in my head. Yet, it wouldn't matter either way. The one person that I once found myself needing to listen, is never going to hear me. I know that now. *I give up.*

I've only got another week, at worst, left here and then I can argue my case to move on and be placed back in a group home, hopefully Safe Harbor. I've got to put this summer behind me, bury it so deep that it'll never have the chance of hurting me again. Just a faded memory at most. Brody originally didn't want to keep me around, and I'll make good on his wish by the time our last check-in arrives.

"Apparently, Evie's going out of town with her mom before the school year starts," Lux explains quietly. I stare at him rather blankly, like all the lights have been snuffed out within me. "So Hank and Brody thought it'd be a good idea to throw her a birthday party a week early before she leaves."

I honestly couldn't care. Throw her a birthday, don't throw her one—whatever. It's not them throwing her a party that bothers me, oddly enough. It's the fact that Brody not only clearly forgot my birthday, but that he's throwing Evie an early party on my *actual* birthday.

I nod at Lux to let him know I hear him, but say nothing as I start down the hall.

"Where are you going?" Lux calls, scrambling to his feet to follow me. "Sailor, you don't have to go back out there."

Stopping abruptly, I turn to him. "I know."

But misery loves company, right? If nothing else, Brody and I can keep making each other miserable in the time we've got left.

Lux searches my face, for what I can't be sure. "Sailor."

"I need to do this." As much as I want to forget, I need to remember this moment, or at least the feeling. Then I'll have learned. I'll know better than to let anyone in, to let them close.

"I don't think—"

I turn away from Lux before he can finish his sentence, and head back out to the party. It's in full swing, the guys playing with Evie while Brody and Hank both nurse bottles of beer. Kelly remains out at the grill, but I can read the tension lining his frame.

Great, maybe he'll decide to have another *conversation with Brody to rip him a new one. I can't wait to accidentally overhear that one too!*

Cova's the first one to spot me, face stricken with concern. I ignore it—the worried glances, the whispered attempts to check in as I walk by. I hardly feel the brush of hands as I tune out the world. Instead, I let Evie rush delightedly into my arms, plastering on a smile and settling in to play into her every whim.

At least one of us should have a decent birthday. So far, hers is looking pretty great.

As someone who's been on the wrong end of a birthday

where she's let down, I don't wish that upon her or anyone else. Evie adores Brody, for whatever reason. As long as he continues showing up for her, I'll play my part in this little charade until I'm no longer needed.

"And, and, and then Benny pulled my hair," Evie finishes telling me with a deep breath.

I swear she didn't take a single one while she explained her playdate with the kids across the street from Hank's place earlier. I nod, though I barely heard half of what she said. "Wow," I manage.

Banks comes to the rescue, holding up a balled-up fist. "Did you give him one of these?"

Evie scrunches her nose at him. "One of what?"

Banks huffs, like he can't believe she doesn't know. "A knuckle sandwich!"

"No!" Evie giggles, shaking her head back and forth. Pushing up in my lap, Evie holds her head high, grinning. "I pushed him into the mud."

"Attagirl!" Griffin holds out his fist, and she bumps it with her own. Despite myself, I laugh.

"Alright," Brody announces. He stumbles a little as he gets to his feet, and I eye the beer in his hand. "I think it's time for cake and presents."

Evie claps her hands excitedly, and I help her to her feet. She shoots off like a rocket across the room and I follow after her, only for Brody to stop me.

"Hey, Sail?" I take a step back, cringing at the alcohol on his breath as it washes over my face. "I forgot a present in my bedroom, will you grab it?"

If it means getting away from you, sure.

Giving a curt nod, I leave the room, trying to shake off the weight of too many eyes following after me. *They just need to leave it alone.*

To leave *me* alone.

I push Brody's bedroom door open a little too hard, the knob smacking the wall with a resounding thud, bouncing off and coming back my way. I stop it with a raised arm, eyes skimming the room. A gift bag filled to the brim with rainbow tissue paper lies haphazardly on the floor in front of his bedside table, like it had been knocked over. *Or totally forgotten*. What a shock. I roll my eyes as I cross the room and kneel down to pick it up.

Only to stop short at the sight of Mom.

I almost don't recognize her in the framed photo sitting next to Brody's bed. In the picture, she's a younger, healthier version of herself, and next to her, curled up into her side, is a Brody who can't be much older than Evie is now. He looks so tiny the way he's tucked against her, his arms wrapped around one of hers as she holds a book out in front of them. But instead of taking in the story she's obviously reading, Brody's chin digs into her arm as he gazes up at her, looking like she hung the moon.

A tear slips down my cheek. Was this what Mom saw, when she looked at him? The kid she used to read to? The little boy she all but raised, until she had to raise me instead?

A sticky note rests in the corner of the frame and I squint to read it.

I'm sorry. -Dad

Their dad?

Sorry about what?

Paper crinkles underneath my foot and I tear my gaze away from the frame. Grabbing the corner of Brody's bedsheet where it hangs to the floor, I lift it up and peek under the bed to make sure nothing fell out of the gift bag.

Instead, a weathered shoebox catches my eye. I reach for it before it fully registers what I'm doing.

There's a light knock on the door. "Sail..." Lux's words die on his lips.

I don't look at him, keeping my eyes firmly on the box in my hands. "Will you take the present out? I'll be right there." He doesn't move. "Please."

Every footstep matches the heavy thudding of my heart, and I swallow thickly, bracing myself. He presses a kiss to the side of my head, a light tug in my chest letting me know I'm still very much alive—that I can feel.

Then he's gone, the door clicking quietly shut again behind him. Only once I can no longer make out his steps do I open the box. Inside, a stack of letters and photos lies in disarray. One letter in particular catches my eye, Mom's name scrawled across the envelope, our address written below. There's no postage stamp in the left-hand corner.

With trembling hands, I open it up and begin to read, my stomach sinking with every word.

THE WAVES BREAKING across the shore lull me into a false sense of peace. Dropping the now empty beer bottle at my side, I hiccup as I throw myself back into the sand. The wooden boards of the pier block my view of the night sky and I frown. *I should have chosen the sky.*

But would the sky choose me? I giggle to myself, tears skimming the sides of my face and running into my hair. It kind of tickles.

"SAILOR?"

"SAILOR!"

I squint up at the underside of the pier. *Who's yelling?* They're kind of ruining my mood. *Rude.* The voices get louder, and someone curses. *Oooh, that does not sound nice.* I giggle to myself again. They should be put in time out.

You know who else should be in time out? Brody. The smile falls from my face, tears completely obscuring my view. Yeah, he deserves a time out for *sure*.

"Sailor?" The voice is much closer now, and then someone sucks in a startled breath. "Guys, I've got her! She's over here!"

A face appears above me, and I swipe at my tears until I can make out who it is. "M-Milo?" I hiccup, tilting my head as I try to take him in upside down.

"Hey, Sail." He crouches down, greeting gently. "Whatcha doin out here?"

"Umm..."

What *am* I doing? Wiping the last of my tears, my hand flops down at my side, bumping the shoebox and I flinch at the jolting reminder. I push myself upright, then almost topple back over again, my head swimming.

"Woah there." Milo reaches for me, arm coming around my back. "Here, let me help."

"*Thank God*," someone breathes in relief from somewhere behind us.

Someone drops down in front of me, and I find myself pulled into a tight hug. I barely have time to inhale the familiar scent of spiced cologne before Lux is pulling away, staring at me with those storm-filled eyes. His face is strained as he takes me in, eyes dropping to the stuff at my side before looking back at me. Gripping my chin with trembling fingers, Lux says, "Do you have any idea how scared we were when we realized you were gone?"

He's not really asking, so I don't bother answering.

After reading the letter Brody wrote to Mom and clearly never sent, I'd dropped it back in the box and scooped the whole thing up, swiping a six-pack of beer on my way out. Brody uses it all the time to cope, so why can't I. Maybe stick my head in the sand, just the same too. Then maybe it all wouldn't hurt so much.

With no real destination in mind, I started walking. I needed to get away. I needed to breathe, because after reading that letter, and all the others buried at the bottom of the box, I haven't been able to.

It doesn't seem like Lux has been able to either, if the heavy rise and fall of his chest is anything to go by. Tears fill his eyes, the pain written all over his face and I swallow thickly. *I did this to him*. He's scared because of me.

Lux shakes his head. "No. No, Sailor, I'm scared *for* you."

Oh, did I say that out loud?

I pull away from him and his jaw clenches in response. See, this is why you can't let anyone in. It hurts too much. You can't predict what they'll do, what they'll say. Except that Lux must've known. It was clear in the way he watched me so closely as the night wore on, the way he held me just a little tighter any chance he got, the way he questioned me coming back. I've been so worried about trusting others that I've never really taken the time to think about what it could mean for others to put their trust in me.

I promised him...

I wasn't supposed to run.

I broke my promise.

I messed up.

The next time Lux speaks, his voice is gentle. "Can you tell me what happened?"

I don't know if I can. A sob rips out of me, and I grab at my neck. Lux's eyes soften as he realizes what I was reaching for. But my necklace is still gone. Just like any semblance of peace I thought I was finding this summer, with Lux, with the others.

God I'm ready to leave this town. Even as I think it, I feel nauseous at the thought—or maybe that's the beer.

"Sailor?" Cova crouches beside Lux, her eyes searching my face. "What is it?" I look down at the box, and she follows my gaze. "What's all this?"

"Brody's secrets," I whisper. Who knew a man so dense could be carrying wounds this deep? I don't know if that surprises me more than what I read.

A hand grabs mine, holding it firmly in theirs, and my eyes trail up to find the mischief gone from Griffin's eyes. *He looks so sad.* "Whatever it is, Sail, it's okay. We'll face it together."

Tears fall down my face at Griffin's assurance. With his free hand, he reaches up, gently wiping away the tears. I close my eyes, unable to face his kindness. *I don't deserve it.*

I don't deserve them.

"Brody has a daughter." The words rush out of me so fast, I'm not sure if they're able to decipher what I actually said.

Griffin's thumb pauses on my face. "He has a *what*?"

I open my eyes to find all of theirs wide, mouths open. Finally, from behind Griffin, Banks gestures gruffly to the box. "Can I see?"

I shrug, since it's not like it really matters anymore. They all gather around Banks as he opens the box. Lux remains in front of me, eyes intent as he watches me closely, like he knows I've shut down.

I may not have run from Siren's Cove, but the distance has never felt greater.

It's better this way.

I can't stay here.

I think I'm going to be sick.

Banks lets out a low whistle, holding one of the photos up of a young, brown-haired girl with bright blue eyes. Other than her coloring, nothing in her features truly stood out to me when I stared at her, nothing recognizable that would scream she's a Lehmann. I'm sure at first glance, many would say the same about me.

But what do I know? Maybe she favors her mom's side.

"Brody's never mentioned her," Banks says at last.

I shrug my shoulders. "He's never really mentioned me either, right?" They only knew what they did about me because of Lux and Kelly.

I take a breath. "That's not all." I look past Lux, out at the dark water. "There's letters. From their dad. My grandfather." The sudden darkness in my tone must be obvious, because everyone pauses. But rather than digging for the letters, they all seem to brace themselves, some sitting, others remaining on their feet.

"What did they say?" Cova asks at last.

"They're filled with apologies." I laugh to myself, but I don't really feel it. I grab blindly for another beer, to chuck out into the water or down in a few gulps, I'm not sure. Tatted hands appear in front of me, and gently pry the bottle away. My shoulders sag in defeat. "Apparently their dad is sorry for not believing my mom when she accused a friend of the family of raping her. And for how he turned his back on her when she got knocked up later on. Not because it was out of wedlock—god forbid—but because the child she was carrying was half Black."

I shake my head, immediately regretting it as everything blurs around me, my stomach churning. I don't know if it's from the alcohol or the grief, but it's not like it matters. I close my eyes and continue, "He said he carried too much of the ways he was raised to recognize how *ignorant* it was of him to shun his only daughter. Oh, and he regrets not being there for my mom when she took her final breath, which is more than what his own son can say."

Even with all he wrote, all he claimed to be sorry for, there was still nothing about regretting not being there *for me*. Even with recognizing his own prejudices, it ran too deep in that man for him to shake.

Cutting ties with her family was probably the best thing Mom ever did for us.

"Sailor." Cova's hands curl gently around mine. I can hear the pain in her voice, like she feels my pain as her own. My eyes flutter open, finding tears tracking down her face. "I'm so sorry."

"*What do I do with this?*" I whisper, pain searing my throat.

"What do you *want* to do?" Milo asks gently.

My eyes drop down to the still open box, the little girl smiling up at me in one of the photos. Somewhere out there is a little girl, probably missing the man in her life that's meant to be there to protect her, play with her, watch her grow. Who she's meant to laugh with, and run to when things get hard. Who's supposed to hold her up when her world feels like it's falling apart. Who's meant to love her unconditionally and make sure she *feels every ounce* of that love, every day of her life.

And instead, she's just a picture in a box.

Heat rolls through me, igniting into an inferno that flares across my skin, the flush spreading fast head to toe. Releasing a deep shaky breath I announce, "I need to talk to Brody."

To face the music and finally put this chapter with him to rest. Because Cova was right. Having a relationship with someone is a privilege, not a right.

And he has none.

"Okay." Milo exchanges a look with Cova, but he doesn't try to talk me out of it. "But in the morning, okay? Let's get you to bed so you can sleep tonight off and tackle the problem with a clear head tomorrow."

Sleeping tonight off might be good. But a clear head to face tomorrow? Not likely.

Griffin squeezes my hand gently. "What do you say, Sail?"

I nod my head and Lux rises to his feet, helping me up. I stumble a little but stay upright, watching as the others collect my things. I really didn't bring much with me, just the shoebox and the drinks.

"I'll get rid of these." Banks slides the empty bottles back into the pack and starts for the parking lot, the others falling into step beside him.

Before they make it out of earshot, I call out to them, "Thanks for looking for me."

They stop almost as one, looking back at me. There's a moment of silence, stretching out across the sand, before Griffin speaks.

"We'll always look for you, Sailor."

His words flicker inside me, the faintest lick of warmth, but I can hardly feel it with the ice coating my veins.

THIRTY

I SIT at the edge of my bed, my fingernails biting into the palms of my hands as I hold the shoebox close to my chest and try to make myself move.

When Priya first drove me into Siren's Cove at the beginning of the summer, I thought my biggest problem would be simply surviving a couple of months with Brody while I drowned in grief, counting down the days until Priya would come to retrieve me once she and Dani realized this wasn't going to work out long term.

Instead, I found friends I wasn't looking to make, faced off with a best friend I thought had abandoned me for good, and was willing to try *one last time* with an uncle I thought I'd given up all effort in fighting for when it was clear he'd never fight for me.

But everything I thought I could bury and move on from with some time and distance has surged from the darkest depths of my memories with a rage I can no longer swallow. It took a lot of convincing to have the guys leave me to face this on my own.

This fight with Brody is mine—no one else's.

As a little girl, I never had all of the right words to say, but even with the ones I used, that had never been enough for him.

I've never been enough for him.

But I think I see it now. Everything Cova and the guys have been trying to tell me all summer. That I'm worth more than the amount I've summed myself up to be after all these years I've fought for Brody's time and attention. He's just never been able to see my worth.

And that's on him.

Releasing a deep breath, I tighten my grip on the box. *I can do this.* Lifting my chin high, I leave the bedroom, following the sound of rummaging out to the kitchen.

I find Brody with his back to me as he digs through the refrigerator. "Hey," he says, without looking up. "Did you guys get into some beer last night? I could have sworn we had another six pack in here."

I stop short at the question, my hands shaking. *Unbelievable.* Of all the things...

"That's what you notice?"

Brody stops rifling through the fridge, straightening up at the tone of my voice as he turns to face me. His eyes search my face before falling to the shoebox in my white knuckled grip. The color drains from his face.

Shakily, I place it on the counter, watching him as I do. He licks his lips but doesn't say a word.

Choosing the bigger fight, I ask what I really want to know. "Is she yours?"

"Look, I don't know what you saw—"

"Is she yours?" I ask a little louder over his quick scramble of excuses. *It's always an excuse—always.*

"I haven't seen the woman in years—" He pushes on like I haven't spoken. *What else is new?* He never could hear me. No, he's always chosen *not* to hear me. A choice he's made time and time again. I've never been more certain than I am right now.

Raising my voice over his explanation I could care less for, I ask again. "Is she yours?"

"She just she started sending me these letters and pictures, as if—"

"*Brody*!" I shout, because I just can't hear one more lie out of his mouth. *Enough is enough.* I can't take another second of it. "Is. She. *Yours?*"

He swallows thickly, unable to meet my eyes. Staring at the box, he admits, his voice barely more than a whisper, "I don't know."

"You don't know, or you don't *want* to know?"

He rubs at the back of his neck with a shrug before scooping up a pack of cigarettes on the counter, tapping the corner against the palm of his other hand. "Does it matter?" *Tap, tap, tap.*

The question comes out so soft, so unsure, that I almost think I make it up—that I can't be hearing him correctly.

"Does it—?" All I see is red as heat erupts through me. I swipe out, knocking the box to the floor, the contents spilling at our feet and he stops all movement, eyes wide. "Of course it *matters*!" I scream. "*All of it matters, Brody!*"

The words start pouring from my mouth, my heart bleeding right before him. "What is it about this girl—about *me*—that you just can't seem to care enough about? I mean, *my God*, your selfishness knows no bounds."

He stumbles back against the fridge, as if it'll hold him up as I bring his world to a screeching halt. Snatching up one of the photos, I slap it down on the counter before him. "Here is another moment in your life, where someone is trying to get your attention and you decide, what? To turn the other way? You can't keep running away from every problem in your life and go on to act like nothing's happened!"

"I don't know what you mean. That's not—" he starts, but I cut him off, slapping my hand down on the counter again when all I really want to do is hit him.

"STOP LYING!" Pain tears through my chest as it becomes harder to breathe, everything I couldn't release when I was seven and ten and thirteen boiling out of me all at once. "It's the truth and you know it. You act like you don't have a clue what's going on around you even when it's right in your face. Then you act shocked—asking questions you already have the answers to."

Brody swallows thickly. "Sailor."

"Why don't I matter to you?" Tears spill hot and fast down my face as I stare at him, waiting for answers I'm certain I'll never actually receive.

Brody's mouth opens, but nothing comes out.

"Did you even know yesterday was my birthday?" I ask, a lot quieter now. I'm too tired to yell anymore. It's not like it makes a difference. "Not like you've ever remembered any of them, of course, but you know, seeing as how I'm living under your roof now I was just curious if maybe Priya or Dani relayed that to you since you're suddenly so adamant in wanting to keep me. Or has that changed—what with it being a new week and all?"

Needing to push his buttons—to get *some* sort of reaction from him—I continue, "Have you even realized that you bailed on plans *you made* with me the other day?"

"I...shit." He rubs at the back of his neck. "Sailor—"

"But it doesn't matter, right?" I whisper. "I don't matter. Not to you, anyways. You could never choose me back then, and when it comes down to it, you can't choose me now."

"It wasn't—"

"You're so far gone with the drinking, the smoking, the women, that you can't lift your head up long enough to see what you're doing to the people around you. What you're doing *to me.* " I hold his gaze even though it nearly brings me to my knees as I admit, "I'm done, Brody. I can't continue letting you hurt me. You and me? We're finished."

I turn on my heels and head for my room, only stopping when his footsteps close in behind me. Despite everything, I feel one wild, irrational surge of hope. *Maybe he isn't finished talking. Maybe he wants to fight this out—to understand. To fight for me. For us.*

I hold my breath.

But the front door opens and closes quietly, a resounding echo in the house.

And I'm alone.

I thought I knew rage, but this one sweeps through me with a vengeance so potent I choke on it. Deep filled sobs rack through me, and my throat burns as I scream. My eyes find the photo frame I broke earlier this summer and I tear it off the wall. Chest heaving, I reach for another frame, and another, hurling them down the hall. Glass shatters across the wood floors, frames breaking in a multitude of pieces. Blood drips from my hands as I tear at the memories, but there's not a single cut that runs as deep and painful as the ones Brody has carved across my heart.

I did everything. I've laid myself out to him. I've spoken my truth. I've tried with him even after I swore I'd never do that again. And. It's. Still. Not. Enough. *I'll never be enough.* Not then. Not even now.

My hand sweeps the wall for another frame through my tear-filled haze as I continue to sob, only to come up empty. Swallowing past the immense strain in my throat, I wipe at my tears until I can see the wall before me, now as bare and empty as I feel. Broken glass bites into my skin as I drop to my knees, my eyes glazing over.

I wonder if Brody will try to ignore this too.

WHEN SHADOWS BEGIN to stretch across the bare wall, I slowly rise from the floor. Photos lay torn from their frames, glass covering every ounce of the hall. I leave the mess, stumbling further down the hall to the bathroom, the light clicking on automatically. I grip the sink, dried blood caked across my skin. Raising my hands up to my face, I blink until my reflection comes into focus in the mirror. There's blood smeared across my face, my eyes bloodshot and nose red from crying. My bun has fallen sideways atop of my head, curls escaping in disarray.

I turn away, unable to bear my reflection. Breathing fast, I push out of the bathroom and head for my room.

Whatever I promised, it doesn't matter. *I should just grab my things and go.*

I start for my bags when a little pile of presents catch my attention. It hits me, suddenly, that most of the people at the party last night thought we were celebrating *my* birthday. I hesitate, for only a second, between grabbing my things and heading out the door—or taking a seat, and letting myself see what the people who *do* care about me wanted me to have.

I take a seat.

The first gift I reach for is heavy, and my brow furrows as I lift the box. Trying to forget what happened with the last box I opened, I hold my breath and peel off the lid. Inside is something flat and rectangular, wrapped in white tissue paper with a little card sitting on top. I pick up the card, my eyes scanning Cova's familiar handwriting.

> Sailor—
>
> You might've not wanted any friends, but we sure found one in you.
>
> Thanks for a summer full of unforgettable memories.

Tears swim in my eyes as I place the card aside and unwrap the tissue paper to find a scrapbook nestled inside. I pull it out of the box with shaking hands and open it to the first page, my breath hitching at the sight of a group selfie. I only vaguely remember taking it, the guys corralling Cova and I into a photo that first day we went to the beach. Cova was so annoyed with the guys—they'd been a sweaty mess from tossing around a football earlier that morning, all covered in sand from roughhousing. Banks "made it up to her" by tossing her over his shoulder, and dunking them both in the ocean as he washed off so as not to "offend her." Of course, that only sparked a water fight between the two that seemed to call to the others, and before I knew it, Griffin was ushering me into the water to fight at his side.

Despite everything, I smile softly at the memory. It was a pretty good day.

Turning to the next page, then the next, it's an onslaught of memories—many I had no idea were being captured. But here they are anyway, page after page of laughter and sunlight and friendship, with little trinkets glued down and notes taped in from the guys and Cova. I trace a fingertip over a photo of me laughing, the image blurring as my eyes somehow manage to fill with tears once more.

I look happy.

I swallow with the realization. When I'm with the others, I *am* happy. I've shedded so much of the pain and anger I brought with me into Siren's Cove over the past few weeks. But then I stumbled across Brody's secrets and I was yanked right back to being a person I know for sure I don't want to be.

I don't want to carry that weight anymore.

I want to be happy.

Closing the book, I bring it to my chest, holding it tightly as I wipe at the silent tears rolling down my face—a complete juxtaposition to the screaming sobs from earlier. Was it only just hours ago that I tore into Brody before destroying the wall?

The wall.

Something tightens in my chest.

Those aren't just Brody's memories. They're Kelly's and Lux's and Banks and Griffin's and Milo's, too.

What have I done?

With one last glance at my bags, I rise to my feet. I can't fix everything, but I can at least go find a broom. I start up the hall only to stop short at the sight of Lux at the other end, the destruction of my pain laid out before him. I watch him with bated breath as his eyes sweep across the mess before rising up to meet my weary gaze.

"Lux." I whisper, my voice raw. He immediately closes the space between us, glass crunching under his shoes, and cups my face.

"You're bleeding."

Maybe on the inside, but on the outside... "Not anymore."

He shakes his head, refusing to accept it. "Come on," he orders, going to grab my hand before realizing I'm holding tight to the scrapbook. His eyes shoot back up to mine and they soften.

"I love it," I admit quietly.

Tapping at the middle of my chest with a finger, he swallows thickly. "Hold onto that feeling, always."

My bottom lip wobbles. *I don't know if I can.*

As if reading the struggle across my face, he gathers me in his arms, holding me close. It's in the warmth of his arms that the tension slowly bleeds from me, and I sink into him.

THIRTY-ONE

THREE WEEKS LATER

"BRODY, IT'S KELLY." *Again.* "We're worried about you, man. I need you to call me back."

I hover at the sliding glass doors leading out to the back porch, shoulders hunched as Kelly paces back and forth outside, his phone gripped tightly in his hand.

Kelly, the guys, Dani—they've all been trying to get a hold of Brody for two weeks. When I didn't show for group night at the center, Dani decided to pay a visit to the house. Of course she chose to make her appearance as Lux and I were in the middle of cleaning up the hallway.

Greeting your caseworker at the door, all cut up and emotionally drained does not bode well, especially when that caseworker is Dani Marshall. She threatened Kelly with my immediate removal from the home, demanding that Brody return to the house to face his own consequences. But as every call went unanswered and every text unread, even my anger was eventually replaced with concern.

Did something happen to him?

Did he do something?

The thought of Brody harming himself, beyond his typical

drinking and smoking, had never crossed my mind before. But if I've had my own thoughts in the past, why wouldn't he?

I'd told Brody that we were done, but I didn't mean it like this. *God, please don't let it be like this.*

Kelly comes to an eerie stop in his pacing at the weight of my eyes, and he musters what he probably hopes is a reassuring expression. "We'll find him." In what state, who knows, but I have no doubt Kelly will move mountains to make sure Brody's found. As complicated as their relationship is, I know he loves Brody as much as Mom did. Like his own little brother. "I put some feelers out with my army buddies."

"What if we don't find him? At least, to deal with DCF?" My stay has already been extended by two weeks. Decisions of my immediate future pending as we try to track down a man I could just see taking off long enough to not have to deal with me, then returning like nothing happened. It'd be a great way for him to clean his hands of me without ever having to get them dirty.

But he wanted me, at least for a little while. *Didn't he?*

That question is something I still can't quite answer.

Hell, almost everything involving Brody is confusing and hard to swallow. I've been contemplating asking Priya for help in setting me up with one of those online therapists. Since the incident in the kitchen and my meltdown that followed, I haven't been doing so well. Lux, of course, has noticed and has been keeping closer to me than usual. So I can't keep a meal down—sue me. I've nibbled here and there.

"We'll find him," Kelly insists.

"But if we don't..." I step outside, determined to face my possible impending reality. "They'll place me back in the group home." Whether it's one here or back in South Carolina, I don't know. Summer is wrapping up, school will be starting soon.

"Would you want that?" Kelly asks quietly.

I swallow thickly. "No. Not anymore."

I want to stay. To live here, with my friends, with Lux.

He puts a hand on my shoulder. "We'll figure it out, Sailor."

I take a deep breath. It's just the two of us. I might as well ask the question that's been weighing on me for so long. "Kelly, why did Mom choose Brody to look after me?"

Why didn't she just choose you?

Kelly sighs, taking a seat on the steps. I sit beside him and wait. "Your mom figured that when the time came, you two would need each other. She hoped that Brody would get his head on straight, especially where you're concerned. It'd give him a chance to make up for all his past mistakes. And for you? Well, Brody's all the family you have left, at least by blood. She wanted you to always have a piece of her." He takes a slow breath, and lets it out even more slowly. I wonder if he hears Mom's voice in his head, too. *Don't forget to breathe.* "Even at the end, she never gave up on him. I don't think she ever could."

I wipe my eyes before any tears can fall. "I miss her so much."

He puts an arm around me. "I do, too." I rest my head on his shoulder, my eyes only just closing when Hank's voice suddenly fills the backyard.

"Hey, Kelly. Sailor."

I sit up, watching from under hooded lids as he makes his way from around the side of the house, stopping in front of us. He shifts from one foot to the other, rubbing his hands across his shorts. Kelly tenses underneath me.

"You know where Brody is." It isn't a question.

Hank sighs. "Yeah. Yeah, I know where Brody is." He pulls something from his back pocket, holding it out to me. It's an envelope with my name messily scrawled across the front. "Sailor, this is for you."

I take it from him, gripping it tightly as I stare unseeingly across the backyard. "He's gone, isn't he?" I know it with every fiber of my being. *Where could he have gone? This is his home.*

"For now, yeah," Hank admits. I feel sick. When he speaks again, it's in a voice I've only ever heard when he's talking to Evie. Calm. Quiet. Almost kind. "You should really read the letter."

Right. Okay.

With a shaking breath, I open the envelope, pulling out the folded up letter. *God, I'm sick of letters.* If the ones I've come across so far regarding the Lehmanns are anything to go by, this can't possibly be any better. My hands tremble slightly as I unfold it, but I make myself read.

Sailor,

I don't know where to start, but I'll try my best. You're probably wondering what my best even looks like and I got to be honest here, kid, so do I.

I messed up. With you. Your mom. With everything.

She was relying on me to step up and take care of you, and I failed. I realized it that day in the kitchen AND over the course of the summer. So many of the things you said—your honesty. I didn't know how to handle it. I didn't know how to handle you.

I've never had anyone need me the way you've needed me.

And when you landed on my doorstep, it hit me. Not just how much you look and act like your mom, though I'll admit that was hard enough, but...all I could suddenly see was the little girl you once were, begging me not to go. Do you remember that night? Of course you do. I'm sure you do. Anyways, I kind of hoped that if I acted like everything was okay, then we'd be okay. Leave the past behind us.

But I think the past haunts the both of us.

The little girl isn't mine, by the way. I reached out to her mom, took a DNA test. It came back negative. I couldn't understand why it upset you so much, why you'd care. Maybe we could talk about it? If you'd want. I know you probably have a lot to say, and I want to listen. Or maybe, now after everything, you've got nothing left to say to me. I think that scares me most of all. Here I spent all this time pushing you away that I've probably done it for good.

I need you to know that I love you. I've had a funny way of showing it, and the thought that you've never felt loved by me at all, well, shit, Sailor, THAT is what I'm sorry for most of all.

I've checked myself into a nearby rehab center. There's some things I've never dealt with—that I don't know how to. I'm hoping this place will help. Lux told me how you tried taking a page out of my book the night of Evie's party and I can't have that for you. I'd never forgive myself if you head down that road, Sailor.

I've never been really good at keeping any promises to you, or myself for that matter, but this time, I swear—I'm going to clean myself up, figure my crap out, and if you're willing, I'd like to work on our relationship. I don't know how long I'll be gone for, but by the time you read this, I'll have hopefully worked something out with Dani so you can remain there at the house. Stay here in Siren's Cove. You should enjoy your senior year with the people who really care for you.

Take care of yourself.

-Brody

I STARE DOWN at the letter, vision slightly blurred as the tears fall down my face, my chest rapidly rising and falling. God I want to believe him—to believe *in* him. But...

"I dropped him off at the center myself," Hank explains quietly. I turn to face him and Kelly, who watches me with concern. "He told me not to give you the letter until he'd made it at least two weeks into the program. I think he wanted to prove he was serious about his decision." *Only time will tell, right?* Actions always speak louder than words—especially where Brody is concerned. I don't know if I can hold my breath on this one.

"He also wanted me to give you this—says he's sorry he couldn't be the one to give it to you himself." Hank digs in his pocket, retrieving a small black pouch. I plant my feet firmly where I stand, nauseous at the idea that there could possibly be one more thing to handle. When I can't get my feet to move, Hank closes the distance between us and carefully drops the pouch in my hands.

Pulling open the drawstring, I tip the bag into my palm.

The cold bite of the chain nearly makes me crumble.

My necklace. He fixed my necklace.

I hold it up in the light, the siren's tail dangling from one end, and can't help but smile. I bring it to my chest, holding it close, and my eyes fall back to the letter.

Maybe there's hope yet.

AS IT TURNS OUT, Dani met with Brody, and I'm now in Kelly's informal kinship care. It's a temporary arrangement, involving a lot of paperwork and more frequent visits from Dani while Kelly works on getting licensed as a foster care provider, but it means that if rehab doesn't stick and Brody goes back on his word, I still have a place to stay.

Permanently.

Kelly stepping up soothes the tension that's lined my body with all of Brody's back and forth. I have a real shot, a second chance, at calling somewhere home for good. I never thought it would be Siren's Cove, but life has a way of surprising you.

"You once told me that there'll be people who'll fight for you and others who won't," I say to Kelly long after Hank left, the two men exchanging a gruff handshake and Hank leaving me with a gentle pat on my shoulder. Coming out of the day with less resentment for *Hank* of all people was not on my bingo card. "But there's one thing I don't think either of us have really considered."

Kelly looks up at me from where he's stirring something on the stove for dinner. "What's that?"

"Sometimes the people who don't fight for you could simply be because they don't know *how* to, not because they don't want to."

It's something I'd been thinking about ever since I read Brody's letter. From what I've seen of Brody, the pieces of his childhood I've put together, I don't think he ever had someone demonstrate to him all that he could be. Mom was the closest thing he had, but after she left, there was no one there to believe in him. He's a prime example of how one can't possibly know how to show up for others when no one has shown up for him. The alcohol, the cigarettes, the women, the permanent frat guy persona—all of it was just him trying to feel wanted. To feel good.

If I hadn't had Priya in my corner from the moment Mom got sick, or I'd tried to get through this summer without Dani or Cova or the guys or Lux, what kind of vices might I have turned to?

Kelly smiles softly at me like he could read my thoughts. "You're pretty bright for a girl who only just turned seventeen."

I shrug. "Mom always did call me an old soul."

"Yeah." Kelly meets my gaze, his eyes warm. "Your Mom did tend to be right."

Kelly's been opening up about Mom in the last few days, sharing his fondest memories from their past. It's nice to hear someone other than myself talk about her. It reminds me that I'm not the only one who remembers her, that knows her life mattered. And in telling the stories, I feel all the more closer to her. Like I'm standing next to the sun.

Priya comes to visit, too, just like she promised she would at the beginning of the summer. It's sort of surreal, seeing her. The girl she meets when she comes through the door of Top Fin isn't anything like the girl she'd left here back in June. Seeing me among the brightly-colored racks of surf gear, smiling and laughing with my friends, seems to ease something in Priya, and her smiles come more and more easily over the course of the afternoon.

Before she leaves, I ask her about finally getting connected with an online therapist and my first session is scheduled for next week. Until then, I've been putting the journal Priya gave me to good use.

Any time I've had it open, head buried in the pages and pen scrawling across the lines, I can feel the guys watching. I've smiled to myself on more than one occasion at Griffin's incessant need to ask what I'm writing, only to be deterred by the others cuffing the back of his head in warning.

Some of them try to act more nonchalant about it, but as the summer winds down, I know it's starting to wear on them as to what's next for me.

Like right now.

Cova and the guys are spread out across the backyard for a game night. Lux sits stiffly on the porch steps, his hands flexing open and closed, the strain of his knuckles clear from just inside the house. Banks glances at him every so often, pausing in tapping away at his phone before returning to the screen. Griffin and Milo attempt to play a round of cornhole they pulled out from the shed, and Cova's tucked away at the table, her face in a book, but I've yet to see her actually turn the page.

Slipping outside, I wander over to Lux and sit at his side. I pull out my journal, opening it to the first page and handing it over to him. He sucks in a sharp breath and any pretense of the others keeping it cool go right out the window.

"What? What is it?" Griffin throws down the bags in his hand, eating up the distance between us in a few quick strides.

Lux turns the journal around so the others can read what I wrote at the top of the page. They crowd together, smiles ripping across their faces as they read—

> *Register for classes at Siren's High*
> *Prom with Lux ?*
> *Grad bash with Cova, Griffin, Milo, and Lux*

"I, um." I clear my throat. "I was wondering if you guys could help me pick out my classes for our senior year."

My words break them out of their trance and a cacophony of noise erupts from them, so loud and full of joy that I startle in surprise.

Griffin sweeps me up into his arms before anyone else can snag me, my feet dangling off the ground as he spins me around, and my head falls back as laughter spills from my lips. I grip his shoulders, shrieking at him not to let me fall, but just like with whatever lays ahead of us, I know he's got me.

"I knew you couldn't live without me!" Griffin's smile lights up his face. Smacking a kiss on my cheek, he gently puts me down. "It's okay. I wouldn't be able to live without you too, snickerdoodle."

I return the kiss and he pretends to swoon into Milo's waiting arms. "You got me there, muffin."

"Group hug!" Cova shouts.

Arms come around me from all sides, the warmth easing the last of any tension I carried this summer.

"Oh, this is going to be epic!" Griffin exclaims from somewhere in the middle of the pile, sounding slightly smushed, like his face is half-buried in someone's—Arm? Shoulder? From the muffled *oof*, I think Cova's received the brunt end of his excitement. Ideas for the upcoming year start pouring from his lips faster than any of us can keep up with until Banks cuts him off.

"Griff. Take a breath man. You're gonna pass out."

I giggle, automatically curling my hand around the much larger and tatted one that takes hold of mine. A flutter stirs in my stomach as I peer up at Lux, who's found his way through the clump of limbs to my side, his dimples making a rare appearance and I glimpse the little boy I've always adored.

Brody was right to say that I've never felt loved by him, but here with these guys, and Cova, they make up for everything I had been missing—everything I was so sure I didn't need.

I've never been so happy to be wrong.

With a gentle squeeze to Lux's hand as he holds tight to mine, I lean into him and remember to breathe.

ACKNOWLEDGMENTS

This book was forged by heartache, female rage, and a cataclysmic moment that pushed me completely over the edge. These experiences inspired me to pick up a pen for a much-needed outlet. And so, aside from thanking myself first and foremost for publishing my first novel (because hell yeah, I did that), I should thank my own 'Uncle Brody' for being exactly who he is and all that he'll never be. If things had played out differently between us over the course of my childhood, this story wouldn't exist.

To my editor, Shelly Jay Shore, your in-depth exploration of this book helped me to elevate Sailor's story in ways I hadn't thought to tap into. I'm incredibly grateful for how you left no stone unturned, pushing me to become a better writer. I've come a long way.

Most importantly, and deeply impactful to this book existing in its entirety is my time spent as a Writer's Roadmap Mentee. Tomi Adeyemi, thank you for seeing me. For believing in me. For unlocking that magic I needed so greatly to tap into. What an extremely pivotal moment in my life and career. I am forever grateful. Thank you.

To my community who has lifted me up, championed this story, provided support in ways only they could, and often heard me ramble, thank you. Truly. Specifically, to the Creative Cottage Coven for being a positive and safe space, to the *Sazonada* crew for their help with translations, and to my early Beta readers: thank you for your feedback.

I especially need to thank Luisa, Nathalie, Sammi, and Tatiana. Your friendships have been immeasurable. Thank you for the countless FaceTimes, the sending back and forth of audio notes that rivaled podcasts, and the trauma-bonding. Y'all are my ride-or-die, and I appreciate you riding with me through this journey.

And to my Mom for supporting my love of books all my life, thank you for reading with me as a kid and enabling my reading habits even now. I especially appreciate your support of this story, for listening to me babble (even when you didn't fully comprehend what was going on), and for celebrating every small win. I love you.

Lastly, to the readers. I always knew I'd share my work with the world, and as I began exploring Sailor's story, it became clear this would be the first. Wrestling with the grief, rage, and heartache of family relationships has largely impacted my life. I never felt that I mattered enough to my own family; their absence often upset and confused me, especially when it felt like it should've been obvious in the ways I needed them. Or even more painfully, when I sometimes outright asked for their presence as a child. Their inability to show up for me carved wounds across my soul that I will always carry the scars of. If you resonate in any way with Sailor's story, especially her relationship with Brody, I'm sorry, I see you, and I hope you heal from all the things that have brought you pain. Thank you for picking up this book, for giving it a chance. For giving me a chance.

May we walk away from bridges we didn't burn.

ABOUT THE AUTHOR

Sydni Lynn is a previous Writer's Roadmap Mentee, writing emotionally raw stories with themes of found family, love, sacrifice, and the mixed-race experience. Her more controversial takes on writing include a love for cliffhangers and challenging the status quo on happily ever after's. When Sydni isn't writing, she's trying to keep up with her never-ending TBR stack and K-Dramas, exploring ways to advocate for diverse stories, and staying rooted in community.

www.ingramcontent.com/pod-product-compliance
Lightning Source LLC
LaVergne TN
LVHW020706110826
845149LV00012B/2129

* 9 7 9 8 9 9 8 5 8 8 8 0 8 *